A FISTFUL OF
RAIN

ALSO BY GREG RUCKA

A FISTFUL OF RAIN

Greg Rucka

BANTAM BOOKS

A FISTFUL OF RAIN
A Bantam Book / August 2003

Published by Bantam Dell
A Division of Random House, Inc.
New York, New York

Book design by Lynn Newmark

Library of Congress Cataloging-in-Publication Data
Rucka, Greg.
A fistful of rain / Greg Rucka
p.   cm.
ISBN 0-553-80135-X
I. Title

PS3568.U2968F57 2003
813'.54—dc21
2002043793

Manufactured in the United States of America
Published simultaneously in Canada

10 9 8 7 6 5 4 3 2 1
BVG

For David Hale Smith

My agent, my advocate, and my dear friend

In a heart there are windows and doors

You can let the light in

You can feel the wind blow

When there's nothing to lose

And nothing to gain

Grab a hold of that fistful of rain

—Warren Zevon

A FISTFUL OF
RAIN

PROLOGUE

This is the song I can never write.

There has been rain, and clouds like blood blisters have parted to a startling blue sky. The water, now in puddles in the street and clinging in drops to blades of recently cut grass, shines with the sudden sunlight, creating a glare that hurts the unshielded eye. Late afternoon, and there is a chill, but it's not enough to drive the girl and her mother inside, because they are working together in the driveway. There is newspaper spread out over oil-stained concrete, two paring knives, and a black felt-tip marker, used to make the design. The pumpkin has already been lobotomized with a jagged zigzag cut, imperfectly executed by eleven-year-old hands. Seeds and guts are piled in a heap.

The girl, with pumpkin innards sticky on her hands and deep beneath her fingernails, works ferociously, trying to make the perfect face. She imagines the work completed, with a candle burning inside, knows how it should look when everything is done. But her hands frustrate her, refusing to execute the design in her mind, and in her impatience, she makes mistakes.

The mother encourages and cautions, urging the girl to watch what she is doing, to not lose the knife, to not press too hard, to get it right because there's no second chance. The mother separates the pumpkin seeds into a shallow bowl as she speaks, saying that they will toast them later, then sprinkle them with salt. They will make a good snack, she tells her daughter.

The front door opens, and the brother steps out, pulling on his jacket. He ignores his sister and his parent as he passes them, a teenager too old for Halloween now that he is too old to wear a costume. He carries the tension of the home in his shoulders and back, and grunts the barest acknowledgment to his mother when she demands he be home for dinner. The girl doesn't look up from her work, battling with the knife, trying to cut the perfect toothy grin. She hears her mother complain softly about that boy and the trouble he gets into, but the refrain, like so many others in the child's life, has become background noise, and doesn't penetrate.

And so they work, daughter and mother, crafting a face that once was used to ward off spirits, but instead will beckon strangers to their door.

Then there is a new sound, the motor in the garage as the opener grinds to life, and the girl looks from her work over her shoulder, to see her father behind the wheel of the truck. He is waving his hand with a cigarette between his fingers, saying something lost behind the engine, and there is anger on his face. In the cab, beside him, as far as he can be without leaving the confines of Detroit Steel, is her brother, everything about him wishing he was somewhere else. When the girl looks at him, the boy looks away, but not soon enough to hide the water in his eyes.

The mother rises, wiping her fingers on her jeans, telling her daughter to gather her things and to get out of the driveway. Her father has come home, he has had a hard day, she tells her daughter. He is tired.

The girl thinks that every day is a hard day for her father, that every day he is tired when he comes home. But she doesn't speak, because she is feeling something familiar, and when she feels it, she knows it's best to stay quiet. It's an ephemeral sensation, less distinct than fear, and she has come to recognize the feeling as her friend, because it speaks of danger. She gathers her pumpkin in both hands, begins to carry it from the driveway to the porch.

She hears her father's voice above the truck's, louder now, and she almost relaxes. His shouting is another part of the background noise, and the girl who smells autumn and rain and pumpkin knows that were he closer, were she in the truck with him, she would smell beer behind his cigarette. Her mother responds using words that regularly earn her brother detention at school. There is the creak of a door opening and the slam of it shutting again, and her brother's voice joins, but not for long.

The girl is setting the pumpkin on the porch when she hears the pickup's engine rise to a roar, as if shouting to drown her mother's curses. She hears the sound of tires spinning freely on wet asphalt, but only for an instant. She hears the stainless steel bowl of pumpkin seeds clatter over concrete as a tire brushes it, and she hears her mother's voice stop, as if pulled from her body and thrown aside.

The engine falls silent.

The girl feels weightless and dizzy, and doesn't remember turning to look at what has happened. She doesn't know if she is running or walking or floating to the entrance of the garage. She cannot hear the sound of her father emerging from the cab of his truck, and she cannot hear the words her brother is shouting at her as he takes her shoulders and tries to turn her away.

Most of all, she cannot hear the sound that her mother is making, caught between wheel and the ground.

When she looks down the length of the driveway, she sees a spread of blood merging with the rainwater in the gutter.

The sunlight vanishes behind a freshly loaded cloud.

It starts to rain again.

CHAPTER ONE

The hangover was waiting for me when the plane from Sydney landed in Los Angeles. Which was as it should be, because I'd started drinking in the Red Carpet Club, and hadn't stopped until well after the International Dateline.

The looks the flight crew and fellow passengers rifled at me when I got off the plane had me thinking I'd been a less-than-model passenger, that I'd perhaps done something mortifying, but no one said a word, and I wasn't about to ask. There was no vomit drying on my clothes that I could see, and I still had my pants on right way round, so whatever it was, it couldn't have been that bad.

Certainly it couldn't be any worse than what I'd left behind in Australia.

The vise really began tightening at each temple as I was waiting to pass through customs, and it was a bad one mostly because I was still tagging after the drunk pretty closely. The world was dull and dizzying, and maybe that was why I got pulled from the line, but then again, maybe it wasn't. I took it without protest, just the way our manager, Graham Havers, had taught each of us in our little band to take it. Celebrity status has perks, but it also means that there's always someone looking to take you down a peg or ten. It's not as if musicians—or more precisely, musicians who play "popular music"—are known for living a Seventh-Day Adventist lifestyle.

The search was thorough, and the agents were, too. They asked if I had any contraband, specifically drugs. They asked it repeatedly, trying to trip me up. They had me turn out my pockets. They shook out my jacket. They patted me down. They even tore open my packet of cigarettes, checking each tube of precious nicotine to make certain it was filled with tobacco, nothing more.

When they'd finished with my bags I started to take off my shirt but the supervising agent stopped me, saying, "What are you doing?"

"Isn't this what you want?" I asked. I impressed myself by not slurring. "I mean, isn't this what, you know, what you want?"

His eyes went to flint. "No."

"Oh," I said, and tucked back in. "Well, then, my mistake. Right? My mistake?"

"I'd say so."

I got my things together and he held the door for me out of the little examination room, letting me pass through. I impressed myself again by not wobbling.

"I've made a few," I told him.

"I'm sorry?"

"Mistakes," I said. "I've made a few."

I had to stop in a ladies' room before switching terminals, and I gave until it hurt. When I emerged, there was a photographer waiting outside—he must have picked me up coming through customs—and he shouted my name when I emerged.

"Mim! Bracca! Hey! Gimme something I can sell!"

I got my hands up before I heard the whirring of the speed-winder, one to shield my face, one to let him know just what I thought of him and his Minolta, and then I was shoving through clumps of fellow travelers, and that was the end of the encounter, such as it was. It made me feel a little better; if he ever bothered to develop the roll, he'd have some lovely close-ups of the calluses on the fingertips of my left hand, and of the middle finger on my right.

The flight was delayed due to fog in San Francisco, which has happened to me more times than I can remember, and which never makes any sense each time it does. I'm flying Los Angeles to Portland, why the hell does fog in San Francisco factor into that equation?

Between that and the security I was on the ground another six hours before boarding. I sucked smoke in the Cigarette Ghetto near the gate, an outdoor area ringed with stone benches and overflowing ashtrays, wishing I had one of my guitars with me. Of the five I'd taken on tour, four were being shipped back separately. The Telecaster was traveling as luggage. I spent most of the wait dozing, the kind of drunken nod-off that's punctuated by alarming jerks of the head as you realize you might have slept through something important.

Somehow I managed to get on board at the right time, and once I was safely in my new seat, I fell asleep—or more precisely, passed out—again. I missed the safety spiel, which was probably just as well, because I had a dim memory of getting maudlin during it on the last flight. It wasn't like I was denying myself lifesaving knowledge; I'd flown so much in the past year that I'd suffered nosebleeds from all the recycled high-altitude air.

It was the jolt-bounce-slide that accompanies every wet-weather landing in Portland that woke me, and I came to cotton-mouthed and with the headache worse than ever. I was finally sober, but I still wasn't certain that was a good thing.

The terminal was mostly empty, and filled with the strange muted sounds that airports and hospitals share in the dead hours. I stopped at the restroom again, gargled with water from a drinking fountain, and by the time I was actually walking the concourse, I was doing it alone. The kiosk near the security checkpoint had an LED reader, and it welcomed me to the Rose City, Portland, Oregon, and told me it was 1:16 in the morning Pacific daylight time, on October 22, a Monday.

That seemed important to me, but before I could remind myself why, my eye caught something else, locked behind the secured gate of a closed newsstand.

The new issue of *Rolling Stone,* face out on display, between stacks of *People* and *Entertainment Weekly*. Nice cover photograph, typical crap *Stone* fare, vibrant color, big logo. Three twentysomethings standing on a rugged beach, wind snapping hair and fabric. Two women, one man, all of them staring at the lens, all with their own expressions.

Vanessa front and center, wearing her stage outfit, the outfit she wanted the world to think she wore every day, and not just during a gig: black leather pants that took her ten minutes to pull on; white half-tank with a small mushroom cloud parked between her breasts, cut off above the navel, revealing the stomach of someone who had starved herself for two days before the shoot; black bra straps showing a calculatedly feminine touch of lace; bright red lipstick highlighting her pout, leaning in at you, one hand in her hair, as if about to make an offer no red-blooded male could refuse. She can't be older than twenty-four, you think, looking at that shot. Truth is, Van's creeping up on thirty faster than she'd care to admit. If the wind has made her cold, it's not like she's noticed.

Over Van's right shoulder, Click, the self-proclaimed token black man of Tailhook. Lean, looking someplace in his mid-twenties, head shaved, eyebrows pierced, tattoos visible creeping up the sides of his neck from beneath the collar of his Portland Winterhawks team jersey. His blue jeans torn as if they're one wash away from losing the key thread, the one thread that's holding that decrepit denim together. On his feet, mismatched Chuck Taylor All Stars, red on the right foot, green on the left. Each hand balled in a fist, like he's ready to fight, but not eager. Like he'll trade blows if that is what's expected of him, nothing more. No malice on his face, just a trace of apathy, or maybe boredom.

And over Van's left shoulder another woman, black ringlets styled like dreadlocks framing her face. Brown eyes on you, mouth closed, looking like she's afraid she might swallow a bug. Lines of small hoops running from earlobe to cartilage on each side, starting big enough to fit a thumb tip, ending small enough that maybe a Q-tip wouldn't slide through. Standing on a rock to give her a much-needed boost in height, so that with the assist in elevation her head is almost but not quite level with Click's shoulder. Black tank top revealing blue-black tattoos on each arm—right side a tribal band, left a howling wolf. Baggy olive-drab cargo pants, and black Doc Martens. Made up to appear as if there's no makeup at all. Her arms crossed over her chest, only because she doesn't know what else to do with them when there's no guitar for her to hold.

Me.

Christ.

My bags were spinning lonely on the carousel when I went to claim them, and I put the strap to my duffel over my shoulder and took my guitar case in my hand. The flight case the guitar had traveled in looked none the worse for wear, but I was still relieved to have the Tele back in my possession. There's no one I'd take a bullet for, but I'd jump in front of a bazooka to save my Telecaster.

Once outside I lit a smoke, then looked for the car. I didn't see it anywhere, and was starting to get peeved when I realized that there wasn't going to be one waiting, this time.

It bothered me that that bothered me.

So I went to the cab stand instead, where a Rose City Taxi driver was already opening his trunk in preparation for my fare. I put my bags in the back, laying the guitar case on the top, and the driver went around to his door, and I went around to mine. It was cold and raining, light but steady, and it felt nice. I stood there with the door open, enjoying the weather, and it was then that I realized why October 22 mattered, why it was significant.

It was the day we'd left on our tour.

It had taken me a year to come home.

Almost.

As it happened, a man with a gun kept me from my bed for a little longer.

CHAPTER TWO

He waited until the cab had pulled away, until I was up on the porch and out of the rain.

I set down my bags, began searching my duffel for my keys. The lights inside were off, and that annoyed, but did not surprise. Mikel was supposed to be keeping an eye on the place, but my brother had his own home, a condo in the northwest part of town, and certainly wasn't obligated to sleep at my house. Making the place look lived-in would have been nice, though.

So I was on my haunches, searching my bag for a set of keys I hadn't used in months, and with the rain, I didn't hear him coming up behind me at all.

"Excuse me?"

It sounded strange, muted, but it also sounded familiar, and in the moment before I turned my head, it didn't worry me. I'd heard that nervousness before, a thousand times, the timid question posed by an awestruck fan: *Is it really you?*

I'd found my keys, and straightened up, turning, trying to hide annoyance and find my pleasant meet-and-greet face. I said, "Yeah, look, you'll have to forgive me but I just got home and ..."

Then I stopped, because I was facing him, and I wasn't liking what I was seeing one bit. Best I could figure, in a strange neuron click of clarity, was that he wasn't just a fan.

He was a stalker.

He had longish hair, dirty blond, and green and brown cammo pants and a black sweatshirt with a hood, but the hood was down. His face was vaguely familiar, the way all faces smear together when you've seen millions of them from stages all around the world. He seemed big to me, but everyone seems big to me, and when I'm surprised on my porch by a strange man, that's always going to be factored in for free.

He also had a gun, and that just added to the whole effect.

It was so utterly surreal, all I could say was "You've got to be shitting me."

The man raised the gun, to point it at my head, and said, "Come here."

My response was instinctive and contrary, and if I'd thought for a moment, I'd never have said it.

"Hell no," I told him.

"It's not a choice, bitch."

He started coming forward, and the whole strangeness of it ended abruptly, and it became terrifying, instead. I went for my door, which was stupid and I fumbled it, jabbing my key pointlessly at the lock and missing. Then he was on me, and I heard the keys drop as he rammed the gun into my neck, wrapped his bare hand around it. The gun felt blunt and cold, and his grip felt hot and wet, and the cloud of fear that had been gathering coalesced into real panic.

"You come with me *now*," he hissed into my ear. "Or I'll blow you away."

The only coherent thought I had then was that I was going to die, probably horribly, and that it wasn't fair because I wasn't even supposed to *be* here, I was supposed to be in New York City, and if Van hadn't handed me my walking papers I would be, and then I wouldn't have to be raped and murdered on the steps of my own home.

"Please don't do this," I said softly, and it didn't sound pathetic to me, just sincere.

His answer was to pull me away from my door and off my porch. He turned me, walked me down the path from my house to the street, between the big apple trees in the front yard, to the sidewalk. Every house was dark, and there was no motion but us and the trees that shivered in the falling rain.

It seemed to me that I could probably scream for help once before he killed me, and that didn't seem like a very good option at all.

Cars were parked along the curb, neighbor vehicles, and he walked me across the street, past a beat-up Chevy to a big Ford truck. The truck had a hardtop over the bed, something to keep it closed and dry, and he told me to open it, and then he told me to climb inside.

"Please don't do this," I said again. "You really don't want to do this."

"You don't know what I want," he said. "You better just hope I don't want all of it. Get in, all the way to the back, then turn around."

I had to go on hands and knees to get inside. The bed was lined with a hard black plastic, and the sound of the rain hitting the hardtop was loud. When I reached the far end I turned, watched as he moved his gun into a pocket, keeping his hand on the grip. He looked away from me, back across the street, as if checking on my house, and I could see he was trying to work something out, and I figured that was probably good for me, because if he already had a plan, I wasn't going to have a chance at all. Not to say I had a chance to begin with, but to tell the truth, my fear had begun to ebb, as if it couldn't keep up with the bizarreness of it all.

I wondered if I'd really sobered up, or if I was still drunk.

The man returned his attention to me, and when he spoke, the fear came back in a cascade.

"Give me your clothes."

"They're not your size," I said, meekly.

His sweatshirt stretched around the barrel of the gun as he thrust it farther in my direction. "You think I'm joking? You think this is some fucking joke, you split-ass bitch? Get out of your fucking clothes."

I just stared at him. I couldn't bring myself to do it.

"You want me to hurt you? You want me to hurt you and do it myself?"

I shook my head. The muscles in my jaw were starting to tremble.

"Do it. Now."

It took effort, and it took me finding a justification, it took me telling myself that this couldn't be what I thought, that he wouldn't do this here, not in the back of his truck parked two doors down from my own home, that there had to be something else he was after. Something more than his power and my humiliation.

He wouldn't do this here.

Even so, my fingers copied my jaw the whole way, numb and clumsy as I fought my boots, my belt, my buttons and zippers. I struggled out of my clothes, and I thought he would leave me my underwear, but he wanted that, too. The hardtop trapped the cold, seemed to increase it, and it made me shiver.

When I was naked, he reached in and took my clothes.

"Lie down and don't move," he said, and then he slammed the gate on the truck.

I heard the driver's door open and close, felt the vibration run through my skin. The engine started, the smell of exhaust in the trapped space. We lurched into motion.

I closed my eyes, and wished I was home.

It was dark and still raining when the truck stopped and the engine died. I heard the driver's door open again, heard the footsteps splashing around to the back of the vehicle, then the key scraping the lock. The gate came down.

"Get dressed and get out," the man said, and threw my clothes at me.

Surprise didn't stop me. I dressed, fast, not bothering to tie my boots, just getting covered and then sliding along the bed. I dropped off the gate, onto the street, looking around, and as soon as I was out, the engine started again. I could see the man behind the wheel as he pulled away, and he wasn't looking back.

It seemed like all of me was shaking, and for a moment, I was sure I would fall, that my legs wouldn't hold me. I felt the rain on my face, and I searched the darkness, trying to find some sense of where I was.

I was right where I'd started.

CHAPTER THREE

My front door was unlocked, and I blew through it, slammed it shut behind me, throwing the locks and switching on the hall light. The alarm panel on the wall said that the system was in reset, and I stabbed at it, desperate to get it to arm, but it refused to change its message. My guitar case and duffel were both in the front hall, and my keys were on the table beside the door. I didn't understand, and I didn't try.

The phone in the kitchen gave me a dial tone, and I called 911, and tried to be coherent. I said things like "gun," and "naked," and "truck." The dispatcher told me someone was on the way, and told me to stay on the line, and I thought that was fine and dandy, because the phone was cordless, and that meant I could get a bottle of Jack Daniel's from the pantry and put some of the drink into me.

That helped, but not much.

The white cop's name was Dunn and the Asian cop's name was Watanabe, and they were the ones I spoke to, because they were the first to arrive, coming in two different cars and reaching my door within thirty seconds of each other. They were by no means the last, and within ten minutes of the call, I had seven officers of the Portland Police Department swarming in and around my house, moving throughout the neighborhood.

Dunn sat me in the kitchen and asked me to tell him exactly what had happened, and I did, I told him all of it, as best as I could, as coherently as I could. When they'd arrived, both he and Watanabe had worn looks of earnest concern, even excitement.

When I was finished, the looks were gone.

"Were you hurt?"

"No, not ... not really. Scared out of my mind, but not ... you know, not hurt."

"He didn't assault you?" Watanabe asked.

"No. He made me give him my clothes, but that was all."

"If we took you to the hospital, would you consent to a doctor running a rape kit?"

"No, what? Why? He didn't rape me, he didn't touch me. He never touched me after he put me in his truck."

"He put you in his truck, he made you strip, he drove you around, and he took you back here?"

"Yes, that's what I'm saying, that's exactly what I'm saying."

Dunn asked, "Can you describe the truck?"

"It was a Ford, a big one."

"What color?"

"Blue, maybe green? It was dark."

"You didn't see the license?"

"It was an Oregon plate, that's all I know."

Dunn spoke on his radio to someone, telling them that they were looking for a big Ford truck, blue, maybe green. I didn't hear the response he got.

"And you say your things were inside when you got back?" Watanabe asked. "Is anything missing?"

"No, not that I can tell. I haven't had a chance to look."

"But it doesn't look like anything's missing?"

"No, but I haven't had a chance to look."

"I understand that." He glanced around the kitchen. "It doesn't look like there was a break-in."

"It happened outside!"

Dunn and Watanabe nodded.

"When was your last drink?" Dunn asked.

"I had a drink, I had a drink when I was on the phone with the dispatcher person."

"Before that?"

"I told you," I said, and I really did try not to sound shrill, but I was seriously starting to fray. "I'd just gotten home, I'd been on tour. I just got back from Australia."

"You were drinking on the flight?"

"That was hours ago!"

"How long have you been on tour, Miss Bracca?" Dunn asked.

"A year, almost exactly."

"And this house has been empty all that time?"

"No, I've been home a couple times, and I had my brother checking on the place."

"What's his name?"

I hesitated, then figured if my brother had done something so bad they knew who he was, they'd certainly already know his name.

"Mikel," I told them. "With a *k* and not a *c* and an *h*. But I don't see what that has to do with anything."

"We're just trying to be thorough."

"My brother didn't force me to strip in the back of a pickup truck!"

"We're not saying he did."

"You're saying you think I'm making this whole thing up."

"There's no physical evidence here, Miss Bracca," Dunn said. "There's nothing missing, you don't appear to have been injured; in fact, you maintain you weren't. We've got cars out in the neighborhood, they're looking around, but all we've got right now is you, and frankly, it just doesn't make a lot of sense."

"I'm not making this up," I said, more to myself than anyone else.

"You're describing a kidnapping, that's serious stuff. And then what looks like the start of a sexual assault. But it doesn't track, it doesn't execute."

I stared at the cops opposite me. "Why would I make this up?"

"We're not saying you're making this up."

"There was a *man* with a gun, he made me take off my *clothes—*" But Watanabe interrupted me, holding up his hands, trying to soothe. "Miss Bracca, we're taking a report, and we'll put out a description for this guy, have a car stay in the area. But this doesn't really sound like a stalker, or even a break-in. It sounds like maybe, just maybe, this was a guy thinking he had a mugging or something, and then he realized who you were, and he realized how far over his head he'd gotten."

"You don't believe me."

"We certainly believe that you believe something happened," Dunn said.

"So that's it?" I asked after a second.

"We'll file a report," Dunn said, and from his tone I could tell he was moving into wrapping-up mode. "Keep an eye out, and there'll be a patrol in the area. You should have some detectives calling you to follow up tomorrow."

"And that's all?"

"Miss Bracca, I understand your frustration. But there's really no evidence of any crime having been committed."

I nodded, not because I agreed. It wasn't enough to say that I'd been terrified and humiliated, and trying to convince either of them that it hadn't been just some mugging gone wrong, that it had been a stalker, seemed suddenly like a very egotistical claim to make.

And I was tired and out of cigarettes and still feeling a little hung-over. The clock on the VCR was telling me it was four minutes to five in the morning. That just made it all seem even more surreal.

They were on their feet, and I realized they'd already said good-bye. I got up and shook each of their hands at the door, and they gave me new smiles, not professional now, and they each told me it had been a pleasure to meet me.

"Love the new song," Watanabe said. " 'Queen of Swords,' I just love that song."

"It's a great tune," Dunn added.

I was too drained to be angry, or even annoyed. Cops come to my house to take a report, they turn it into a fan event.

"Thanks," I said, and smiled right back at them, the way I always do when the people I meet stop being people, and turn into fans. "Thanks a lot."

They left me alone, real happy to have met a rock star.

CHAPTER FOUR

For a minute after the cops pulled away, I just kept watching the street from the living room window. Rain was still falling lightly, my apple trees drooping from the weight of the water. Not much more to see beyond that. Silhouettes of parked cars in front of houses still sleeping, and a darkness that was heavy and wide. Irvington has few streetlamps.

The house creaked, then went silent again. It was a new noise to me, and I had to think it through before deciding that it was nothing to be alarmed about. My home had been built in 1923 in what was called locally the Portland craft style, and which I supposed up in Seattle was referred to as the Seattle craft style. It was barely two stories, a portion of the attic having been converted into the master bedroom with a bath. There was another full bath on the ground floor, near the guest room, and then the kitchen and the living room, some pantry space. The basement had been finished when I purchased the place, and I'd left detailed instructions on how I wanted the space converted into a music room, but I didn't know if the contractors had done as asked. I didn't feel much like finding out.

I'd closed on the house only two weeks before the tour had begun, and since then had been home only three times, the longest for a stretch of seventy hours back in July. We'd returned for a show out at the Gorge, about ninety miles east of Portland, one of those multiband, all-day affairs hosted by the local alternarock station. The gig had sucked, but those radio-hosted megashows always do—too many bands all vying for the limelight, and never a chance to get a decent sound check, so you never know what you're going to be stepping into. When you play live and loud, there are monitors set up on the stage—essentially small speakers— positioned so the musicians can hear themselves. Kinda crucial.

That day the monitor mix had been awful, and after the sixth song the jackass on the board still couldn't get it right, and we had no idea how we were sounding, but each of us was pretty certain "awful" might come close. Van finally stormed off the stage after "Broken Nails," giving the finger to everyone in the audience.

The crowd had loved us anyway. They'd have loved a mechanical monkey clapping cymbals.

But that had been almost four months ago, and between travel, setup, and the show, I'd been in my home only long enough to sleep and do laundry, and even that had been difficult, because the contrac- tor and the electrician and the plumber all wanted to talk to me about the work I was having them do. I'd barely even seen my brother, spending most of my remaining time with Joan and Steven.

Which was what made me remember that Steven was dead. Not remember, really; more, bring back the reality of it, solidify the fact. Claimed by that modern classic, complications brought about by can- cer of the throat and mouth.

I felt supersize guilt. I hadn't talked to Joan since the day after he'd died, since I'd told her I wouldn't make it to the funeral. I'd have to see her. I'd have to explain myself.

I already knew that I wouldn't be able to.

The headache was still with me, though now I didn't know if it was from the drunk, the lack of sleep, the pure terror of the truck ride, the frustration of the police, or all of the above.

The house creaked again.

Maybe it hadn't been a big deal, maybe the cops were right, it was just a mugging gotten out of control, a criminal biting off more than he could chew, then not knowing what to do with the leftovers. A mistake, nothing more. Maybe the thought that I would be stalked at all was ludicrous. I wasn't the one pouting and preening onstage, I wasn't the public face of Tailhook. That was Van, always was, always would be. If anyone was looking to sniff a pair of panties, they'd go after hers, not mine.

I didn't want to be alone.

I let the curtains drop back over the window and grabbed my coat off the bag still in the hall. It took me a minute to search the drawers in the kitchen before I located my car keys in the back of the knick-knack drawer, along with my garage opener. I couldn't remember where anything was, and that only made me feel all the more disconnected with the space, all the more anxious to get out.

The garage was off the side of the house, pushed back about twenty feet from the street, freestanding, and my Jeep was where I'd last left it. Mikel might have used it, but he had his own car, so I figured he'd left mine alone. I climbed in and tried the engine, and the battery was weak on the ignition, but it caught after a long crank. The tank read just below half. I backed down the drive, switched on wipers and lights, closed the garage door after me, and headed the twelve blocks to the Plaid Pantry on Broadway, telling myself I would get some cigarettes and that was all.

The lot was illuminated and mostly empty, and I parked right out front. The clerk behind the counter looked up at me from his reading as I came inside, eyes on me all the way to the wall of refrigeration. I spotted the beer and pulled at the handle, but the door didn't budge, locked.

"Not until seven," the clerk said.

I glared back at him and he shrugged and resumed his reading, and I gave the door another protest tug, then got myself a can of Coke, instead. Portland goes dry from two-thirty until seven in the morning, no alcohol can be sold, and trying to convince the clerk to make an exception wouldn't work, no matter who I was. Portland PD is serious about its alcohol enforcement, if not about its stalker laws.

Paid for the soda and two packs of Spirits, and it took the clerk until he was handing me my change before he raised an eyebrow and asked if he knew me.

"Where'd you go to high school?" I asked.

"Grant. You go to Grant?"

"No, I was over in Hawthorne."

"Huh."

"Oh, well," I said, and went back out to my car. I opened one of the packs of smokes and lit a cigarette, then decided I still wasn't going to go home, so I got out of the car again and went to the pay phone next to the entrance, trying to decide who I should call. Joan was pretty much straight out. Foster mother dispensation would get me a lot, but the guilt payback would be brutal, and I couldn't do that to her.

So I started dialing Mikel's number, thinking that, at the very least, I could determine whether or not he was renting out my home to any of his more disreputable friends.

It took four trills before he answered.

"Mikel? It's Mim," I said.

"Mim?"

"Your sister."

He cleared his throat, coughed, rustled. I imagined him switching on the lamp, wondered if he was sleeping alone, or if Jessica was in bed with him. "Jesus, it's not six yet. What time zone are you in?"

"Your time zone. Listen, brother dearest, and understand I ask this only because the cops put it in my head, but do any of your dope-fiend buddies own a big Ford pickup, maybe green, maybe blue?"

"Cops?" he asked, immediately alarmed.

"Yes, they wear uniforms and carry guns and—"

"I know what a cop is."

"And I'm very proud of you for that. Answer the question, Mikel."

"I'm not sure what the question is."

I spoke slowly. "Do any of your drug-taking, dope-dealing, party-all-night friends own a big Ford pickup?"

"No. Why the hell are you even asking?" He coughed again, then added, "Wait, did you say you're in my time zone?"

"I'm at the Plaid Pantry on Broadway and Sixteenth. Cold, tired, in the rain, and frankly still scared out of my mind."

"What happened?" The hint of annoyance that had crept into his voice disintegrated. "Mim, are you okay?"

"I got home tonight and some guy pointed a gun at me and he made me get in his truck and ... and it's fucked up, it's seriously fucked up, and I called the police, and they didn't believe a word I said—"

"Go back inside," Mikel said. I could hear him moving, getting out of bed. There was nothing else in the background though, so I guessed that meant he'd been sleeping alone. "Go back inside and wait for me, all right? I'll be right there."

"I'm all right now," I said. The lie didn't even sound believable to me.

"You're always all right. Go back inside, I'll be about ten minutes."

"Mikel," I said, but he'd already hung up.

It took him closer to fifteen minutes before he parked his Land Rover beside my Jeep. I'd spent the time drinking my Coke and smoking my cigarettes, standing by the pay phone, and when Mikel hopped out he was wearing a scowl, but he didn't say anything until after he'd wrapped me up in a big hug, and I gave it right back, pressing my nose into his chest. I hugged back harder than I meant to at first, but it felt good and it felt safe.

"I told you to wait inside."

"And I always do what you tell me," I told his chest.

He let me go and looked me over, showing me the worry in his eyes. Mikel is three years my senior, just touching thirty, and every day he looks more like I remember our father, big and strong. We have similar features, but I got my mother's body type, which makes me pretty small. Mikel's got straight black hair and an angular face, blue eyes, broad shoulders. He looks like he could be in construction or some sort of physical labor, but that would require too much work, and one thing Mikel hates is work.

When pressed, he tells people that he's in computers, doing Web design and software work, but that's only half-true, and certainly doesn't earn enough for a Land Rover. What earns enough for the Land Rover is selling pot and X and coke to the hip urban professionals who live on the west side of the river. He doesn't use. He doesn't take anything stronger than caffeine, ever. But he's more than happy to sell.

He was dressed very Gap casual, hastily assembled, a sweater and corduroys.

"You should have waited inside," he said.

I shook my head, not wanting to explain my reasons, not wanting to say that the clerk had figured out who I was, and that had I gone back into the store I'd have been trapped in twenty minutes of pretending to be nicer than I really am. Maybe it was selfish, but maybe I was entitled a little bit, and it wasn't something I wanted to defend.

Mikel sighed, world-weary with his sister's strangenesses. "What happened?"

"Not here," I said. "I don't want to talk about it here. I want to sit down someplace warm and drink coffee and feel safe."

"You have breakfast?"

"They fed us on the plane, just before we landed in L.A.," I said. I didn't add that I'd thrown it up shortly thereafter.

"You up for some Strong Bread?"

"The one on Sandy. Not the one near your place."

"Why not the one near me?"

"Because I get recognized more at the one near your place."

"Poor little princess," he said, but he said it with a smile, and I wasn't sure what was teasing and what wasn't.

CHAPTER FIVE

The sky was lightening, but the rain was still falling when we reached the Cameo Café. I parked behind him about a block from the restaurant, and we scurried from the wet into the warmth and noise. On weekends it can take up to an hour to get a seat at the Cameo, especially in good weather, but even though it was noisy inside, the restaurant wasn't full, and Mikel and I got a table near the back. It's cramped inside so that when it's really hopping, even someone of my size feels that she has to walk sideways to work her way between the tables, but once you get a seat, it's pretty comfortable. The grill is right behind the counter, so all conversation is accompanied by the sizzle and smell of cooking food.

One of the Korean women who run the place dropped menus in front of us and gave us cheerful good-mornings along with two mugs of watery coffee. I drank mine greedily, as Mikel doctored his own cup with cream and sugar.

"So what happened?" he asked.

It was harder to tell it to him than it had been to tell it to the cops, maybe because I knew how he'd react to certain parts. I told him about my stalker who the cops were certain wasn't a stalker at all, and he listened, fiddling with his silverware and watching me intently the whole time. His face tightened when I told him about the back of the truck, but it smoothed when I told him what the police had said.

"They don't believe me," I finished.

"I'm not sure I do, either," Mikel said, slowly.

"How can you say that? Jesus Christ, Mikel! The guy could have raped me!"

"Well, don't take this the wrong way, but why didn't he?"

"I don't believe you just said that."

"Stop being such a Drama Queen and think about it. It doesn't make much sense, does it, Mim? You said your stuff was on the porch, yet it's inside when you come home? You say you got kidnapped and stripped at gunpoint, but you don't have a mark on you?"

"Would you rather that I'd called you from the fucking hospital?"

"Mim, you've been lying your whole damn life. You can't expect me to take this one at face value."

I got up, but he reached out for my wrist as I was squeezing around the table, taking hold, his fingers digging into me.

"Don't run away from me," Mikel said.

I yanked free. My voice was tight when I spoke. "I'm not lying. I'm not a liar. It *happened*. And I'm not going to sit here and have you tell me it didn't."

Mikel glanced around, then back to me. "For someone who doesn't want to be recognized, little sister, you're making a very big scene. Sit back down."

I checked, saw that he was right, that heads had turned my way and were staying there.

"Sit down, Mim."

"You're a bastard." I sat down.

"I am well aware of your feelings about our father."

"You're more like him every day," I said.

It was a bald-faced lie, but it scored a point, and it forced silence for almost a minute.

"You said the alarm was off?" he asked.

"Not off, in reset."

"See, that I believe."

"Oh, just that?"

"Well, that's my fault." Mikel looked at his menu, then back to me, embarrassed.

"How is that your fault?"

"I had it shut off in August."

"I was out of town and you had my damn alarm shut off?"

"The contractors kept setting it off when they were working." He sat back, getting defensive. "I'm on the contact list. Whenever it went off, I got called."

"Because you're supposed to be looking out for me!"

"I *was* looking out for you. Every time there's a false alarm, there's a fine, Mim. It went off six separate times—that's over two grand in fines—before I called and had it disconnected."

"But they finished, the contractors finished."

"Yeah." He frowned. "I forgot to have it reactivated."

I stared at him, and then the waitress came and we each ordered breakfast, Mikel asking for the Korean scramble, and I asking for the Strong Bread pancakes, which are full of all sorts of wholesome grains which are supposed to make you strong, at least according to the menu. They also sell Strong Bread by the loaf, but it's harder to justify putting syrup on a loaf of bread, so the pancakes were the better choice.

The waitress left and Mikel excused himself, telling me he'd be right back, and then he headed outside. He was pulling out his mobile phone as he went through the door. It didn't mean he was working a sale, but I couldn't help assuming that he was.

I drank a second cup of coffee and half a glass of apple juice and tried not to be angry at Mikel. But when he came back to the table I was still feeling sulky.

"Sorry about that," he said, taking his seat.

"Business good?"

"Wasn't business."

"Doesn't answer the question."

He shrugged.

"You should stop."

"Why? To protect your good name?"

"Maybe to protect yours," I shot back at him. "You're gonna get caught, and you'll end up like Tommy."

"I'm never going to end up like Dad. I don't drink, I don't use, and I'm pretty fucking smart, if I may say so myself."

"Smart would be not dealing."

He looked at me pointedly. "See, and I'd think smart would be not using."

"I don't use."

"You're still drinking."

"Look, if you've got somewhere to be, I don't want to keep you."

"Mim, you're being an ass."

"I wouldn't want you to miss an opportunity," I said.

"Now you're being a passive-aggressive ass."

"I just don't want to inconvenience you."

He stared at me for a long moment. Then he raised his hand, leveling his index finger.

"Rock Star!" Mikel bellowed in his best evangelical imitation. "I know thy name, demon, and it is Rock Star! Begone from this place!"

A couple people at the counter heard him and glanced over at us.

"Stop," I said.

Mikel turned in his seat, as if trying to find a waiter, raising a hand, snapping his fingers silently. "Pardon, *garçon*? A bottle of Cristal, if you please?"

"Knock it off, Mikel."

"A dozen white roses with which to adorn her hair." He turned back to me, really amused, the grin making creases around his eyes. "The purest mountain spring water to bathe her fair and adored flesh."

I tried to glare him into silence, to really ratchet it up, but his smile did it, and I cracked, started giggling. Our plates came and I poured syrup on my pancakes and Mikel dumped most of a bottle of Tabasco on his scramble, and I waited until the waitress had departed before speaking again.

"I'm *not* a prima donna," I told him.

"You want me to cut that for you? I'd be happy to slice it into perfectly uniform bits, then feed them to you with a caviar spoon."

"You don't even know what a caviar spoon looks like."

"For one such as yourself, such a failing on my part is inconceivable. I shall throw myself into traffic at once, of course."

"But who will I get to cut my pancakes?"

He laughed again. "Okay, I'll let you feed yourself. But if Vanessa asks about the syrup, I'm telling the truth."

"Fuck Vanessa," I said, with sincere bile.

Mikel stopped his fork halfway to his mouth. "What'd you do?"

"I didn't *do* anything."

"So why should I rush out and fuck Vanessa? Not that I'd mind, of course."

"She sent me home."

"You're not back on a break?"

I shook my head, used my fork to cut a not-very-uniform piece of pancake. "They're in New York. She's replacing me with Oliver Clay."

"Who's Oliver Clay?"

"You haven't met him. He's a session guy, out of Seattle, we used him for backing tracks on 'Energize' and 'Tomorrow-Today-Tonight.' He's taking my place for the rest of the tour."

Mikel ate a bite, then a second one, studying me. I pushed my pancakes around, suddenly not wanting them.

"At least I don't have to worry about Van telling me to watch my figure," I said.

"What'd you do?"

"Nothing, I told you."

"You have a fight?"

I shook my head.

He set his utensils down, leaned forward, lowered his voice. "Mim?"

"It's exhaustion," I said. "They're making the announcement some-time today. Saying that I'm taking the rest of the tour off."

"Exhaustion."

"Yeah."

"Miriam?"

"Don't want to talk about it," I said.

He didn't move, keeping his head close, and I kept looking at my plate, at the islands of pancake and the sea of syrup. I knew what it was he was thinking, I knew he suspected. He quit drinking in his late teens, and I could feel his judgment, and I thought about calling him a hypocrite.

We finished eating, but the conversation went shallow, mostly Mikel asking questions about the tour. We'd hit Japan before Australia, with two nights in New Zealand in between, and he was curious about Christchurch. He knew a couple of software people who'd had pro-tracted stays in New Zealand while working postproduction on a se-ries of films, and apparently all of them had raved about what a great place the country was.

"Nice crowds," I told him. "Nice hotel. Venue was cool, very mod-ern. Great acoustics. I broke three strings on the Tele the first night and had to finish the second set using my alternate, but I don't think anyone but me and Fabrizio noticed."

"Fabrizio?"

"My guitar tech. Nice guy. Fat little guy. But nice."

"That's all you can say about New Zealand?"

"That's all of New Zealand that I experienced. If you want more, I can try to remember the hotel room décor and what I ate for dinner each night."

We finished eating and the check came, and I snatched it before Mikel could, and he tried to go all big brotherly on me.

"Give it."

"No." I dug around in my jacket for my wallet.

"Give it here, Miriam."

"Are you rich?"

"I'm comfortable."

"Yeah, well, I have been told that I am stinking rich," I said. "My treat."

It was hard for him to argue with that. We paid and went outside, and the rain had stopped. The sky was the color of a muddy sheet. Mikel waited while I lit a cigarette, then asked what my plans were.

"Home," I said. "Sleep."

"You sure you want to go home?"

"Don't know what else my choices are. I mean, I either go home, or I never go home, right?"

"I'm just asking if you're up to it."

"I'm upper to it now than I was before I called you. Daylight makes it better, I think. I should probably do some shopping, get some groceries in."

"I'll keep you company."

I glanced at him suspiciously. "Overprotective much?"

"Only when you let me."

"Mikel."

"Let me keep you company," he said gently. "We'll go shopping, I'll go back to your place with you, I'll look around, we'll call the Scanalert people and tell them to turn your system back on. It'll make me feel better."

I thought about protesting, but didn't really want to. I didn't want him to see that I thought he was being really sweet, either, so instead I shrugged and headed back to my Jeep, telling him I wanted to go to Fred Meyer. He followed me down Sandy Boulevard, and when I checked in my rearview mirror, I could see him behind his wheel, watching my progress and the traffic, all the while talking on his mobile phone. He caught me looking at the light and gave me a grin.

I grinned back and shook my head. For all his many faults, I adore my brother.

He almost makes up for our fuck-awful parents.

*   *   *

We stopped by the bank first, so I could get some cash out of the ATM, and I checked all my accounts, not just my savings. It was the first time I'd actually seen my balance in months, and I was a little surprised at the numbers. According to my checking balance alone, I was maybe a very rich girl, indeed.

The machine only let me withdraw four hundred dollars, and I took it to the Fred Meyer on Broadway. Freddy's is a mammoth combo-store, groceries and clothing and household supplies, and a couple of them even have electronics and jewelry departments, and I've never been in one when it wasn't busy, no matter what time of day or night. Freddy's also has the slowest checkers in the world, which doesn't help things. But for one-stop shopping in the Portland metro area, it can't be beat.

We were there about an hour, getting everything I needed or might need to reactivate my life at home. It would have taken less time, but I got cornered early in the cereal aisle by three teens, two girls and a guy who should have been in school. Either the news hadn't broken yet or they hadn't heard, because they immediately started looking for Van and Click, as if we all three did our shopping together.

I asked them their names and introduced them to my brother. We talked about how amazing Van and Click were, and then I told them that I had to get back home because it was past my bedtime. They laughed.

"You're my favorite," one of the girls told me. "You kick total ass."

They went away, toward baking supplies. Mikel was smiling slightly.

"It's not a thing," I told him.

"You can be very nice when you want to be. Very gracious."

"They're not asking for much."

"Suppose that depends on where you're standing."

I dropped two boxes of shredded wheat in the already full shopping cart. The baking supplies aisle was down below our position on cereal, and I could see the three kids picking out bags of chocolate chips. One of them was looking back at me, speaking to the others, and she waved when she saw my look, so I waved back, then turned away.

"I'm twenty-six," I told Mikel. "I own a house, I could buy five or six others just like it. I own more guitars than I could ever need, more amps than I can possibly use, I've got a platinum American Express card life. I don't have to look at the prices when I'm shopping for groceries at Fred Meyer, because they will *never* stock something I can't afford.

"That's all because people like them like Tailhook enough to pay eighteen bucks for an album, or eighty for a seat at a concert, or twenty for a forty-five-minute compilation of very bad, very overproduced music videos."

Mikel was listening, his head down a little, as if to keep it closer to my own. When Tailhook had left on tour, we'd been popular, but nothing like we were now. Our third album, *Nothing for Free,* had just been released, and we didn't have any idea how it would do. Certainly neither Click nor I had ever been stopped while doing our shopping. It had happened to Van, but only rarely, and only at home, because we were, by and large, a local band.

"Never bite the hand that feeds you," Mikel said.

"Not even that." I glanced back down the aisle, saw that the three of them had gone. "You want to know what that was all about?"

"They wanted to tell you how much they like you."

"Yeah, but do you know why?"

"It's a way of saying thank you?"

"That was about how they want to be my friend. They shake my hand and tell me their names, and I tell them mine, just to remind them I'm a real person, too, that we should act like real people act when they first meet one another. And then it's small talk, weather, music, movies, shit like that.

"Then there's the pause—and there is *always* the pause, Mikel— the moment when there's nothing else to say, because they're done, and they're waiting for me."

"To do what?"

"To say something like, hey, you guys seem totally cool, why don't we go get a pizza together. Or, hey, you know what would be fun? Let's go back to my place and watch DVDs. They want to be more than fans. They want to be special to me, and that's when I offer them my hand again, and I say thank you so much for saying hello, and have a very good life. Most of the time, they go away happy."

"Most of the time?"

I started pushing the cart again, heading to dairy. "Sometimes they don't get the hint. Sometimes they get cranky—'you wouldn't be where you are without me.' Or 'you love all the attention, don't pretend you don't get off on it.' But maybe ninety percent of the people who stop me, all they want to do is say, hey, thanks."

"I couldn't do it," Mikel said, after a couple seconds. "I couldn't keep it up."

I was trying to decide between low- and nonfat milk. I went with the skim, placing it next to the cereal, so they could get used to each other's company.

"You should see Van do it sometime," I told him. "She's very smooth, always smiling. I've seen her in a Virgin Megastore signing autographs for six hours straight, no breaks, no pauses. Always makes eye contact, always says, 'May I sign that for you, please?' and then always says, 'Thanks so much for coming to see us.' She's better at it than I will ever be."

"You seemed pretty smooth to me."

"No," I said. "But it's nice of you to say so."

We filled the back of my Jeep with the groceries, and when we got back to my house, I put the car in the garage. We unloaded the bags into the kitchen through the back door, and while I sorted and stored my purchases, Mikel took a wander through the house. I was still at it when he came back into the kitchen, and he picked up the phone and used his PDA to find the phone number for Scanalert, and I heard his half of the conversation. He had to give them his name and then a password—"Renderman"—to verify his identity, and then requested that they switch the system back on. He hung up happy.

"Done," he said.

"Just like that?"

"Just like that. They just throw a switch or something."

We finished with the unpacking, making light conversation. I finally remembered to ask about Jessica, and he told me that they had stopped seeing each other during the summer, that he was going with a girl named Avery now. I felt bad that I hadn't known about the switch, and he told me about the new girl, and how she was a dancer, and how much he thought I'd like her.

"You need a dancer for a video, you should get her," he said.

"I'm not in the band anymore," I reminded him. "Even if I was, I wouldn't have any say in it."

"You could talk to Van."

I shrugged, thinking that the way Mikel went through women was just another residual of our shared childhood. I couldn't remember ever having had a romantic relationship that lasted more than a month myself, and the only one that lasted that long had been almost ten years ago, during high school. But Mikel's news sobered me; it had looked like the thing with Jessica was serious.

I'd bought beer even though Mikel had given me the hairy eyeball while I was doing it, and as I put the last of the six-packs in the refrigerator, he dropped the bomb. It was probably part of the reason he'd insisted on accompanying me, and he must have been waiting from the moment we'd finished breakfast, but it had taken him almost three hours before he could do it.

"Tommy's out."

I stared at my newly stocked refrigerator shelves, at a box of Land O Lakes butter. I wasn't certain I'd heard him right.

"What?"

"He's out," Mikel said. "Got out three months ago."

I did the math in my head, closing the refrigerator door. "That's not right, he's supposed to be in for another five years."

Mikel had been folding the paper grocery bags, making a stack of them on the counter. He smoothed the last one down, shaking his head.

"Paroled?" I asked. "If he was paroled there should have been a hearing, Mikel. I should have been notified. I should have been able to attend."

"He wasn't paroled," Mikel said. "He's out, he's done. All finished."

"He was supposed to do twenty years."

"There's this thing, it's called a buy-back or time-served or something like that. For every day of good behavior in prison, the state takes a certain amount off your sentence. It's how they deal with overcrowding."

"That's not right."

"He did fifteen years, Mim. That's a long time."

I was practically spitting. "Fuck that. Mom's still dead."

"And he's still our father."

"No, my father's dead."

"I'm not talking about Steven—"

"Good, you better not."

He took a soft breath, looking away from me. I waited, then decided I didn't want to wait for what he might have to say, and found my cigarettes. I lit one and flicked angry ash into the sink.

"He's been staying with me, Mim. He'd really like to see you."

"He's *what?*"

"He didn't have a place to stay. He's staying with me until he can get on his feet."

"Ex-con Tommy living with my drug-dealing brother? Are you out of your mind?"

"It's not like that. I'm just helping him out. He's having trouble finding a job, you know, with the economy the way it is."

"Hard to get a gig when you're an alcoholic killer," I said. "I'm really torn up for him."

"He was in prison for fifteen years for what he did," Mikel said. "He's not the same man he was when it happened, he's not the same man he was when we were in that house."

"Bullshit."

"Maybe it's time you stopped inventing history, Miriam, and saw Mom a little more for who she was, rather than this sainted martyr you want her to be. Maybe you ought to give Tommy the benefit of the doubt."

"You saw it happen," I said, softly. "You saw it, too."

"I know that, but—"

"You saw it, too!" I screamed at him.

It pushed him back a step, surprised him. I smoked more of my cigarette.

"He'd like to see you, just to talk with you." Mikel picked up his keys from where they were lying on the counter. "I think if you can give total strangers twenty minutes at Fred Meyer, then he's not asking all that much."

"You're leaving?"

"I've got shit to do, you're tired, and I don't want to get in the way of your drinking."

"Hey, fuck you, big brother."

He started down the hall, to the front door. "I'll give you a call tonight or tomorrow, to check up on you. You might want to call Joan, let her know you're back."

I caught up with him at the front door, as he was moving onto the porch.

"He's staying with you?"

"I told you already."

"Right now, Tommy's there right now?"

"I don't know about right now. He's been picking up construction work where he can, so he heads out pretty early."

"Do me a favor? When you see him?"

"What?"

"Make a point of telling him I hope he burns in hell," I said, then slammed the door on him.

CHAPTER SIX

cracked a beer, then fetched my flight case from the hallway. The alarm panel said the system was "ready," so I armed the system, and when the panel sang its three-tone alert, I actually felt safe and tight in my house. Then I took the case down to the basement, to the music room.

The contractors had done as I'd asked, sealing the windows and replacing the entry door with a heavier, reinforced version. There was padding now down over the concrete, and acoustic tile on the ceiling, and my gear was there, too, my amps and other guitars—the ones that hadn't come on tour with me—and my keyboard. In a pinch, the space could serve as a passable recording studio.

I worked the combination on the flight case and snapped the locks up, then checked the Tele. It had traveled fine, secure in its bed, dry and happy and cool to the touch. It wasn't my first guitar and it wasn't my newest, but it was my favorite electric. Leon Fender and George Fullerton started making Fender guitars in 1950, and their first model was called the Broadcaster, but they had to change the name because the Gretsch company made drums also called Broadcaster. They renamed their guitar the Telecaster, and it's been pretty much the same instrument ever since; the only real difference you find is in the quality of workmanship and materials, who did the building, what was used to construct the guitar.

My Tele was made in 1954, body of ash, neck of maple, black pick guard, still fitted with its original hardware, a gift from the label after *Nothing for Free* went gold in the U.S. They'd given Van an emerald and gold necklace from Tiffany, and Click a set of Keplinger snare drums. The Tele was almost fifty years old, now, and to this day I've never met an electric that plays as sweetly. It had the original pickups, but the input jack had been replaced, and the fingerboard refretted, a custom job that made it less collectible but let it play like butter under my fingers. Fabrizio did some other minor work on it while we were on the road, as well. Before each show, he would string every one of my guitars, replacing the old ones with the new. He was utterly tone-deaf, and relied on an electronic tuner, and each and every time he handed me a guitar, it was perfect. I'd fiddle with the tuning heads just for show, but he and I both knew it was garbage.

Holding the Tele and thinking of Fabrizio, I realized that Van hadn't even given me the opportunity to say good-bye.

I put the guitar in its stand, next to the Gibson SG, got out the soft cloth and gave every instrument a wipe-down, then put the case and cloth away in the storage closet. I had to move a couple boxes to make room, and when I was shoving things around, one of the boxes tumbled. Copies of the press kit from *Nothing for Free* spilled onto the floor, black-and-white photos of the band sliding across one another like a monochromatic tide. I swore a lot and bent down, trying to gather them all together again. There were another three boxes in the closet just like the one I'd toppled, each filled with the same promotional material, and I still had no idea on earth why they'd been sent to me rather than our manager, Graham.

Things back in their place, I headed upstairs. The beer was dead, so I exchanged it for a fresh one in the kitchen, drank it while I smoked another cigarette, looking out the window at the backyard.

The lawn was more crabgrass than anything else, and the rosebushes all needed a desperate pruning. Maybe I could get a recommendation for a gardener from one of my neighbors.

I finished the cigarette about the same time I finished the beer, so I opened another two, then dragged myself upstairs to my bedroom. I put both beers on the nightstand. The bedroom smelled of fresh carpet and the hint of fresh paint, and, again, carpentry, but nothing more. The pictures on my bureau were all the same. There were three of them—a small picture of myself with my mother, taken at one of my barely remembered birthday parties, when I'd turned either five or maybe six. Another one, larger, of me and Mikel, taken a couple years back at a bar. The last one a backstage shot taken here, at the Roseland Theatre in town, after a Tailhook show, of me standing between Steven and his wife, my foster mother, Joan. In the picture, I'm shining with sweat and holding a bouquet of flowers, and Joan and Steven each look like they're proud enough to burst.

I unpacked my bag, throwing my dirty clothes in the laundry basket and my clean clothes in their drawers. I undressed, took a beer with me into the shower. I stayed under the water long enough to finish it, got out when it was empty, and dropped the bottle in the trash. There was condensation on the mirror, and I swiped at it and stared at my reflection, seeing my mother. She'd been a small woman, too, and for some reason I couldn't conjure a memory of her hands ever being warm. She'd been thirty-two when she died, barely six years older than me, and showing more age than she should've, thin-faced and already creasing.

No wrinkles on me yet, nothing that would take three hours in a makeup chair to hide. I looked myself over, checking from every angle I could manage, and remained pretty pleased with the results of my survey. I hadn't been vain before meeting Van, and I didn't like to think I was, now, but being with her for so long had taken its toll. We'd been a band for less than a month when she shared with me her Thesis of Rock Stardom, which essentially came down to this—for guys, it's how you sound *first,* then how you look; for women, it's how you look, *then* how you sound, and even then, it's more about how you look. It was fine if Click wanted to chow on cheeseburgers and sit on his can watching TV, she'd say; you and me, girlfriend, we've got a date at 24-Hour Fitness.

I wondered if the man with the gun had liked what he'd seen. I wondered if he'd gotten off on it, and then thought I was probably damn lucky he hadn't.

And for a second, I wondered if any of it—the man with the gun, the back of the Ford, the drive around for nothing—had happened at all.

Mikel was wrong about a great many things, and he certainly was no authority on trust or The Truth, but he was right in at least one respect: I am a hell of a liar.

I'm so good at it, half the time, I don't even know I'm doing it myself.

I came back to my reflection, the water still on my skin, and began toweling off. Honestly, I thought I looked pretty good. Hell, I thought I looked better than pretty good, I thought I looked great, and I told my reflection as much, and then added some unkind things about Van and vanity and how it was appropriate that the one was named after the other. I wasn't quite sure which one I meant, but I was very passionate about the whole thing, and my reflection, if anything, seemed even more sincere about it than I.

There was another beer waiting, and I went to keep it company, and a little later decided that there were more downstairs, and I could have a couple of those, too. I thought about putting on some clothes or a towel and then decided, my house, my rules. I negotiated the descent okay, and I made it to the kitchen just fine, but I had some trouble getting back up the stairs.

Actually, I had a lot of trouble getting back up the stairs.

I remember making it to the bedroom. I remember a bottle breaking on the bathroom tile. I remember that there was blood, and that upset me.

I don't really remember much more than that, honestly.

CHAPTER SEVEN

I suppose what happened in Sydney started in Christchurch, but it probably started long before that. And the sad thing is, the Christchurch gig was amazing, maybe because so much had threatened to go wrong.

We'd played in a smaller venue than expected, only three hundred people at capacity, and the hall had been crammed, completely SRO. The audience stood shoulder to shoulder, the air-conditioning on the fritz, and the stage monitors that we use to hear ourselves play had suffered what the head sound tech called an Apollo 13. By which he meant a catastrophic failure he had no idea how to fix.

Given all of these things, we should have stunk on ice. But it was a small stage, and we used it, and Van and I danced around the lip and clambered all over Click and his kit, and we improvised, and we played like hell, but most of all, we had much fun.

God, we had so much fun.

And when it's like that, the audience knows it, and they don't care that the only fresh air is coming in through the opened windows and the propped doors, they don't care that they're getting bumped and knocked from every direction, they don't care that their feet are killing them. They want the music, the show, and when they get it, they're someplace else, someplace better.

Those nights are magic.

They called us back three times, and at the end of the third encore they were still on their feet, and making so much noise that applause and cheering chased us all the way to the green room. Graham was waiting, and his expression confirmed it; we'd blown the doors off the place.

"This is it," he said, rushing from Van to Click to me, handing a towel and a bottle of water to each of us. "This is the memory I'm keeping, the one for my deathbed. This is my moment of triumph."

We shared in our glory between gulps of water, laughing, praising, remembering the moments of brilliance, the near-disasters, the fantastic saves. Graham ran the circuit, slapping shoulders and pouring drinks. I'd finished one of my fifths of Jack Daniel's onstage during the show, but the rider in my touring contract specified two to be supplied at each venue, and Graham handed me the remainder without my even having to ask. My rider also specified two liters of Arrowhead water and a carton of American Spirit Yellows, hinge-lids. I liked the fifths because they were easy to carry and easy to stow onstage. The Arrowhead normally got finished while onstage, too, like it had this night. Of the cigarettes, I'd keep a pack or two, then give the rest to the crew.

"Mimser," Graham said when he gave me the bottle, "I'm calling Prudential, fuck that, I'm calling Lloyds of London first thing tomorrow, on my honor, I'm calling them and insuring your hands! I saw smoke tonight, *smoke* coming from those strings."

I laughed around the mouth of the bottle, fell into a chair. Graham leaned in and smooched my sweaty forehead, then headed for Click. Click was halfway through rolling himself a cigarette, and when Graham uncharacteristically gave him a hug, tobacco went spilling out of the paper and onto his lap, and I laughed again, Van joining, too.

"The hell are you on, man?" Click demanded.

"A beer, a beer for the beat." Graham was spinning around, searching for a bottle. Click's rider was the simplest of the three of us—he'd specified nothing but a carton of Bridgeport India Pale Ale, and he'd done it as a joke, because it was a local Portland microbrew, and he figured to give the promoters a headache. It did, I'm sure, but there was always a carton waiting for him. He was sick to death of the stuff.

"Nah, I'm good with water, Graham, and you need a tranquilizer."

Graham whipped around again, clapping a hand down on each of Click's shoulders, once more disrupting the rolling process. "This is the love, Click, and you must accept it. You were outstanding tonight, you could have gotten the dead to their feet the way you were playing tonight."

"You are *so* high," Click told him.

"On life!" Graham said, gave Click one last pat and moved, finally, to Vanessa, where she was sprawled in a chair, her shoes already off, finishing her second bottle of water. Her rider specified that the water be Evian. It also specified a bottle of Grey Goose vodka, a bottle of Glenlivet, and a dozen fresh-cut red and white roses. She'd drink the water, but never drank the alcohol. She wouldn't give it away, either; she'd dump the contents either down the drain or down the toilet, and once or twice I caught her using it as a perfume.

The roses normally figured into the encore, when Van would go to the edge of the stage and give a couple to whoever had caught her eye during the show. It was the code—a fresh young male carrying a couple roses, red or white, got access backstage, and often access to even more than that.

Graham opened a third bottle of Evian for her, swapping it out for Van's empty, then crouched down beside the seat, his hands in front of him, cupped, as if he would catch whatever she might spill. Van took another swig from the bottle, then looked to Click, then to me, grinning. She was still a little out of breath from our close, and perspiration still shone on her arms and face. She looked at Graham and the grin got bigger.

"You may praise," she said, regally.

Click and I laughed, and Graham didn't miss the cue.

"I think a shrine, Vanessa. A shrine dedicated to you, a shrine befitting a goddess. You have ruined Christchurch for the next girl, there is no one to follow you."

"You were practicing that one," she said mildly.

"I was. I was, but I think it captures the essence."

"It wasn't bad."

"I'll swap you insurance for a statue," I told Van.

"Fuck that, I'll take either of yours for the walking dead," Click said.

Graham got to his feet, looking at all of us, touching one hand to his breast, faking the wound to his heart. "All I do for you, and yet you mock. Do I not care for you? Do I not provide for you? Do I not love you?"

We all told him that yes, he loved us very well, indeed, and we laughed more, and set about getting cleaned up and ready for the first wave of backstage passes and VIPs. As our manager, Graham is required to be our greatest advocate, but even his hyperbole knew some bounds; seeing him like this, tonight, was different, and only reinforced the sense of triumph.

The parade of visitors started, and we played nice with them all for another hour or so. Most of the flock went to Van, but Click and I had enough attention that we couldn't duck out without being rude. You never know who'll be coming backstage; we've had politicians and movie people, we've had local celebs who act like we should know them, and people who've won contests who act like we shouldn't. Sometimes someone from the label shows, or someone hooked into the Big Money, and they've got to be treated like insiders. So it's part of the job, to be nice backstage, and after a show like this one, it's even easy, and pleasant.

The last were two girls, late teens, with passes won at a local record store, and Click and I did our best to keep them engaged, getting them to talk about themselves, as Van finished with her clump.

Then Graham was at the door, telling us we had to get back to the hotel, and I walked the two girls out, giving them a handshake, thanking them for coming. Graham went with them down the hall, to make sure security got them out the rest of the way without trouble, and that left one person alone, outside, a good-looking white kid in his early twenties, holding three white roses.

"Hey, you," I said. "What's your name?"

He actually checked over his shoulder to see if I was possibly talking to someone else before giving me an answer. "Pete."

I nodded and stepped back, searching for Vanessa, who was getting the last of her things together. "His name is Pete," I told her. "He's waiting outside."

She grinned at me, a little caught, a little conspiratorially, and I thought what the hell, it's been a good night, I'll make it easy.

I leaned back out into the hall. "Hey, Pete—we're getting ready to go back to the hotel."

"Oh," he said. He did a bad job of hiding disappointment.

"You want to hold on a minute, you could probably ride back with Van."

It took him a second to parse it, to trace the thread to its inevitable conclusion. Then he said, "Oh," again, but this time it was far more enthusiastic.

"Be a second," I said, and closed the door.

"Thanks," Van said.

"Cute."

"God, yes."

"He a keeper?"

She shrugged, pulling her bag onto her shoulder. "I'll let you know in the morning."

Pete was enough of a keeper that he was at breakfast the next morning in the restaurant, looking dazed to be seated between Van and Graham. Click was there, too, but I didn't realize I was running late until I saw our tour manager, Leon, with them, as well. I caught the last of the day's marching orders, and then Van told Pete to go with Leon. I downed some orange juice, listening to their idle talk.

"Well?" I asked Van.

"Throwing him back," she told me.

I nodded and switched to coffee, doctoring it with way too much sugar, just for the added jump start. Click was working on an omelet, and Graham was futzing with his PDA.

"You hungover?" Van asked.

"Just a headache," I told her.

"Not coming down with something?"

"No, just a headache." I looked closer. "You've got a hickey."

Click and Graham both focused on her, and Van's hand flew to the side of her neck, alarm all across her face. Then she saw me grinning and picked up her butter knife, making a stabbing gesture.

"Not funny, Mim!"

"No, especially if he's not a keeper."

"Shut up, drink your coffee."

"Yes, my mistress."

Graham stowed his PDA, pulled out his briefcase, and started distributing photocopies.

"Came this morning. You are looking at a mock-up of the article that will run next week in *Rolling Stone*. Complete, I might add, with an image of Tailhook on the cover."

Conversation stopped for most of a minute as rustling paper and moving silverware took over the audio. The packets were ten pages, including a copy of the cover photo, stapled together, black-and-white. I skimmed, more interested in combating my headache than finding out how good or bad I looked, but Click and Vanessa both put full attention onto theirs.

"I'm 'The Body,' " Van announced after a moment. "Me, body."

"Not just any body," Graham said. "*The* Body."

"This'll be in color?"

"That's what I'm told. The article is mixed, some b/w, but your shots are color."

"The body?" I asked.

Van showed me the page she was looking at, a picture of her relaxing in a chair, head craned back but turned toward the camera, laughing and stretching. Her belly was bare, showing the hoop through her navel, the tone of her muscle. Not overtly sexual, but attractive. It was captioned with the words "The Body."

"Which makes Click?"

Both Click and Graham answered. " 'The Spine.' "

I went to my copy and flipped through. The picture had Click from the waist up, wearing his Winterhawks jersey, looking straight on at the camera with his hand-rolled cigarette drooping from a corner of his mouth. His smile in the shot was amused at the attention.

I flipped to what they said about me, and when I saw that I'd been labeled "The Brains," I laughed out loud. Then I saw the picture they were using.

I wasn't certain it was me at all for a couple of seconds. I just didn't think I looked like that, that I could ever look like that. The second thing was that I had no memory of it being taken, no recall of the moment when the camera turned on me to catch me in the pose.

It wasn't a studio shot, it was a candid, probably taken during the two weeks the interviewer had been in our shadow, and it looked like I was backstage someplace, alone, sitting on one of the metal gear boxes. Before a show, or maybe after, because I had my concert clothes on, the cargo pants and the tank top. The Tele in my hands, eyes closed, my head back, not exerting myself, just relaxed, just playing, maybe even singing. Light on me and shadow all around.

I'd never looked that good, that sexy, in all my life.

"Pretty hot," Graham said. "Pretty hot, indeed."

"You look three seconds from orgasm," Click observed.

"You've never seen me three seconds from orgasm. How would you know?" I told him.

"My imagination is active. It looks entirely sexual, it looks like you're getting off."

"Were it that easy."

"You've had a long-term relationship for a while now, haven't you?"

I held up my right hand. "Yes, the five of us are very happy together."

"That is a picture that will be on lockers," Graham told me. "That is a picture that gets reprinted, Mimser. *That* is a picture that immortalizes a rock star."

I wasn't sure what I felt about that.

From the look on Van's face, she wasn't, either.

The second night in Sydney, all of us—the band, the crew, everyone—went to a party at a club called Home. The party was thrown by the label, celebrating not just the *Rolling Stone* cover, but also the debut of our new single. "Queen of Swords." It had entered the *Billboard* Top Fifty at twenty-two, as they say, with a bullet, and it was a big fucking deal, because it meant we'd finally smashed out of the alt-rock circle, and now had a genuine mainstream hit on our hands.

I was drunk when I arrived at the party, having polished off the second fifth of Jack in the limo on the way over, and Graham had to shepherd me across the floor and to the VIP room before he could get to the serious business of glad-handing the reps. I stayed on a couch, watching pretty girls and handsome men and avoiding conversation, and at some point someone handed me another bottle, and I got to work on that until I couldn't work on anything anymore.

Sometime later, Graham helped me into my hotel room, got me onto my bed and the boots off my feet and the wastebasket by my head.

"Just put it in the goal, baby," he told me.

*   *   *

The next day was hell.

We had a live set to be played on local radio, and that had to be canceled, but there were two television appearances to do, and there was no way out of those. Graham had slept in my room, dozing in the easy chair by the desk, and every time I'd woken to vomit or use the bathroom, he'd been there.

The first television spot was live, for an audience, and when I saw myself on the monitors, I knew the makeup chair hadn't been enough. I looked awful, and even though my hands knew what to do, Van froze me out during the set, and even Click kept his distance. The worst part was that after we'd finished playing "Queen of Swords," the host wanted time with Van in the chair, and that meant that Click and I had to stay on the stage, beneath the lights. It took supreme effort to keep from being sick again.

Then we changed studios and did another set. This one went a little better, but not much.

As soon as we were finished, Graham carted me back to the hotel, and put me back to bed. The good news was that we had the night off. The bad was that we were flying to New York in the morning, to do an MTV gig, and that we were all supposed to meet in the lobby at six.

I thought that maybe, just maybe, I might be sober by then.

I was, but not enough that I realized what I was seeing when I reached the lobby the next morning. I had my bags and my flight case for the Tele, and I came out of the elevator and into the lobby with the dawn just starting to stream in through the hotel's windows, bouncing harsh off the marble floor. Beyond the service counter there was a little sitting area, and they were all already there, Van, Click, and Graham, seated around a little coffee table.

Click saw me making toward them first, and he reached out and tapped Van's bare knee through her torn Levi's, said something. She and Graham both looked my way, standing up, and Click followed to his feet a second later, slower.

None of them had any bags visible, and I supposed it could have meant that they'd already loaded them, but even as I thought that, I knew it wasn't the case. A weird tightness crawled across my chest, as if trying to squeeze, but from the inside, and I could feel my heart beating, not like it was faster, but as if it had suddenly grown larger, as if each pulse threatened to rupture my chest.

Van had one of her trademark tank tops on, a black one with a silver logo in its center. The logo was an image of a stylized, almost Art Deco, woman, standing in a swirling *G,* and beneath the letter was the word "Girlfiend." It was the name of a lesbian boutique in Los Angeles, on La Cienega, though Van didn't wear the shirt because she was advertising a preference; she wore it because it made the boys crazy. Her skin was clear and her eyes were bright, and her hair professionally unruly. She hadn't bothered with makeup, and when she smiled, her lips seemed to almost pale away against her face.

"Mim," she said, and for a moment I thought that I could get forgiveness without asking. Then the smile went away, and I wasn't going to see it again.

"This is ominous." I tried to make it sound flip. It didn't.

"We've got to talk about some changes." She was watching me closely, not quite staring, but really focusing. Then she gestured at the seat that Click had vacated and added, "You want to sit down?"

I looked at Graham, but Graham wasn't having any, focusing instead on the leather portfolio he was holding in his hands. Click barely gave me eye contact before looking away to Vanessa.

"You're canning me?" I directed it at Van, trying to keep my voice strong. It came out too loud, and bounced around the lobby. Early risers glanced our way.

"Why don't you sit down?" Van motioned at the chair again, then fell back into hers.

I stared at her, but she was only giving me her profile now, facing the empty seat. Neither Graham nor Click made a move or a sound.

I had to set down my bags to take the chair, and it was clumsy, and humiliating.

Van waited for me to get settled. "You were really fucked-up yesterday."

"Are you canning me?" I asked again.

Van shook her head slightly, as if to say that I had her wrong, that wasn't what this was about at all. "Been a long tour, Mim."

"Why won't you give me an answer?"

"Gonna be even longer, now that we've added all those European dates." She glanced past me, around the lobby. Out the windows, you could see the harbor and the opera house. "I'm not sure you're up to it."

"What—I don't even understand what ... what are you *saying*, Van?"

She focused on me again. "Your drinking's way out of control."

Heat flared in my cheeks and neck, and I realized the humiliation I'd been feeling had simply been the orchestra tuning up, going through their scales. We'd hit the overture now. I opened my mouth and couldn't find my voice enough to respond.

"We're worried about you."

"You bitch," I said.

"Mim, you were so drunk the second night in Melbourne you barely made it through the encore."

"My playing stands," I said. "My playing is solid, this is not about my fucking playing!"

"You don't need to shout."

"I can't believe you're doing this! You didn't have shit to sing before I came along, you were an actress with a rhythm section, that's it! Now you're cutting me loose because I drink? At least I'm not chasing dick onstage, Vanessa!"

She pinked up, and maybe was rethinking her choice of setting for the scene. "What I do in my time has never gotten in the way of the band."

"You're full of shit," I said. "This isn't about my drinking, that's just your fucking excuse. This is about that fucking *Stone* piece, that's what this is about."

"What?"

"You don't want me eclipsing your light. You don't want anyone looking past you and your bass to see me on guitar."

"Jesus, are you *still* drunk? You're not threatening me, Mim, and you never have. You *can't,* it's not *in* you. I've never argued that you weren't the better musician, the better writer. I've never pretended that wasn't the case. But if you were up front, Tailhook would never have come this far. Because even though you can play like fire, you're a crap showgirl."

"Fuck you—"

"This is about the band!"

The shout shut me, and everyone else in the lobby, up.

Van wiped her mouth with the back of her hand, lines digging in around her eyes. "Graham has a check for you. What you're owed from the last four gigs. He's got a ticket for you, too, back home, the flight's in a couple hours. I've talked to A&R and the label, and they know the situation, and I've told them that we're replacing you for the rest of the tour."

"You tell the press that I got canned because of a drinking problem, I will personally run a truck over you first chance I get."

"Jesus, Mim, I'm your *friend,* I would never do that!" She shook her head slightly, as if she couldn't believe I could be so hurtful. "There'll be a statement, saying that you're wasted from the tour, that you just need some time off. We'll be back home in June, and we'll talk then, see if we can't give it another try."

I stared at her, disbelieving. Graham had come over to my side, was crouching down on his haunches, opening the portfolio. He took two envelopes and tried to hand them to me, and when I wouldn't take them, dropped them in my lap. He murmured something to me, but I didn't hear it.

"You're really doing this," I said to Van.

"It's done."

"Who're you replacing me with? You replacing me with Birch? That beanpole son of a bitch?"

"Birch is busy."

"Who?"

"Oliver Clay. He's meeting us in New York day after tomorrow. That's when we're making the announcement."

The urge to cry was sudden and almost irresistible. "No, no way."

"It's Clay."

The finality in her voice was clear, but I tried one last time. "Don't do this to me, Van. Please don't leave me behind."

"You've got a flight to catch." She stood up. "We'll have your gear sent on as soon as we're back in the States."

I just sat there, watching as she walked away, toward the restaurant off the lobby. Graham followed close behind her, casting me a pitying glance. Click came around behind me, and put his hand on my shoulder, gave it a brief squeeze. Then his hand was gone, and when I looked up at him, he was walking away, too.

I felt the weight of everyone in that lobby staring at me as I got my bags together and went outside to catch a cab.

CHAPTER EIGHT

The sunlight came, assaulting me. It pulled at my eyelids, trying to scratch my corneas, and when I rolled to get away from it, my right hand lingered, not ready to come with me. I pulled, felt pain slicing through skin, and forced myself to look.

I was in bed, my bed. There was blood all over the pillow next to me, and my palm was stuck to it, flat. I lifted my hand, watching as the pillowcase followed the motion, and then the fabric ran out of play, and I was lifting the pillow, too. The pain came back. I gritted my teeth and pulled again, and the weight of the pillow peeled the accidental bandage free. Fresh blood began leaking to the surface.

The rhythm sections of several collegiate marching bands were working on a quick time in my head. When I tried to sit up, they went batshit, really going nuts. My stomach didn't appreciate it, either, and told me it wanted to leave, now.

I went to the bathroom and threw up, mostly dry heaves, and something that looked like it wasn't meant to actually be outside of me. When it was over I leaned back against the counter, staring at the shower stall, feeling shaky and hollow. The room smelled of vomit and stale beer, and there were shards of broken glass on the floor, and smears of blood. A bath towel was in a lump by the door. Blood had dried in mud brown on the white terry cloth, and I had a feeling it wouldn't ever come out.

Seeing the towel reminded me of my hand, which was still seeping. I reached up and pulled another towel from the rack, and just that left me breathless and queasy again. I wrapped my hand with the towel, went back to staring at the shower stall door. There was no water visible on the glass, and I tried to use that as some sort of benchmark for how long I'd been out. A while.

I was wearing a pair of sweatpants I'd forgotten I owned, and a T-shirt. There was some blood on the T-shirt, on the right sleeve, which I figured must have gotten there when I'd pulled the thing on. I couldn't remember doing that, but I couldn't remember trying to clean up spilled blood or getting into bed, either.

Somewhere, downstairs, the phone started ringing. There was a phone up here, too, but I didn't hear it. I was in no hurry to find out why. I was in no hurry to move.

I just wanted to curl up on the floor and die.

It was evening when I woke again, and I was cold from the tile, but this time my first urge wasn't to throw up, so that qualified as progress. I hadn't turned on any lights, and it was almost dark. I sat up and heard glass tinkling as I brushed it with my leg. My head throbbed, but it was endurable, though maybe this lack of illumination helped. My eyes didn't take long to adjust, and when I thought they and the rest of me were ready, I pulled myself to my feet using the counter, then picked my way to the light switch by the door.

The downstairs phone was ringing again. Or maybe it was ringing still.

Using the light from the bathroom, I made it to the switch in the bedroom, and turned that one on, too. Drops of dried blood peppered my new carpet, recounting my travel from bathroom to bed, and then the return trip. I perched on the edge of the mattress and unwrapped the towel from my hand, slowly. It stuck, like the pillowcase had, but not as much, and there was almost no fresh bleeding when it came free.

The downstairs phone went silent, and I looked for the upstairs one, to find out why it hadn't been participating, and discovered that I'd yanked the unit free from the cord at some point. Maybe it had been in response to it ringing. The other option was that I'd tried to make a call or four, and the thought of what such conversations would have been like almost sent me back to the bathroom.

After a while, I got up and found some slippers in the closet. I put them on and made my way downstairs, to the pantry. In the corner, I found the dustpan and brush.

It took me most of two hours to clean up the mess. When I'd finished, I had the broken glass out of the bathroom, the tile cleaned, the sheets on the bed changed, and the towels in the trash. I used the towels to cover all the empties I'd gathered. There were ten of them, not counting the broken one.

While I was cleaning up, the phone started ringing again. If someone wanted me badly enough, they could come and get me.

I took another shower and put a real bandage on the cut in my palm. The laceration didn't seem to have been so deep as to require much more than that, but once I had the bandage in place, I curled my hand, as if I was holding my pick, just to see if I could still do it. It ached, but I could still play.

I got dressed in clothes I hadn't worn for over a year, and discovered that I'd lost more weight than I'd thought. It's hard to eat well on the road, and I hadn't been nearly as religious about it as Van had, so it was kind of surprising. As I was tightening my belt, I realized that I was famished.

Back downstairs, I looked in the pantry again, at the shelves freshly stocked with boxes and cans I'd purchased with Mikel, and I didn't see anything I wanted to cook, let alone eat. I dug through the drawers and cabinets in the kitchen until I found the Yellow Pages, then found the listing for Kwan Ying's, picked up the phone to dial. The voice mail tone was active, but I ignored it and ordered dinner. I ordered Szechwan chicken, veggie lo mein, veggie spring rolls, hot and sour soup, won ton soup, and an extra side of white rice. The guy who took my order asked if I was entertaining.

"I used to be," I said.

After he confirmed that I'd be paying in cash, he hung up, and I did, too, then picked up the phone again and called the number to retrieve my voice mail. Voice mail makes getting messages easy when you're on the road, and I'd used it a lot in the past year.

The recorded lady told me that I had seventy-eight messages.

Just for kicks, I played the first one. The recording said it had been left "yesterday," which didn't tell me when today was, but made me nervous.

"Hi, Miriam, this is Jamie Rich, I don't know if you remember me. I did the piece on Tailhook for *Spin* last April, we had dinner at Canter's in L.A. I'm calling to see if you have anything to add to the statement Vanessa Parada and Click released this morning regarding your hiatus from the band. You can call me back at—"

I fast-forwarded through the rest of it, deleted it, and then hung up again.

Only seventy-seven of those left to go.

I ate my dinner, such as it was, in the front room, listening to Mark Knopfler's *Sailing to Philadelphia.* All I could really manage was half of the hot and sour soup, and a little white rice. I finished with a cigarette, listening to the whole album through, then hoisted myself and put the food in the fridge before returning to the stereo. I swapped discs and loaded all five slots with Dire Straits, the albums in chronological order up to *Brothers in Arms,* then climbed back on the couch and shut my eyes.

I started crying sometime during *Telegraph Road.*

I fell asleep somewhere in the middle of *Making Movies.*

*   *   *

I woke up to the doorbell ringing, and new sunlight coming through the blinds to warm me. I tumbled off the couch and stubbed my toe on the coffee table and swore and hopped into the hall, and the doorbell sounded off again as I was trying to disarm the alarm.

"Hold your fucking horses," I shouted, and punched the last digit and heard the cheerful bleat and yanked the front door open, ready to tell whoever it was to go to hell.

Which worked out fine, because it was Tommy.

CHAPTER NINE

Hello, Miriam," Tommy said. When I didn't respond, he added, "I was hoping we could talk."

He'd been almost my brother's age now when he'd been sent away to prison, and he was still so big I had to look up to see his face, even though I'd grown and he seemed to have shrunk. His black hair had taken on a lot of gray, and it was in his stubble, too, along his jaw and chin and above his mouth. His eyes seemed smaller, heavier, and there were a lot more wrinkles and creases on him, but they didn't sag, as if he'd earned them while on a diet. He was wearing canvas work pants, and work boots, and three shirts; a white T-shirt visible under a half-buttoned Pendleton flannel, covered by a thicker, quilted flannel, open. A pair of leather work gloves were stuck through his belt, riding at his hip, and a pack of Camels was resting in his T-shirt pocket.

I stared at him, the surprise already drowning in my anger, then stepped back and pushed the door open the rest of the way, gesturing to let him inside. He hesitated, then stepped over the threshold. After I closed the door, I put my back to him and made for the kitchen.

Tommy followed, looking around as he came. I ignored him, set to making coffee, measuring grounds and adding water. The clock on the microwave said it was 8:11 A.M.

"I didn't wake you, did I? I didn't mean to wake you."

My cigarettes were on the counter, so I shook one out and got it going, turning to keep an eye on him. He'd made it as far as the kitchen table, and was looking out the window into the backyard.

"You've got a nice home." It sounded a little cracked when he said it, as if his throat was parched. He turned his head to look at me, to see if he could get a visual response since I wasn't giving him an audible one. When I still didn't speak, he added, "This is a very nice place. Nice neighborhood, too."

I took some more smoke off my cigarette, staring at him. The coffeepot was nearly full, the pump inside wheezing the last hot water into the basket. I turned away to get myself a mug.

"Mikel told me that I shouldn't come by without calling first, that it probably wouldn't be a good idea," my father said. "I left you a message, but I guess you didn't get it."

The coffeemaker gave a dying gasp, pushing out the rest of the water, then rattled. I flicked some ash into the sink, then poured myself a cup. When I looked again, he'd taken the same seat Mikel had on Tuesday, his hands in front of him on the tabletop, one cupping the other.

"It's just that I was nearby. I got a job today, starts at nine, this construction site on Sandy. They're doing a renovation. Since I was in the neighborhood, I thought it wouldn't be too bad if I stopped by. To say hello. To see my girl."

My cigarette had died, and I ran the tap to kill the last of the embers, then dropped it in the trash under the sink. I lit another one.

"No ashtrays, huh?"

I drank some of my coffee.

The chair squeaked as he turned in it, dropping his hands back into his lap. He drew himself up with a breath, as if strengthening a resolve.

"I've heard your music, you know," he said. "Mikel has both of your albums—"

"There are *three* albums," I said.

The surprise was visible on his face, not that there was an album he didn't know about, but that I'd bothered to speak in the first place.

"I don't ... I never imagined that you would have a gift like that." He raised his hands slightly, as if showing their potential, as if they weren't his but were mine. "You remember that Silvertone we got from Sears? I guess that wasn't a good guitar, but you did like it, you'd sit on the couch and pluck on it for hours."

"It was a piece of shit," I said.

"We ran it through the hi-fi, you remember that? To get it to sound through the speakers, because you wanted an amp. The noise was awful. I thought your mother was going to throw us both out of the house."

I glared at him, trying to make him see that he'd crossed a line, that he'd crossed it a while back. Tommy lowered his hands, looked away.

"I just didn't know," he said. "That you could play those instruments and write those songs. And sing, too. You sing."

"Van sings. I do backup."

"Yes, I understand that, but there are a couple of songs where you're singing, and she—Vanessa?—is backing you up, too. I like those songs a lot."

"I can't sing very well," I told him.

His mouth worked slightly, and his head sort of shook and nodded a little bit at the same time. "Well, I liked those songs, the ones where you were singing."

"Thanks, Dad," I said.

The sarcasm hit him like a whip, and there was a brief instant where I saw something flicker in his eyes. Then it died away, and he looked like he had before, sad and lost, like I'd just kicked a three-legged puppy.

"I just ..." He took a breath, started again. "I've never forgiven myself for what I did to you, or your brother, or most of all, to your mother. I don't drink anymore, I don't take drugs anymore. I don't do those things that I used to do anymore. I know you're a grown-up woman, now, and I know you're famous and I know you're successful. But you're also my girl, and I want you to know that I'll try to be your father again, if you'll give me the chance to do that."

"You're not my father," I said. "My father's name is Steven Beckerman, and he died three months ago. He was a musician and he was a singer, and he died from aggressive cancer of the throat. He died unable to do the one thing that made him totally happy. My father taught me how to sing and he taught me how to read and write music. My father taught me how to play guitar, and I still have the first one he ever gave me, and when I play it, I hear him, and that's his legacy, that's what he taught me.

"All you ever taught me was how to drink."

He was silent for several seconds. "I can teach you how to stop."

"Why the fuck are you even here, Tommy?" I demanded. "Did you really figure you could show up and I'd say it was great to see you, all is forgiven? You killed her. You fucking killed her. Mikel may believe your bullshit, but I didn't then, and I sure don't now."

"It was an accident."

"I want you to leave."

He had more he wanted to say, it was all over his face. But whatever he saw in mine kept him from trying again, and he got up from the table. I walked after him to the front door.

"You know, I barely remember that day," Tommy said. "I was so drunk I barely remember anything that day until I was in the emergency room, looking at Diana as they pulled a sheet over her face."

"Shut up."

"What I'm saying is that you may be right."

"Just shut up, Tommy."

"Miriam, what I'm saying is that for fifteen years, I've thought every day about you and Mikel and that accident." He was blinking rapidly, as if there was grit in his eyes. The strain was making his voice climb little by little. "I don't want you to forgive me. I can't even forgive myself."

"Then what the hell do you want? Is it money? Is that why you're here?"

He looked horrified. "What? No—"

"I'll tell you what, Tommy. I'll go and write you a check right now, this very moment, if you can look me in the eye and stop lying long enough to say that it was murder, that it wasn't accidental. None of this, *I can't remember,* none of this, *I was drunk.*"

"Miriam—"

"What do you say? Thirty grand, would that do it? Just pulling a number from the air. I can go higher."

He stared at me.

"Fifty," I said. "Fifty grand, right now, you tell me you murdered her, you fucker."

Tommy reached for the door, headed out. The sunlight was bright, and made me wince. He started across the porch.

I stuck with him, feeling the cold of my porch on my bare feet. "Sixty," I said.

At the end of the walk, he made a right, heading down the block. There was an old gray Chevy parked at the curb, and I thought it was his, but he kept going past it. He'd shoved his hands in his pockets, lowered his head. A wind had risen, tearing leaves from branches up and down the street.

"Eighty, Tommy!" I shouted after him. "Eighty, all you have to do is say it!"

He kept walking away from me.

"I can go as high as a hundred," I said, but it was more to myself than to him.

My father disappeared around the corner. He hadn't looked back.

CHAPTER TEN

Her life was saved by rock and roll.
Here's how.

An ambulance came and took my mother and cops came and took Tommy, and our neighbor, Mrs. Ralleigh, came and took Mikel and me. In her living room across the street, she tried to get me to stop crying, tried to get Mikel to say something, anything. She was an elderly African-American woman who lived alone and would bring us fresh squash and green beans from her garden every fall, and her home smelled strange to me, both antiseptic and greasy all at once.

I kept trying to get up and run back outside, and Mrs. Ralleigh had to keep blocking me from the door, finally wrapping me in her arms and holding me on her couch until I stopped struggling and surrendered to sobs alone.

More cops arrived, and we watched them from the window, Mikel and I, working in the rain. There was one not in uniform, and he crossed over to us after a few minutes, knocking on the door. Mrs. Ralleigh went to answer it, and then they came back together.

"This is Detective Wagner," Mrs. Ralleigh told us.

Detective Wagner sat down opposite us, balancing a notepad on his thigh. He was using a chewed pencil to write with, and I could see he'd made drawings, too, what I know now were diagrams, trying to place positions, but then, I thought they were just doodles. I couldn't tell how old he was; he was ages younger than Mrs. Ralleigh, who I'd always thought was over a hundred, easy.

"Alice says that your name is Mikel," Detective Wagner said. "And that your name is Miriam, but that everyone calls you Mim."

Mikel didn't respond, just kept staring toward the window. I nodded, tried to wipe my eyes. I still had tears coming, and they weren't stopping. When I followed Mikel's gaze, I could see a man taking pictures of my father's truck, of the driveway, of the stainless steel bowl.

"I need to ask you both some questions. Will you let me ask you some questions about what happened?"

Nothing from Mikel, and again I nodded, and the detective came and sat next to me, gave me a pat on the arm, and started to write in his notepad everything I told him. His handwriting was very bad and I couldn't read anything on the paper. Mikel never said a word, and I was rambling, talking about trucks and jack-o'-lanterns and pumpkin seeds and yelling. It didn't matter. Wagner knew what had happened, he'd known it from the moment he entered Mrs. Ralleigh's home, maybe before.

Just like he knew that even as Mikel remained silent and I couldn't shut up, my father was already under arrest for the murder he'd committed.

Mrs. Ralleigh walked him to the door, leaving us in her front room. She and Detective Wagner talked before he left, and I caught bits of it, not trying to overhear, unable to avoid it. Words like "testify" and "trial" were used.

It wasn't until then that Mrs. Ralleigh asked if my mother was dead. The question made me angry, the answer so obvious. When Wagner confirmed that she had died on the way to the hospital, that my father had been arrested in the emergency room, I heard Mrs. Ralleigh say a prayer.

Then she asked, "What do I do with them?"

"We're trying to determine if there's family," Detective Wagner said.

"No, no, there's no one. Diana, she told me that last year, around Thanksgiving. It was just the four of them."

"Someone will be by."

"When?"

"Soon."

"I can keep them for the night. But I'm ... I just don't have it to keep them for longer. I'm too old."

"Someone will come by. Just keep them here for a couple more hours."

Then the door shut, and from the window I could see Detective Wagner as he went down the walk, back into the rain. The cops were still working across the street. He started talking to some of them, then used the walkie-talkie in one of the police cars. He glanced over to Mrs. Ralleigh's house once, and he saw my brother and me in the window.

He turned his back.

We were placed with our first foster family a week later.

I was eleven. Mikel was fifteen. Our father had murdered our mother, and now we were going to live with people we had never met before.

There was no way it could end well.

The Larkins were sweet people, good-hearted, born-again. They wanted it to work. The problem was they already had six kids, and two more with the designation "troubled" was just too much. I was easy. I just wouldn't speak unless there was no other alternative. At least I wasn't acting out, yet.

Mikel was acting out all over the place.

He'd been honing his "troubled youth" act even before our own family had been dissolved, and when we were placed with the Larkins, he went pro. If there was trouble, he'd find it; he got into fights, he stole money, booze, even a car. He robbed Mrs. Larkin blind, taking cash out of her purse when her back was turned, then disappearing for days on end. He got arrested three times, the last for a felony assault, and that was the one that did it; he ended up getting sent to Hillcrest, a juvenile facility outside of Salem.

Tommy had already been sentenced and sent off to the Oregon State Penitentiary at that point. He'd taken a plea, and that decision avoided a trial, which was a good thing, since a trial would only have served to make us all look like the Gresham White Trash we truly were; ignorant, barely literate, and certainly a burden on society. Two kids who were unremarkable at school, one of whom was already building a record; a mother with a string of arrests for drinking and disturbances; a father responsible for a record of his own, alcoholic, known to take drugs, unable to hold down a job; a history of State visits, monitoring the status of the kids; police reports on various domestic disturbances; emergency room bills leading to a conclusion of domestic violence.

So my mother was gone, my father was gone, and now Mikel was gone. The world had shifted onto an insane axis, and everything I'd been sure of turned out to be wrong. The only thing I could say was true was that I'd seen my family disappear entirely over the course of eight months.

So I did the inevitable, and picked up where Mikel had left off.

Three weeks after Mikel went to Hillcrest, I didn't come home after school, and that was the final straw for the Larkins. When I was finally escorted back to their home at four in the morning, I was drunk, with a Portland police officer at each shoulder. I'd gone home with a friend and stolen a fifth of Early Times from her parents' pantry, then lied and said I was going back to the Larkin home. Instead, I'd gone up to Mount Tabor Park and gotten shitfaced. Someone who was nice had found me passed out while walking their dogs and called the police.

All the kids were in bed, but Mrs. Larkin was up, and I remember the look on her face when she answered her door. Her eyes were swollen almost shut from crying and she took me from the officers and gave me a hug like I was one of her own. She didn't ask where I'd been, she just thanked the cops, told them that Mr. Larkin was out looking for me, driving around, but that he'd be back soon.

She put me in the shower, got me cleaned up and into a nightgown. Then she brought me to the room I shared with her two eldest daughters and put me in bed. She knelt beside me and kissed me on the forehead. The other girls were awake, but pretending not to be.

After Mrs. Larkin left, one of the girls said, "You're not very nice."

She was right. I wasn't very nice. There wasn't anything I could say to that.

Less than a month later I was moved to a new family, named Quick, outside of Salem. The move upset me; I was terrified Mikel wouldn't be able to find me.

The Quicks were middle-aged, with the father working for the state government, and the mother one of those über-moms who can juggle three Tupperware parties while organizing the school bake sale. They had two boys, both older than I was, one of them just sixteen, the other fourteen. Upon my arrival there was a family meeting where they all told me they understood things had been hard, and that they were willing to try if I was. I told them that I was willing to try, and they said that was good, and it lasted about three weeks, and then the brothers decided that since I wasn't really their real sister, maybe they could do some of those things they'd been hearing that boys do with girls.

It started with the older brother, Brian, urging the younger one, Chris, to put his hand down my shirt. I didn't know what he was after until he had his hand on my breast, at which point I shoved him, hard, and he fell down, hard, and hit his head on the corner of the bed and started howling. Mrs. Quick scooted in to find out what the commotion was about, and I told her, and she confronted Chris, who promptly denied it. Brian, standing by, backed him up, and told his mother that my attack had been unprovoked.

Two to one, I lost.

If that had been the end of it, I might have been able to take it.

It wasn't.

Realizing that they could get away with it, Brian and Chris proceeded to see just how far they could go. One of them figured out how to pick the lock on the bathroom door with a flathead screwdriver, and soon I was taking thirty-second showers. We'd be watching television and the moment a parent left us alone, Brian or Chris would grope me, or poke me, or, on one occasion, expose himself to me.

And I would shout at them to stop, would shout for someone to believe me, and Ma and Pa Quick would tell me that I needed to stop acting out, to stop trying to get attention. I needed to be a good girl, they told me. I needed to behave.

So that's how this is going to work, I realized, at which point I decided to hell with them. If this was what doing my best was going to get me, they could have my worst, and I gave it to them with both barrels.

That day I came back to the house because I thought Mrs. Quick was going to be at home like she'd said she would be, and I'd be protected. I was in the living room dropping my backpack when Brian and Chris came out of their room and told me they had something to show me.

"I don't want to see," I said.

"You do," Chris said. "You do."

"Just come in here," Brian said. "We've got something we want to show you."

It was the way he said it, it turned something in my stomach to lead. Precognition or instinct or something else, but I knew that if I ended up in their room, it would be very bad for me.

I grabbed my backpack and started for the door, and Brian moved to cut me off. Then Chris was coming in at my right, and they were grabbing me and pulling me and I was shouting and kicking and fighting.

"Grab her pants," Brian shouted. "Grab her by her pants!"

They dragged me, screaming and struggling, after them. Laughing. Like it was funny. I'd lost one of my sneakers, and my jeans were slipping down because of the way Chris was yanking on my pant legs, and I could feel the rug burning my back because my T-shirt was being pulled up by the friction on the hall carpet.

"C'mon, quit fighting!" Brian was shouting at me. "We're gonna fuck, it'll be fun!"

I kicked and pleaded, and it didn't do any good, and then suddenly both boys had let me go, and were staring over me, gone absolutely quiet. Looking like they'd seen their own death, the color just gone from their faces. I twisted and rolled and looked where they were looking.

Their father stood at the end of the hall, holding his jacket in one hand, his briefcase in the other. He'd been in the military, still had the haircut. Black hair with gray scattered through it, as if it was coming in a strand at a time, with no rhyme or reason.

The muscles jumping in his neck.

"What are you doing to Miriam?" he asked them. He set down his jacket and briefcase without taking his eyes from his boys, then moved to where I was on the carpet, lifted me to my feet.

Brian tried to answer. "Nothing, sir, we were just—"

"I heard," their father said. "I heard everything you said."

"But—"

"Don't move. If you move before I come back, God as my witness, I will put you both into the hospital."

Their father put a hand on my elbow, turned me back toward the kitchen. He set me in a chair at the table. There was perspiration on his upper lip. His hand felt like it was shaking when it let me go.

"Stay here," Mr. Quick said.

I nodded.

He was removing the belt from his waist as he went out of the kitchen.

When he returned, the belt was again at his waist, and he was carrying a suitcase and my missing sneaker. He told me that he would get the rest of my things later, but for now he was taking me to a hotel, because he didn't think it was fair to keep me under the same roof as those boys after what they had done, after everything that had happened. He told me that his wife would stay with me if that would make me feel more comfortable, and he told me that he was so very sorry.

Two days later I was placed with a new family.

When I left the Quicks, all I wanted was a place to stay, to be safe, and all I expected was another one of fate's split-finger fastballs right to my head. I figured if I remained with the new family, whoever they were, for more than six months, it would be a miracle.

The new family was named Beckerman, Steven and Joan.

I was with them for almost ten years.

They had a room ready, and the first thing that made me feel like this was going to be a good thing was that it wasn't decorated in pink. It didn't have stuffed animals on the bed. It was a girl's room, not a princess's.

And it had its own stereo, a real one, not a boom box, but an old four-component Denon unit, tuner, cassette, CD, and LP, hooked to two brand-new bookshelf Bose speakers. There were headphones, already plugged to the output jack, and it was like they were sending me a message—this is yours, use it whenever you want, but remember that we're here, too. No cautions about volume. Just, here's the headphones, knock yourself out.

Steven repaired instruments for a living, mostly tuning pianos. Joan taught music at various high schools throughout the Portland district. After hours or on weekends, they gave private lessons. Each of them called those things their jobs, what they did to keep the roof over their heads from leaking. Their jobs, not their work.

Music, that was their work.

They did it together, and I blame them both equally.

June, and school had ended, though I was scheduled for summer school in just a few weeks, a desperate attempt to bring me back in line with my classmates. I'd been with Steven and Joan just shy of two months, and the time hadn't been easy, because as much as I liked the room they'd made for me, I sure as hell didn't trust them. The longest conversation we'd had so far had concerned how I could get a letter to my brother, and if I could go and visit him soon. The answers were yes and no; I could write him all I wanted, but Mikel wasn't allowed visitors for the time being.

So for two months, I'd been quiet and self-absorbed, testing their boundaries, stealing their cigarettes, and getting more chores heaped on me as punishment. I wasn't as bad as I'd been with the Quicks, but I was getting ready to escalate.

They'd done their best to weather it. They'd seen me poking at the various instruments around the house, fiddling the keys on a trumpet, striking notes on the Steinway. Both of them had asked me if I had any interest in playing any of the instruments they had around. The flute, for instance, or the violin, or the clarinet, or the piano.

"No," I'd said.

A lie. But the last time I'd played an instrument had been when I was ten, and though I could still remember the thrill of it, I remembered the rest, too. The weakness of my hands and the failing of the guitar; Tommy's impatience with my inept fingers; my mother's annoyance, her telling me that I shouldn't play so loudly until I could at least play, you know, *well*.

It is impossible to practice an instrument quietly. Music, by its very definition, must be heard.

Dinner was finished, and I had cleared the table, doing my appointed chores. I finished drying the last of the dishes just as Joan was pouring coffee for herself and Steven. They both looked at me, the kind of look that always made me nervous. They looked pleased, and that had to mean that I'd done something wrong.

"Go to your room," Steven told me. He was smiling.

So was Joan.

"Why?"

"Go to your room and see."

Stupid games, I thought. Stupid people. Don't know anything about me. Don't know who I am or what I want and don't even care.

Making it as clear as possible with body language that I was doing them a big favor, I went to my room.

The guitar was on the bed, resting in an open case.

"Yours," Joan said. "Do whatever you want with it."

Steven added, "We'll be downstairs."

They left us alone.

It was a used Taylor acoustic, scratches on its body, gouges in the wood around the pick guard. The steel strings seemed to float just above the mahogany neck.

I sat down beside it on the bed and just stared at it, trying to figure out if I wanted to be bought this easily. It wasn't as sophisticated a thought as that, of course, but that's the only way I can think of it now.

The Taylor won out in the end.

I picked it up, held it the way I had seen Steven holding his guitar. I put my index finger on a string, it was the sixth string, the low E, and I struck the note.

I went downstairs with the guitar held in both hands, by the neck, and found Joan and Steven in the piano room, sitting side by side on the bench. Steven was smoking a cigarette and singing softly along to what his wife was playing, and then she saw me and let the notes trail off, and his voice followed.

I pushed the guitar out in front of me, toward them, and said, "Show me how."

Joan laughed, and Steven got up and went to get his acoustic, and we settled on the couch, and he started to teach. It was just after nine when he began, and he knew what I was after; he didn't talk about chords or sevenths or octaves or diatonic scales. He explained only the barest facts that I needed, just enough to get me playing notes that combined to make music that I could recognize. He showed me everything he was doing on his guitar, never touching me or mine, letting me mimic him. I was clumsy and awkward and my fingers kept slipping. My back ached from this strange new posture, the muscles in my neck throbbed because of the way I was craning my head, trying to watch both of my hands at once. The steel strings dug channels into my fingertips. My left hand, my fretting hand, cramped up.

"Stop," Steven said. "Take a break."

So for five minutes I stopped, massaging my hand, amazed at the blood on my fingertips, blood on the strings.

"It hurts," I told Steven.

"Your fingers'll get used to it," he said.

I picked up the Taylor again, and he made me review everything

I'd learned so far, and it still didn't seem like I was learning anything at all. It just seemed like we were playing with the guitars, having fun with each other.

Joan came back and announced that it was past one, and that she was going to go to bed.

"You go on up, hon," he said. "Mim and I are going to work at this a little longer."

"Don't stay up too much later," she told us.

"We won't," I said.

We were up until dawn.

CHAPTER ELEVEN

After Tommy left, I spent the day getting my life, and myself, back in order. Just checking through the now over a hundred voice mails took most of an hour, and almost every message was like the first had been, reporters wanting a story, demanding a comment. Near the end there were separate calls from Click and Graham, each wanting to confirm that I'd made it home safely. It bought them some grace, but not much.

There were two messages from Mikel, each left Wednesday, one in the morning and one that evening, check-in calls, much like Click's and Graham's. He left his mobile and asked me to call him back, and I didn't. It was clear to me that he'd told Tommy where I was, maybe even had told him it was safe to visit, and I was pretty fucking angry at my big brother.

I rewarded myself with a late lunch of cold Chinese food, another beer, and a trip down to my music room. The nice thing about playing in the basement was that I could play volume. I fed the Gibson through the VOX AC-30 and wailed on that for a while. It's a great unit, classic tube design, and it plays soft pretty well, but when you crank it up you get a lovely, shimmery sustain on the notes, as if the amp is breathing. I wasn't playing anything in particular, just noodling. I switched to one of my Strats after a while, trying to emulate some of the Knopfler I'd heard the night before, but my left just doesn't have the strength his does, and I can never get the same pop from the strings.

The cut on my palm opened again, and I shut everything down and went upstairs to change the bandage, and that's when I saw it had grown dark.

I also saw that my front door was wide open.

It wasn't like I went straight to panic, but I sure as hell accelerated to nervous. The alarm was off, had been throughout the day, ever since Tommy's visit, and I gave myself a mental kick for not having reset it.

I froze, straining to listen. Vague traffic sounds from the street, and the echo of the notes in my head, and now my heartbeat. But I didn't hear anything from the house, didn't hear anyone moving around upstairs.

Had I locked it? I couldn't remember if I'd locked it after Tommy had left. If I hadn't locked it, it was just possible that the door could have opened on its own.

No, it wasn't.

I slid forward and shut the door slowly, turning the knob so it wouldn't click when the latch struck, and looking over my shoulder the whole time, thinking that if it was the stalker, I didn't want him coming at me by surprise. But I didn't see him, I didn't hear him.

I suppose a different woman would have headed to the kitchen for the biggest knife in the rack, gotten herself all set to go hunting, geared herself up to reclaim her home or some bullshit. Someone maybe a few inches taller than me and a few pounds heavier, or who had taken lots of classes in self-defense or martial arts. A different woman would have assessed this situation, would have decided to be sure if her home had been invaded, and then would have gone on to kick ass and take names.

That woman sure as hell wasn't me, and it didn't look like she was going to drop by for a visit, either.

I had no illusions; if it was the stalker, he had a gun. There wasn't anything in my knife rack to beat that. Even if there was, I wouldn't have the first clue how to use it. And somehow, I didn't think plugging in the Tele and blasting some diatonics would save my skin.

But if I could trap him inside while I was getting outside, that wouldn't hurt.

The alarm had a thirty-second exit delay once it was armed. After that, the motion sensors in the hallways would be active, and anyone moving inside would trigger the system. Anyone trying to get in or out would trigger the alarm. At which point the Scanalert people would call the cops.

So if there really was someone lurking around my bedroom and rifling through my lingerie, I could trap him. If he stayed put for those thirty seconds, I'd own his sicko ass.

And thirty seconds, that was enough time for me to get the hell out of Dodge.

I put my thumb on the "arm" button and held my breath for the three seconds it took before the tone chimed and the countdown beeps started. As soon as they did, I bolted. My coat was on the kitchen chair, my keys were on the counter, and I grabbed each without breaking stride, then flew out the back door, slamming it behind me, making straight for my Jeep and keeping time in my head.

At eighteen beeps I was behind the wheel, and by twenty-seven I was screeching out of the driveway onto the street, and when I reached thirty and the alarm was armed, my headlights were splashing across the front of my house, over the fence and trees and the door, and I saw no one, I saw nothing.

"Got you, motherfucker," I said.

Then I saw him, pounding at an angle across my neighbor's yard, heading away from me in a desperate run. He was in the puddle of my headlights for barely an instant, and it wasn't long enough to be sure, but I thought it was the same guy, the same stalker, and I floored it down the street, trying to catch him. So what if he had a gun? As long as he kept heading away from me, I could run the bastard down.

His lead was enough that he beat me to the corner and he flew across the street without hesitating, and my lights caught him again, and again I thought it was the same guy, the same stalker, but he'd shaved his head, now, the long hair gone. I tore into the intersection after him, and there was a horn, shrill and to my right, and I slammed my brakes to keep from colliding with a blue Honda. I hit the horn and screamed some pretty crude outrage, trying to get around the Honda, but there was a Lexus SUV behind me now, and I couldn't go that way, either, couldn't do anything but watch as my stalker raced over a lawn, pulled himself over a fence, and disappeared into the darkness of a neighbor's backyard.

Just like that.

I drove aimlessly for twenty minutes, then found myself on Hawthorne, turning onto one of the side streets. It was just past ten when I pulled up outside the only place that had ever made me feel truly safe. There was a gentle glow from the north side of the ground floor, from one of the music rooms. It made things easier, but it made things harder. If the house had been dark, I probably would have just stayed in the car for a few minutes, then turned around and gone to a hotel, if not home.

I climbed out of the Jeep and cut across the lawn, then up the steps to the door. The porch had been redone while I was away; the last time I'd been by, it'd been the same rotting and sagging boards that had been in place for one hundred years. Now there was new cedar planking, and a new railing to match. The porch swing was still where I remembered it, though, and a puddle of rainwater sat beneath it, a couple of leaves sodden in the water.

There was piano audible through the door, and I listened for a second. Beethoven, and while I couldn't name the piece, it was Joan on the keys, and she was playing the way she did when she played for herself, and not an audience or a student. I pulled back the screen door and rang the bell, and the music stopped abruptly.

The door opened a fraction, then wider when she saw it was me, and Joan stood there, looking tired and a lot older than the last time I'd seen her.

"Miriam. This is a surprise."

I stepped into the hall. "I'm sorry it's so late."

"It's all right, of course it's all right. I didn't even know you were back in town."

"I got back early."

"You must have done. Last time I talked to Mikel, he said you'd be on the road until June. I thought if I saw you at the holidays, I'd be lucky." She closed the door and put a hand on my shoulder, already leading to the kitchen. "I've got some coffee, from Peet's. The kind you like, but it's decaf, if you want some."

"No trouble?"

"It's already made, honey. If it was trouble, I wouldn't offer."

That was a lie. If it was trouble, she'd have done it anyway.

Joan poured us two mugs, then put sugar and milk in mine before handing it over. I took a sip as she watched.

"Good?"

"Just perfect," I said.

"Good," Joan said again, but softly. She moved her mug from the counter to the kitchen table and took a seat, watching me.

The kitchen felt the same, looked the same, but for some cosmetic changes. There were still fliers stuck to the corkboard with thumbtacks, the poster for her Chicago recital in 1972. There was the framed picture of her and Steven and Chet Atkins still hanging by the door, and another, only a couple years old, of the two of them standing with Benny Green. There was a new one, too, not really a picture, but a framed one-page article on Steven and me from *Guitar Player* magazine, the "Pickups" column. It was maybe two years old, now, just after *Scandal*.

Joan saw me looking at it, didn't say anything. Her hair was a little more silver than the last time I'd seen her, eclipsing the brown, and it was shorter, only to her shoulders, when she'd used to wear it halfway down her back, in a braid. She was wearing casual clothes, baggy corduroys and a wool sweater, but the sleeves had been rolled back, to keep out of the way of her playing. She was wearing her glasses, not her contacts.

"You cut your hair," I said, as I moved to join her at the table.

"After the funeral. Why didn't you come home, Miriam?"

I didn't know how to give her the honest answer, so I gave her the one I'd used before, over the phone, when I told her I wouldn't be back for the memorial. I said, "We were shooting a video. I couldn't get out of it."

If Joan's look had been disapproving, the look she'd given me when I was sixteen and had stayed out past curfew, it would have been easier. But now, it was like she couldn't be bothered, and she nodded her head, maybe not believing me, but maybe not caring. She withdrew her hands, sighing.

Then she reached back and turned my palm up. "What happened?"

"Nothing, I cut it on the tour. Broken glass backstage, I picked it up and there you go. Cut myself. It got reopened somehow, I haven't had time to change the bandage."

"It's not too deep, is it?" Concern made her look even older, even more tired. "That's not why you're back, because of your hand?"

"I'm ... I needed some time off. Van and Click are still touring, they're going to finish out the schedule."

"I'm getting the first-aid kit."

"It's not a deal, Joan."

She retrieved the metal box with its scratched white enamel paint and brought it back to the table, flipping it open and telling me to keep my hand still, then began unwrapping the old bandage. When my palm was revealed she used some cotton and antiseptic to clean the dried blood away. Her fingers were long and very strong, pianist's fingers, with neatly trimmed nails. The second knuckle on almost every finger was slightly swollen, going arthritic. Steven used to massage her hands after she'd been playing for a while.

"Thanks," I said.

She murmured that it was all right while she tore the wrapping on a fresh square of gauze. "Looks nasty."

"It's just a cut."

"You should have someone look at it, honey. You don't want it to turn into something that threatens your playing."

"I'll do it tomorrow," I lied.

She used some strips of cloth tape to hold the gauze down. "You're as bad as Steven was."

I moved my look from her hands tending mine to her face, saw the bitterness. Steven had suffered from the sore throat for months before he'd been willing to see anyone about it, and even then, only because he'd started bringing up blood in the morning. By the time the cancer had been found, the only possible treatments for it had been devastating and, ultimately, futile ones. No one ever said so, at least not to me, but the feeling was that he'd just waited too long.

"I'll go to a doctor tomorrow," I said. "I promise."

Joan closed the kit and said, "You're a grown woman, you'll do what you like. You're home until June?"

I grinned. "That's the plan."

She didn't buy it. "Who's filling in for you?"

"Oliver Clay. You don't know him, out of L.A. He's good. He's not me, of course, but he's good."

The joke didn't even get a smirk. "Did you and Vanessa have another fight?"

I shook my head. "I just wanted to come home."

She started to frown, then stopped it before it could take hold, deciding to let this matter drop, too, which wasn't really like her. My coffee was getting cold, and it felt like it was cold in the house, too, as if the furnace wasn't working.

"I heard 'Queen of Swords,' " Joan said, after a moment. "You're doing things with the instrument that Steven would have been thrilled to hear. It's very accomplished playing."

"He wouldn't have thought it was too glib? I kept thinking he'd have told me I was being glib."

"No, he would have been very proud of you. Steven was always very proud of you."

Pressure came thundering hard behind my eyes, and my head began to ache, like I had a migraine. I wanted to say that I hadn't come back for the funeral because I'd been angry and scared. I wanted to say that if I could do it again I would do it right, I would be there for her. That I would know how to say good-bye to the man who, as far as I was concerned, was my father, more than the man who'd given me my genes.

But I hadn't, I'd chickened out and hidden in the Beverly Hilton behind all the bottles I could find.

Joan was looking at the clock on the stove, and getting to her feet, saying, "I've got to get to bed, sweetie. I've got to teach tomorrow, and I have to get up early."

I started to nod, then blurted, "Can I stay? Just in the guest room or maybe up in my old room, please?"

She stopped, looking surprised. "Of course you can, hon, if that's what you want."

I nodded again, more vigorously, feeling shamefully young.

Joan came around to my side of the table, dropping down on her haunches and putting her hands on my arms. It created strange nostalgia, as if the moment now could have been a moment ten years ago, with me in pubescent misery and Joan offering all the maternal guidance she knew how to give. She put a hand on my cheek.

"Sweetie, what's wrong?"

I tried to open my mouth and say something coherent, but there was just too much to say, all of a sudden, and none of it could come out. All I could do was shake my head and try to explain that I didn't want to sleep in my house alone, and she told me that she understood, and that I was always welcome, and that I should always know that.

"You're our little girl," Joan told me.

The sting of guilt stayed with me to morning.

CHAPTER TWELVE

When I came down in the morning, Joan was already up and preparing to head to work. She looked very proper for school—navy slacks and a cream blouse, the uniform of a woman ready to fill fresh young minds with the infinite possibilities of music. She pressed a mug of coffee into my hands, then went back to loading sheet music into her book bag.

"How'd you sleep?" she asked.

"Fine. You're teaching all day today?"

"Fridays are busy. I'm at school until three-thirty, then lessons until eight."

"I was thinking of taking you to dinner tonight. We could go to that Lebanese place you like, Riyadh's?"

"Tonight won't work, honey," Joan said, pulling the bag onto her shoulder. "I'll be exhausted. But tomorrow's a Saturday, and the only lessons I have are done by three. We can have dinner after that, if you like."

"I'll call you tomorrow."

"That would be fine."

I nodded, dumped the rest of my coffee out in the sink. She waited for me, and we walked outside together. It was clear and cold, but there was no wind, so the chill didn't hurt.

The old Volvo was in the driveway, and as I walked her to it, I asked, "You're okay? Do you need anything?"

"No, I'm fine."

"I've got plenty of money, now. I'd be happy to spend buckets on you. It's the least I can do."

She unlocked the door to her car, then stopped, holding the keys, looking at herself reflected in the window. I knew I'd said the wrong thing.

"I don't want charity," Joan said. "That's not what we ever wanted from you."

"That's not what I meant, Joan, I'm sorry—"

"Steven asked for you."

I didn't say anything.

"Would it have been so much to come home, Miriam?" she said. "Just for one day?"

"I couldn't."

"That's a lie. You didn't want to."

"I was filming—"

"That's the excuse. You were his *daughter*, Miriam."

Joan opened her mouth, ready to say more, to say what came next, but she abandoned it, shaking her head slightly instead. She climbed into the Volvo and tossed her bag across to the passenger's seat, then followed it herself. She fitted her seat belt, then the key, but didn't start the engine.

"We'll talk about it tomorrow. Over dinner."

"I'll call," I told her.

She nodded and started the engine, and I watched as she backed out of the driveway, then went to the Jeep. When I reached it, I turned around and looked back at the house.

It was still big and worn and old and wonderful, and yet it just didn't feel the same inside, and I understood enough to know it wasn't only because Steven was gone. Nothing is constant, nothing remains, and the things we rely on go so quickly, quicker when you try to keep them, it seems.

In that house I'd had happiness for a while, but it had gone, and I wasn't going to get it back.

I stopped for breakfast at this fresh juice and crêpe place near my house and ate, trying to decide if I was being brave or stupid heading home. Whichever it was, I pulled up just before nine to see Mikel's Land Rover parked out front. He saw me from the porch and followed the Jeep around the side of the house as I pulled into the garage. He was still going with the Gap casual look, wearing a duster that gave the whole thing a funky cowboy feel.

I got out with a scowl, ready to tear into him about Tommy, on top of everything else, but as he moved to meet me I could see that he was really upset. He got a folded piece of paper out of one of his pockets and was thrusting it at me.

"When did you pose for this?"

"Pose for what?"

"This, dammit." He was still trying to get me to take the folded sheet, and tension was in everything, in his words and in his movements. I hadn't seen him act this way for years, not since before he went into Hillcrest, and it made me nervous, because it reminded me of how Tommy could be. "I got it this morning, one of the Web guys I know e-mailed it to me."

"What is it?"

"It's a picture of you, Mim, what do you think it is? I'm asking if you posed for it."

I took the paper, unfolding it to its eight and a half by eleven, expecting one of the pub shots, or maybe the one from *Rolling Stone*.

That wasn't what I got.

It was color, a little pixilated, and I suppose it might have been possible to find it flattering in some way, but whatever way that was, I didn't see it. It explained perfectly why Mikel was so upset, though, and why he'd been waiting outside my door with it burning a hole in his soul. There are certain things that, I suspect, outrage any sister's brother.

Naked pictures of her circulating on the Internet probably tops that list.

There was no question that it was me, and even though the background was blurry and out of focus, I wasn't. The picture was snapped at an angle, as if from a slight elevation, and I was totally naked, full frontal onto the camera, but not looking into the lens. Both of my arms were up, like I was stretching, and my hands went out of the frame at the top of the shot. My head was canted down, as if I had just seen something on the floor, and it hid enough of my expression that I couldn't tell what I'd been feeling at the moment of capture. My mouth was open, as if I was speaking.

If the picture itself wasn't humiliating enough, someone, perhaps the photographer, had added some postproduction work. A blue border surrounded the image, thicker at the top and bottom than at the sides. In the space above the picture, in red letters, were the words MIRIAM BRACCA OF TAILHOOK. At the bottom, also in red letters, were the words WET, WILLING & WAITING.

The caption more than the image did it, made my face flush hot, and some of that heat leaked into my voice.

"Where did this come from?"

"Off the Internet someplace, one of those naked-celebrity Web sites. Did you know about this, Mim?"

I stared at the picture in my hand, shaking my head. There was nothing in the image that helped me place it in time and space, nothing to tell me where it had been taken, or when. It looked a little like a dressing room, maybe a venue someplace from the tour, but I couldn't tell, and I sure as hell didn't remember parading around a backstage anyplace in the nude. The best I could say was that I'd shaved my legs and pits fairly recently before the shot had been taken.

"It's on the Web?" I asked.

"It's all over the Web," Mikel told me, taking the picture back. "It's on newsgroups and Web sites, you know it is. Shit like this breeds on the Net. I'm asking again, did you pose for this, Mim?"

"You think I *would*?"

"It looks posed, Mim."

"It's not posed, Mikel! It's a fucking Peeping Tom shot!"

"Dammit, if you're lying to me again, I swear to God I'll put you through a wall! If you did this, if you got shit-faced and let some little fucker take happy-snaps of you, you tell me right now!"

The accusation was worse than looking at the picture, and I felt the heat in my cheeks intensify. "How can you even ask me that?"

"Because you're out of control! Because you do stupid shit and then when it's too late you pretend it never happened! And this is serious shit, Mim, this is out there, right now, don't you get that?" He took a couple of deep breaths, crumpling the photograph in his hand. His grip had turned his knuckles white. With his free hand he reached for my shoulder. "Let's go inside."

I didn't move until he'd let go of me, then walked dumbly down the driveway and around to the front of the house. The alarm started beeping as we came inside, and I tabbed in the code, and it beeped its A-C-E tone and then went silent. Mikel shut the door after himself, and I reached around him to lock it again, and he trailed me into the kitchen. I went to the back door, to look out into the yard, and lit a cigarette. In the reflection on the glass, I watched Mikel smooth the picture out on the counter, facedown by my toaster, so neither of us had to look at it.

"Could you have been drunk?" Mikel asked.

I made him wait before I said, "No."

"If you got drunk and don't remember—"

"That wasn't taken while I was drunk, Mikel."

"How do you know?"

"I'd remember."

"Sure you would. If you didn't pose for this, if you didn't let someone photograph you with your permission, then this isn't just a picture of my baby sister naked. This is some fucker spying on you, that's what this is."

"I didn't pose for it!" I shouted at his reflection, then turned and gave him the rest face to face. "Will you get that? None of us do shit like that! Hell, not even Van, and *Playboy* offered her a couple hundred grand to reconsider not four months ago."

He frowned, thinking. "Can you tell when it was taken? Or where?"

"I don't know! Maybe a dressing room someplace, but it could be a hotel room. I can't even make out the fucking background, how the fuck do I know where it was taken?"

"I think that was done on purpose. Looks like somebody used a Gaussian blur to break up the rest of the image around you."

"A what?"

"It's a graphics effect, real easy to do if you have Photoshop or another program like that. Just takes the image and messes it up. Mostly it's done as an artistic effect."

"That's not art."

Mikel looked at the paper lying on the counter, then grimaced and flipped it over again. "You should talk to a lawyer."

"I don't have a lawyer."

"Sure you do."

"No I don't."

"You must."

"If I do, nobody told me."

"Then call Van or Graham and find out, because you definitely need some legal advice, little sister."

I moved to the sink, flicked ash down the drain. It seemed like I'd finally caught my breath. Mikel didn't say anything, probably looking at the picture again while trying not to look at the parts of it that were me, and just the thought of it got my heart racing once more. How many people had seen it already? How many people I didn't know, and—God Almighty—how many that I *did*? Jesus Christ, what if Joan had seen it? Or Tommy?

For a moment, just for a moment, I thought I was going to vomit.

"I don't understand what's happening," I said, turning to face him.
"What do you mean?"

"I mean I get kicked out of the band and I come home and there's a man fucking stalking me and last night he's in my *house*—"

"He came *back*?"

"—and now you're showing me a picture of myself that maybe people all over the world have seen."

"Did you say he came back?"

"Last night. I think it was him. I don't know anymore. I'd been in the basement and the door was open and I set the alarm and ran, and then I saw this guy running down the block, but I didn't really get that good a look at him. It looked like the same guy, he looked the same, but the hair was different."

"Different how?"

"He'd shaved his head."

Mikel scowled. "Motherfucker."

"I don't understand this! I don't understand why this is happening to me!"

The scowl held for a moment longer, and then Mikel seemed to hear me, and it smoothed. "You're famous, Mim."

I shook my head.

"You are, and the sooner you admit that to yourself, the easier you'll find it is to deal with this stuff."

I pointed at the photograph. "How am I supposed to deal with that? How am I supposed to go outside? Fuck that, how the hell am I supposed to get onstage, thinking that maybe everyone in the audience has seen how I trim my bush?"

He winced. "See, that's something I didn't want to know."

"It's not funny!" I screeched.

"No, I know it's not." He came forward, put his hands on my arms. "Look, call a lawyer, okay? Get some legal advice."

I caught my breath, then nodded. Mikel gave me a hug, and I took it, but it didn't make me feel much better at all. I asked him if he wanted me to make coffee or anything, if he wanted to stick around, but he said he had to get going. He left the copy of the picture, saying that the lawyer might need it, and he gave me a kiss on the top of my head, and went out.

I locked up again after he went, then picked up the phone and dialed Graham's mobile number. I wasn't sure if he was in London yet, or if maybe they were in the air, or maybe even still in New York.

The phone rang twice before he answered. "Havers."

"Graham? It's Mim."

"Mim," he said, and he made the one word sound ominous. "You're home safely?"

"I'm home. I need some help, Graham."

"Mimser." He sighed, an echo on the phone. "You know I'm doing everything I can, baby, but Van's made up her mind—"

"It's not about Vanessa, Graham. I need to know, do I have a lawyer in town, here in Portland? Or does Tailhook, at least, have someone I can talk to about something?"

Caution caved to concern, probably more for Tailhook than for me. "You in trouble, sugar?"

"Do we, Graham?"

"Of course we do, he's been on retainer for two years now. Weren't you wondering where five percent was going every month?"

"What's his name?"

"What's this about, babe?"

Normally I didn't mind the "babes" and the "sweeties" and the "honeys" but right now it made me want to reach through the phone and throttle him. "It's about naked pictures of me on the fucking Internet, Graham! Now will you give me the goddamn name and the goddamn number for this goddamn attorney?"

There was a pause, and I was getting angrier, thinking he was trying to determine if I was full of shit or not, then realized he was pulling the listing up on his PDA.

"Fred Chapel," Graham said, then rattled off a string of digits. I didn't have a loose piece of paper anywhere, so I ended up writing the number on the back of the picture. "This is just about you? Nothing about Van or Click?"

"No, Graham." I snapped it at him. "I'm the only one who's being humiliated."

"Hon, I've got to ask—"

I hung up, then started dialing Chapel's number.

The receptionist transferred me to Chapel as soon as she had my name, and without my having to ask. So even though I didn't know who Fred Chapel was prior to five minutes ago, at least I was assured that he and his staff knew who I was.

Fred Chapel came on the line and greeted me like we'd spoken just yesterday, instead of never.

"Miriam, what can I do for you today?"

"I'm in Portland, I don't know if you heard about that."

"Yes, Graham told me. How are you feeling?"

"Can I come and see you?"

"Is it urgent?"

"There are nude pictures of me being sold on the Internet."

"Are you getting a percentage?"

"This isn't a joke."

"It was a serious question."

"Wouldn't a percentage require my permission? And if I'd given permission, do you think I'd be calling you?"

"Can you be here in twenty minutes?"

"I can be there in ten," I said, but I was lying.

I was there in eight.

CHAPTER THIRTEEN

C hapel's office was near the PSU campus in downtown Portland, on the other side of the Willamette from where I lived, just off Market Street. I pulled into the parking garage just before ten and then rode the elevator up to the offices of Chapel, Jones & Nozemack. The offices were nice, comfortable and quiet, and the receptionist behind the desk was extremely pretty, and she recognized me the moment I came in, giving me a big smile.

I wasn't even at her desk before she was speaking into her headset, saying, "Mr. Chapel? Miriam Bracca is here to see you ... yes, sir, right away."

"You took my line," I told the receptionist. "Now I don't know what to say."

She looked immediately and sincerely apologetic. "Oh, I'm sorry."

"No, it's okay."

"You can head on back." She indicated the interior door, still giving me the big smile.

"I don't know where I'm going."

"Just left and down the hall. You can't miss it."

I thanked her and went through the door and left, and down the hall. There were framed posters on the wall, and four of them were Tailhook related—our covers and the European version of the tour advertisement. There were also a couple movie posters featuring actors and directors and writers who lived in the Rose City, and a promotional poster from last year's Rose Festival. Apparently Chapel, Jones & Nozemack were a civic-minded firm.

The office door was ajar, and I knocked on it before pushing it open further, sticking my head inside. The last lawyer's office I could really remember spending any time in had been the Multnomah County District Attorney's, and Chapel's office bore about as much resemblance to that as fish do to penguins. It was clean and bright, with a chrome desk and black leather chairs and black modular filing cabinets, and two walls were windows, giving a view of the river and the eastern sprawl of the city. I could see Mount Hood in the distance, snow-covered and sharp against the sky. The tinting on the window made the heavens look touched with green.

Chapel came around his desk to greet me, extending one hand while using the other to pull his headset off. The headset looked better suited to Mission Control than the legal profession. Fred Chapel himself was maybe in his early forties, but that was a guess, and maybe not a good one, because nothing else about him really indicated a specific age as much as a lifestyle. He was wearing blue jeans that looked either well cared for or brand-new, and a bright multicolored sweater, and black leather walking shoes that I knew had to have come from Europe, because that was the only other place I'd ever seen them. His face was smooth and tanned, which meant he either spent a lot of the winter out of town, or under a lamp someplace, and his teeth were very white, and he smiled like he'd known me forever and was always glad to see me.

"Mim, please have a seat," he said. "You want something to drink? Coffee or water?"

"No. Thanks."

He dropped back into his chair, smiled. "Graham called about three minutes after you did."

"Did he?"

"It's a Tailhook issue as much as it's an issue for you."

"I'd think it's more for me."

"He said you'd say something like that. But you're still part of Tailhook." He extended an open hand. "Did you bring it?"

I hesitated, then pulled the folded sheet from my pocket and handed it to him. Chapel unfolded the paper and looked it over, then raised his gaze past it and looked me over in much the same way, and though there was nothing reductive or objectifying in the gaze, I couldn't look at him while he did it, and so settled on the view of Mount Hood out the window instead.

"Is it possible that the photograph is a fake?" Fred Chapel asked. "Could someone have edited your head from a publicity shot and then grafted it onto the body of someone else?"

"It's me."

"You're positive?"

"If it's a fake, they're working from an original," I said, shrugging out of my jacket. His look was quizzical, then turned to slight alarm as I began pulling off my overshirt.

I let him worry while I got my arms out of my sleeves, leaving the shirt around my neck, revealing the tank I was wearing beneath. I turned in the chair, left and then right, showing him each of my arms. "The ink's the same."

"You've had shots showing the tats," he said, musing as I got my shirt back in place. "Could be whoever did this just edited the tattoos, as well. Doesn't seem likely, though. Can I ask where you got this copy?"

"My brother gave it to me this morning."

"Did he say how he got it?"

"Someone e-mailed it to him."

"Your brother has friends e-mailing him pictures like this of his sister?"

"I think this was a friend asking if he knew about this, rather than saying, hey, your sister's got a great rack."

He didn't smile. "Do you know where the friend got it?"

"Mikel—that's my brother—said it was off of some pay site, one of those ones that does naked-celebrity pictures."

"Do you know the name of the site?"

I shook my head. "But I can give Mikel a call, he'll know."

"Maybe later. One of my assistants is looking on-line right now. When he gets back to me we'll want to determine if the sites are the same. Let's assume for the time being that the picture really is of you, and not a fake, then."

"I've never posed nude for anyone," I said.

"Never?"

I just looked at him.

"Maybe for a boyfriend, for fun? Or as something romantic be-tween the two of you?"

"You're confusing me with Vanessa. She's the one with all the boys. I'm the one who sits in the hotel room with a guitar in her lap and crap on the TV."

Chapel grinned. "You're keeping your sense of humor, that's good."

"Am I? I'm not trying to be funny."

"Can I ask you some questions?"

"You mean more questions? Sure." I freed a cigarette and stopped myself from lighting it long enough to get a nod from him.

He took an ashtray from a desk drawer and slid it over to me. "You have any idea when or where the picture could have been taken?"

"I don't know. I've been in over one hundred hotel rooms this past year, easy. It's not a dressing room, I'm sure of that. I can't remember ever being totally naked in a dressing room. In my undies, yeah, but not in the buff."

"So you think it's from the tour?"

"It must have been."

"Do you take drugs?"

The question surprised me, but only a bit. "I did a few on tour."

"You understand why I'm asking?"

"You're worried that there might be pictures of that, too."

"I'm not judging you here, please understand that," Chapel said. "This is all confidential, between us, unless you tell me you're going to commit a crime. That happens, I'm obligated to act."

"Not planning on it."

"Always good to know. So this is between the two of us. But I want to be prepared if more pictures surface, maybe showing things you'd rather the world didn't see."

"I never did drugs alone," I told him. "Parties sometimes, or with Click, but never alone."

"What about sex?"

"What about sex?"

He gave me the professionally reassuring smile. "I hear you rock stars get a lot of it."

"I'm not one of them."

"You never took a groupie backstage or back to your room?"

"Wasn't my thing. Van's thing, sometimes Click's thing. Never my thing."

"Are you gay, Mim?"

I stared at him.

"Like I said, I'm not judging. Just asking. I told you Graham called."

I fidgeted, feeling the heat come back, rising along my neck. "Yeah."

"I asked him a lot of these questions, too, just for background. He says he remembers you taking a groupie back to the hotel when you were in Montreal. He remembers it because it was the only time he can recall it happening. He also remembers it because it was another woman."

"I don't remember doing anything like that."

"It's important, because if you took someone back to your room, I'm less inclined to think that's a setup, rather than you going with a groupie to her house."

"Well, it never happened," I said. "So you don't really need to worry about that."

Chapel stared at me, then nodded slightly, as if willing to let it go for the time being. "All right, could the picture have been taken with your permission and you just forgot about it?"

I crushed my cigarette out, lit another one. I didn't want to get bitchy, but I felt it, and I knew it was in my eyes.

"I understand you drink pretty heavily," Chapel said. "That's why you're on hiatus."

"That's why Van says I'm on hiatus."

"I understand that there were a couple of instances on the road where you passed out."

"I never missed a gig. I never couldn't play."

"Would you call it passing out or blacking out?"

I snorted smoke at him. "There's a difference?"

"When someone passes out, they don't do anything else. When someone blacks out, they don't know what else they might be doing."

"Sometimes I black out," I admitted.

"So it's possible you could have had a blackout on the road and someone could have taken these shots then?"

"No."

"You sound awfully certain considering that you wouldn't be able to remember."

"I am."

"Why?"

"Because when I drink like that, I drink alone. Consequently, I black out alone."

That stopped the questions for a few moments. Chapel's hand went to the folded photograph on the desk, almost idly, caressing the edge with his fingers. Then he leaned forward and rested his arms on the desk.

"These are our options as I see it. Further action, or possible action toward prosecution, will require discovering who took the picture, and how. I can get a TRO against the Web site, as soon as it's identified."

"TRO?"

"A temporary restraining order."

"I don't want temporary. I want it stopped for good."

"A TRO is the first step in any injunction, so we'll have to start with that. It won't be a problem, you've got multiple grounds—appropriation, right to publicity, public disclosure of private facts, even emotional distress. The TRO will force the site to take the image down. Then there's the issue of damages."

"I don't want money. I want it stopped."

"I understand. But there's the issue of where the photograph came from, how the site acquired it. Until we know who took the picture, we can't move against them. And if they have multiple images, we could have the same problem, but at a different site. I can contact the Portland PD, let them know about this. Oregon has a specific statute for this kind of crime, the 'Video Voyeur' statute—a lot of states have yet to address this issue specifically, so we're ahead there. We can even contact the FBI, since this is obviously an interstate activity."

There was a new tone in his voice, not a lack of confidence, but almost a hesitation, a lack of conviction.

"You don't sound certain," I said.

Chapel made a slight shrug. "We talk to law enforcement, and it really doesn't matter if it's local or federal, we'll get publicity. As soon as that happens, this picture will be everywhere, we're talking millions of people around the world seeing it. A TRO won't stop people from e-mailing it to each other."

I just sat there, trying to fathom a million people looking at the picture. It was too abstract to be humiliating. Sitting opposite Chapel when he looked at the photo was one thing; a million teen boys at their computers was something else. But then I thought of those three kids at the Fred Meyer, the way they'd looked at me then, and the way they would look at me now.

It hit me that I was totally helpless, and I opened my mouth to tell Chapel as much, but then there was a knock at his office door. I turned in my chair as another man leaned through the doorway. He

was younger and dressed a little more formally than Chapel. He gave
me a glance, then looked to Chapel.

"Fred? You should check your e-mail."

"You find the site?"

The man glanced my way again, as if he couldn't help it. "Two of
them. You should check the e-mail. I'll be in my office."

He pulled the door gently shut after him. Chapel was already clicking his mouse, focused on his monitor. I felt the same slow-motion-
can't-stop-it-something's-wrong feeling coming on me, the way it had
when I'd entered the lobby in Sydney to see Van and Click and Graham
all waiting to give me my walking papers. My hands were trembling,
the way they never trembled before a gig.

"How bad?" I asked.

He frowned at the screen. I got out of the chair, started to come
around his desk. Chapel put a hand up, as if ready to swivel the monitor away from me, but I was already at his shoulder, then, and he
dropped the arm, conceding.

The pictures were open in a viewing window on the monitor, side
by side, and it took only an instant to realize why his instinct had been
to hide them from me, only an instant to realize just how bad it was.

What stung was the pose—hand on my hip, hips cocked to the side,
pouting. It would have been a convincing mockery of a Van pose, if
I'd been clothed and not holding a bottle of beer. As it was, it looked
like I was giving the photographer an eager show.

The border—again the blue and red motif—once more named me
as Miriam Bracca of Tailhook, but this time the caption read HERE
SHE CUMS AGAIN.

It was Picture Three, though, that was like a punch in the stomach.

I was lying on my back, on a bed, the sheets mussed beneath me,
and again I was totally naked. The shot was from above, as if the photographer had straddled my body, looking down. My eyes were half-
closed, my mouth slightly open, my hair a mess, and some of it hung
over my eyes, but not enough to disguise my features. My right hand

extended up above the pillows and out of the frame, with the shot cropped just above my knees.

My left hand was resting between my thighs.

The caption read COME MAKE PUSSY PURR.

Chapel hadn't moved in his chair, hadn't even turned to look at me, but I put my back to him, anyway, trying to find something else to see. Mount Hood didn't help; it didn't matter where I looked.

Me with my hand between my thighs. Me with one hand between my thighs and the other over my head, and what's next, a shot with me taking it from behind?

I put my head against the window, closed my eyes. The glass was cold and a relief against my skin.

So now I'm a whore, I thought. Now the world thinks I'm a drunk *and* a whore.

Graham and Click and Van would see these pictures, they'd see them, the people at the label would see them, the reporters and the photographers and Pete from Christchurch and the groupie from Montreal. Joan's students would see these pictures, would trade them back and forth in e-mails, maybe print them out, maybe bring them to school. Would they tell her? Would they laugh? Would she see them, too?

"Miriam—"

I shook my head. I didn't trust my voice, I didn't trust that I could tell him to be quiet, to go to hell. I was thinking of Steven and how at least he couldn't see his daughter like this, wouldn't know that the world had seen it, too. God in heaven, even *I* thought it looked like I was doing myself, that damn pose, that left between my legs, my right above my head, I might as well have been arching into it—

"Miriam—"

I snapped back, launched myself at the desk, grabbing past Chapel for the mouse. I clicked in vain, frustrated, tried to find a way to do what I wanted, but I couldn't make the computer go, and Chapel had to reach for my arm, saying my name again.

"Mim. Calm down."

I shoved the mouse, stepped back, pointing at the screen, at the third picture.

"I'll close them—"

"No!" I snarled. "No, no, my *arm,* dammit, my arm, in the picture."

Chapel looked at me, utterly lost.

I jabbed my index finger at the picture, at my right arm, extending out of the frame. "There!"

He looked from it back to me, then again, bewildered. "I don't—"

"Bigger! Make it bigger!"

Chapel hesitated, but only for a second, then took the mouse and began clicking. He surrounded my arm, clicked again, and it filled the screen. Glorious full color, my arm.

With blood just barely visible, seeping out from beneath it.

Chapel turned, confused and concerned and hoping for an explanation, and I just couldn't talk. The only thing I could give him was my right hand, palm up, the bandage Joan had put on me still wrapped around it.

He looked from my palm to my face, still not getting it, and he said, "I don't understand—"

"Home," I managed.

CHAPTER FOURTEEN

There were three of them, from a firm called Burchett Security: a woman in her early thirties who looked strong and intense and never spoke and frankly scared me; a man in his late twenties who reminded me of the sailors who'd attended the Tailhook shows we'd played in San Diego; and Richard Burchett himself, who was perhaps in his mid-fifties, light brown hair a little shaggy, beard and mustache trimmed, in Levi's and cowboy boots and a St. Louis Cardinals fan shirt.

Chapel told me that they were professional, thorough, and discreet. He told me they knew what they were doing. He told me to trust them.

Burchett and his crew used gadgets that they held in their hands and gadgets that hung from their belts and gadgets that they slung over their shoulders. They wore headphones and waved magic metallic wands. They dismantled outlets and fixtures and searched moldings and pictures and unplugged appliances and utilities. They moved furniture and lifted rugs, and every time they found something, they used a little pin with a hot pink plastic flag on its end to mark the location.

They'd used twelve of those pink plastic flags before they were through.

Chapel sat with me on the back porch while Burchett and his crew did their work, and that was when I told him about my two stalker incidents.

"You were abducted at gunpoint and you didn't think to call me?" He looked like he was on the verge of a seizure. "What the hell were you thinking?"

"I didn't fucking know you existed," I reminded him.

"Tell me you at least called the police."

"They thought I was full of shit. They didn't go so far as to actually say it, but it was pretty evident that that's what they thought. They told me it was probably a mugging gone wrong or something like that."

"A man points a gun at you, puts you in the back of his truck, strips you, and they call that a mugging gone wrong?" Chapel shook his head.

"They wanted me to go to a doctor, have a rape kit done."

"Did you?"

"I wasn't raped. The only time he ever touched me was to get me into the truck." I thought about it for a couple seconds, then said, "Maybe that's why, you know? He wasn't about me, he was about the cameras. Maybe that's what he was doing, why he was in the house last night."

"Maybe, but then why the whole bit with the truck and the clothes the first time?"

"I don't know."

"You called the cops after last night?"

I shook my head.

"You should have called the cops as soon as you were out of the house."

"They didn't seem to take me real seriously the first time."

"You should have called them, anyway."

"So we'll call them now."

"You could, but with the discovery of the cameras, we'll have the same situation we were talking about at the office. Unless you've changed your mind about the media."

"No, I haven't."

"Then we don't call the cops at this juncture. We'll see what Rick finds, take it from there."

I didn't say anything, and he went back inside, to follow Burchett and his people around, leaving me alone. After a few minutes I went down to the music room and grabbed the Taylor, then returned to the porch. It seemed best to stay out of everyone's way.

I played for a bit, but nothing sounded right, and after a while I gave up. Once I started thinking about the pictures again, about all the people who had seen them, and all the people who would see them, and it was enough to start me feeling good and sorry for myself, and it almost brought tears.

But it brought a memory, too, of being maybe seven or eight years old on a late summer afternoon, the coolness of our tract home in Gresham. Tommy, still in his work clothes, caked in a mix of dried sweat and cement dust. He'd bought a six of Coors and a pack of Marlboros, and dropped himself on the couch to smoke and drink and listen to music on the hi-fi, and I was sitting with him, my head against his chest as we listened to Gordon Lightfoot singing "The Wreck of the Edmund Fitzgerald."

And Tommy had gotten all weepy at the end of the song, and I'd asked him why someone would make a song like that, about something so horrible and sad.

"Because sometimes making a song about something sad is the only way to understand it," he'd told me.

It made me wonder if Tommy ever had a song he wanted to write.

*   *   *

Chapel and Burchett came outside together a little before three that afternoon to give me the joy.

"We're done with the sweep, miss," Burchett told me. "If you want to see what we've found?"

"Not if I'm going to be photographed doing it."

He grinned big. "Made sure that won't happen, miss."

"You should see," Chapel told me. "It'll help you decide what you want to do next."

I had several ideas of what I wanted to do next, but I kept them to myself, since mostly they consisted of violence and alcohol, not necessarily in that order. I got off the steps and dusted my butt off, then nodded for them to lead the way.

We went through the kitchen, where Burchett's colleagues were packing their gadgets into shiny metal containers not unlike my flight case. The scary woman watched me as I followed Chapel and Burchett, and I wondered what her problem was, then wondered if it was that she'd seen the pictures, and so didn't ask.

Burchett led the way to the music room in the basement, and we started there, working the same path they'd presumably taken in their search. He pointed out each pink flag, even though they were easy enough to spot. It was an alarming education.

One flag in the music room. One flag in the downstairs bathroom, in the medicine cabinet over the sink, so that anyone looking—or grooming—in the mirror would be seen. One flag in the downstairs guest room, positioned so it could catch anything or anyone that happened onto the futon. Two flags in the kitchen, presumably in case things got exciting while I was fixing a late-night snack. Two more in the living room. Two in the master bathroom: one of them angled to catch anything happening in the shower or tub; the other one, and Burchett was impressed by this, set in the outlet between the mirrors over the sinks.

The last three flags were all in my bedroom. One directly over my bed. One in the wall just over the headboard. The last one in the outlet by the bureau, to catch me in the mornings when I picked out my day's lingerie.

"And you know what the irony of this is?" I said to them, standing in my bedroom, looking at all of the little flags. "I fucking hate pink."

Chapel smiled thinly, but Burchett laughed out loud.

"Fred says that some pervert pulled a gun on you when you got into town Monday morning. Says he got you into his truck and had you give him your clothes, that right?"

"Yeah."

"And you think that same guy was in your house last night?"

"Maybe, I'm not sure."

"Any sign of a break-in?"

I shook my head.

Burchett scratched his beard, craned his head back to look around my bedroom again. "You started renovating about when?"

"When I left on tour."

"And they finished when?"

"Last month, the beginning of September. I'm not positive of the date."

Burchett looked at Chapel. "That's when this was done, Fred. Our pervert must have gotten himself onto one of the crews working here, maybe working with an electrician. Hell, he could *be* the electrician. Gives him access to the whole house, lets him wire everything just the way he wants. He probably got a copy of the house key from the contractor or someone."

"Then why the hell did he do all that stuff Monday morning?" I asked.

Burchett reached for the Leatherman on his belt, snapping out the Phillips head, then leaned past me and began unscrewing the cover to the outlet by my bureau. Chapel and I waited, watching. It didn't take him long, and he hummed while he worked. Johnny Cash, "Ring of Fire."

When he removed the cover, he pointed to a portion of the wall, just above the lower outlet. There was a black smudge on the paint, a teardrop shape.

"Scorch mark," Burchett told us. "The camera shorted. He must have been trying to replace it."

"And if he'd been listening for news of when she was going to return home, he'd have known she was on her way," Chapel said.

"But he got me outside," I said. "He wasn't inside."

Burchett began replacing the plate over the outlets, his brow furrowed. "Maybe there were two of them, working together. You get one in the house when you come home, the other is outside waiting. He sees you, panics, thinks he can't let you go inside. That would explain why he dropped you off here when he was through. All he wanted to do was keep you occupied for an hour or so."

"There's the little detail where he had me strip for him."

"Yeah, but he didn't touch you, right? And if he has your clothes, you're less likely to make a break for it, irrational modesty being what it is. He takes your clothes, you're going to stay put until the danger is so great your modesty comes second. For most people, by the way, the point when their modesty stops being first is normally right after too late."

"Could the partner be the one you saw last night?" Chapel asked.

"I don't know. Maybe. But if one of them was fixing the camera Tuesday morning, then why'd he come back last night?"

"Well, could've had another short, maybe. Might've forgotten something, something that he thought would incriminate him."

"Or maybe he wasn't here to work on the cameras," Chapel said.

Burchett frowned at him, then glanced at me. He looked embarrassed, and it took me a second longer to realize why, that he'd been thinking the same thing Chapel had, but hadn't wanted to say it.

So I said it for them both. "You think last night he came here to rape me."

"We don't know that," Burchett said, replacing the Leatherman in the pouch on his belt. "Got one more thing to show you."

"I think I've seen enough."

"We're almost through." He smiled reassurance at me, then opened my closet and stepped inside, sliding my clothes down along the rod and revealing the access door into the attic space. He shoved it open and crawled through, then called back for me to follow. I ducked and shimmied after him.

It was dusty and dim, the only illumination the sunlight slanting through the small vent at the front of the house, and it smelled of insulation and wood and stale air. Cobwebs hung off the rafters, and I swiped at them uselessly as I got to my feet. There was just enough room to stand, hunched, if you were short like myself or Burchett. Chapel, when he came through, stayed on his knees.

Burchett had moved forward and when I reached his side, he indicated the vent. Through the slats I could glimpse the street out front of the house, the tops of the apple and elm trees in my yard.

It took me another second before I could make out the antenna, short and stubby and rubber and black, attached to the underside of one of the slats. From outside, in the shadow of the house, it would have been invisible. Burchett had crouched and was fumbling beneath the crossbeams, and then he came up with what looked like a thin rectangular box, also black plastic. It had another antenna attached to it, even stubbier than the first, and a row of three lights, all of them off. A power cord ran away from it, disappearing in the insulation at our feet.

"The transmitter," Burchett explained. "Broadband wireless; you can get one at just about any computer hardware store for a couple hundred bucks. All of the cameras in the house send to this little guy here, you see? Then this fella, he beams the signal to another unit somewhere, maybe only a couple blocks from here, maybe up to a mile away, and it downloads the signal onto tape or maybe even direct to a hard drive."

"Tape?"

"The cameras, they're video, Miss Bracca, not still-image. Those pictures of you, they're not photographs, they're video captures. This guy is taking videos of you, selecting the image he wants, pulling that, and cleaning it up. You see?"

I did see, and it alarmed me enough that I shot a glance back to Chapel, where he was wedged just inside the access way. From his expression, I knew that he'd seen it, too, was probably a lap ahead of me.

"There's a fucking *tape*?"

"It's possible." Burchett looked at the unit in his hands, then back to me. "What do you want me to do with it?"

"Is it off?"

"Yes, ma'am. We did a frequency trap before disconnecting it, so there's no need for it to ever get switched back on." He moved the box to his left hand, went into the coin pocket on his Levi's with his right, coming out with a thin and short metal tube that he held between his thumb and index finger for me to see. "This is one of the cameras. Not much to look at."

There was a bead of glass on one end of the tube, two tiny wires running from the other. In the light I wasn't sure, but the wires looked white and black. The whole thing wasn't much longer or thicker than a matchstick.

"Easy to place, easy to hide, gives a stable enough image," Burchett continued. "You have the right software, you can clean up whatever it provides pretty nice. Not terribly expensive, either. The technology's gotten to the point that this is bush-league stuff."

"Hurrah for technology," I said.

Chapel finally spoke up. "Rick? How long to get this stuff out of her house?"

"Take us maybe an hour to disconnect everything, get it all pulled and all the little holes spackled so that you can't much tell they were ever here."

"Then do it," I said.

"Then what?" Chapel asked.

"Then what *what*?" I asked.

"There's a question of the tape."

"Potential tape," Burchett said. "Miss Bracca got home four days ago, that's nearly a hundred hours of video if the perv who did this kept it all. That's not likely, Fred. Gets expensive."

"Just one tape is a problem, Rick. None of us wants to see a 'Bracca Uncovered' video hitting the Web."

"No, don't suppose we do."

"Then I want to know who did this. And I want to make sure they don't have anything damaging to my client."

"More damaging," I said, but I said it softly, and neither of them heard me.

Burchett was nodding. "With the frequency, we can track back to the receiver. But we'll have to move on that fast. Our perv here most likely already knows his system's gone down. He might guess we're on to him."

"Then get on it."

"We could call the police."

"No," I said. "No cops, no publicity. Bad enough the pictures are out there, I don't want the whole world seeing me like that."

"Rick, you'll have to handle this yourself," Chapel said.

Burchett smiled, nodded his head at me as if tipping the brim of a hat, and I realized what it was that made him so disarming, and that maybe made him as good as Chapel said he was. A man he might be, but in that gesture, you could see the kid who wanted to be a cowboy when he grew up.

As if to prove me right, he said, "We'll get saddled up."

Burchett left with the scary woman, leaving the other guy to remove all the pink flags and the cameras they marked, and Chapel told me that he needed to get back to the office, but that I should call him if I wanted anything.

"You going to call Graham?" I asked him.

"That was my intention."

"You're going to tell him about the other pictures?"

"I don't see how I can't."

I nodded, not liking it. It was stupid, maybe, but I knew what would happen as soon as Graham got the news. He traveled with a laptop, and it wouldn't take long before Click and Van saw the pictures. Click would be bad enough, but the thought of Van staring at those images was hard to take. She'd see it not so much as my humiliation, but proof that she'd been right about me all along.

Chapel left me with his home number, and the number for his mobile, as well as the number for Burchett. He told me he'd get in touch as soon as he heard anything, and that I shouldn't worry, things were well in hand, now. I walked him to the door, and when he was gone I went to the kitchen and got myself a beer, not really giving a damn what the remaining member of Burchett Security might think of that behavior.

I was halfway through the bottle when I realized just how set up I had been, and that brought some dark thoughts running home. Whoever had done this, they'd done it with a lot of time to spare. They'd done it easily, and covered themselves well.

Which made me think it had been an inside job, someone working with the carpenters or the electricians or someone.

There was only one person who had been inside while I'd been on tour, who could come and go as he pleased.

There was early rush-hour traffic on the bridges crossing the Willamette, and it took me close to twenty minutes to get from my place in Irvington to Mikel's in the Northwest Hills. His condo was in a cluster of similar units, designed to look like Victorian town houses, off Westover. It was high enough that, on a clear day, you could see all of Portland spreading out to the east, with Mount Hood's snowcap glistening in the far distance, and to the north, the broken top of Mount Saint Helens.

On a clear day. Not today, not with the evening clouds rolling in, heavy with payloads from the Pacific.

I parked on the street and strode to his front door, trying to think of what I would say if Tommy was there. Probably tell him to get the hell away from me, that I didn't want to see him, that what I had was for Mikel's ears alone. I'd seemed able to bully Tommy pretty successfully once already, so maybe it would work a second time.

All of the tenant spaces were empty except for Mikel's, which was filled by his Land Rover, so I knew he was home, and I figured none of his neighbors were, yet. Tommy hadn't brought a car when he'd visited me, but that didn't mean he didn't have one.

I knocked and didn't get an answer, so I knocked again, harder, and still didn't get an answer. It was starting to tick me off, to make my suspicions seem all the more grounded.

All of his alarm about the picture when he'd shown it to me, his need to hear me say that I hadn't posed. I'd taken it as concern, but maybe it wasn't concern as much as guilt. Maybe the cops had been right all along, that Mikel had let one of his friends crash at my place. And maybe that friend had made me his personal hobby, his cottage industry.

"Dammit, Mikel, open up!"

I pounded harder and even threw the toe of my boot, just for the added noise. No response.

I stopped banging the door, mostly to give my hand a rest. A wind had kicked up, making the trees along the hillside whisper. Distantly, I heard the whistle of an Amtrak train sliding into Union Station.

"Fucker," I muttered, and tried the knob for the hell of it, and it turned easy, and the door came open.

From where I was standing in the doorway, I could see somebody's leg at the end of the hall, sticking out from the living room. A whiff of alcohol and vomit, the scents of my bathroom, brushed my face.

I moved a couple steps forward, across the threshold. Everything in my chest felt like it was compressing, crumpling under pressure.

"Mikel?" I asked.

This time, when he didn't answer, I knew why.

My brother lay on his side, the way he must have fallen, and there was dark blood down his front and his back, seeping into the white carpet. His eyes and his mouth were open, and I knew he had been in pain when he died.

I took it in, then saw the rest. The empty cans scattered on the carpet, the overturned chairs, the broken lamp.

My vision started to swim. I put a hand out on the wall, caught myself, tried to remember to breathe. The alcohol and puke smell was stronger. Something cracked, vibrating in my body, through my chest. Like I was the wishbone at somebody's dinner party, like I was the losing end.

I heard myself moaning, though whether that was in my head or out of my mouth, I'm not sure. The wind outside got louder.

And again, it started to rain.

CHAPTER FIFTEEN

Somehow I kept it together long enough to make it home, but I was fighting panic when I came through the door, and I nearly forgot to turn the alarm off before it started screaming. I shucked out of my jacket and went into the kitchen, and I cracked the seal on a new bottle of Jack and drank from it standing there, pulling again and again until the burn was too much and I had to stop for air.

I didn't even bother with a chair, just slumped to the floor, bottle in my hand, feeling eleven again, feeling the world spinning out of control once more.

Not again, I thought. Not again, please not again.

I was in the backyard, face up to the falling rain, a new bottle in my hand, when the cops arrived. I'd been out there for an hour or so, singing to myself, and when I heard the car stop and the doors slam, I knew it was them, and decided to be a model citizen and go around front to meet them.

At the side of the house I leaned, turning my head so I could peek around the corner. The car was one of the Portland PD unmarked ones, white but glowing a little orange in the light from the street. It had a radio antenna mounted on the center of the trunk.

There were two of them at the door, up on my porch, a man and a woman. Both of them were white, and I couldn't tell their age. The man was saying, "... know who she is, right?"

"I don't fucking care who she is," the woman said.

The man grunted and leaned on my doorbell again.

I said, "Over here."

They turned and looked at me, doing a good job of not acting like I'd surprised them. Objectively, I must have looked like a drowned rat, my T-shirt and jeans soaked, my hair stuck to my skull. The woman came off the porch first, reaching into an inside pocket, the man following her.

"Miriam Bracca?"

"You found her," I said, and pulled at the bottle again.

The woman hid annoyance by flashing her badge. "My name's Hoffman. This is Detective Marcus."

"Sure," I said. "So, did you find him?"

Marcus glanced at Hoffman, but Hoffman didn't take her eyes off me. "Find who?"

"Tommy."

"Tommy?"

"My. Dad."

"Why would we want to find your dad?" I thought Marcus was trying to sound very casual, but that it didn't work, and that he sounded cagey instead.

" 'Cause he killed my brother," I said. "Killed my mother, too, but that was a long time ago. Mikel, that was new. I think he did that today."

They watched me, so I took another drink from the bottle.

"Maybe you'd better come with us," Hoffman said, and she came forward to help, but I backed up and waved her off.

"Why? I haven't done anything."

"How did you know Mikel Bracca was dead?"

The woman had to be an utter fucking moron. "Because I saw him. I went over there this afternoon to talk, well, not talk, to yell at him, but he didn't answer the door and it was open, so I went in and he was there and he was dead."

"Okay, yeah," Hoffman said. "You're going to come with us."

"I'm not," I said, indignant.

"Yeah, you are," she said, like she really wasn't very interested, and she took handcuffs out from beneath her jacket and her partner was now at my side and taking the bottle out of my hand, and when I protested, he didn't care, and when I tried to back away farther, he tried to grab my arms. I flailed and fell back with a splash, and the bottle fell and didn't break. Then they were both helping me up, and my hands were behind my back and I couldn't move them and that hurt.

"I want my lawyer," I said.

"I'll just bet you do," Marcus said, and he led me to their car.

CHAPTER SIXTEEN

They made me kiss the Breathalyzer, and ran a wet cotton swab over the backs of my hands before putting me in a cell to sober up. I passed out, only to be roused by an officer who dragged me to an interrogation room upstairs. It was cold, and even though my clothes had mostly dried, I sat there shivering. The drunk had gone, leaving me with a thickness in my head.

Marcus came in first, carrying two paper cups of coffee, one in each hand, and a legal pad clamped beneath his arm. Now that I could make him out, he looked parked in his late thirties, not unattractively so. He was maybe five foot ten or eleven, not as big as Tommy or Mikel, but with the kind of broad shoulders that Van went nuts for on a guy. The suit he was wearing was dark, charcoal and black, with a black tie and a white shirt, and even after what was probably a long night, he looked neat and pressed.

Marcus gave me a grin as he reached the table, offering me one of the cups. I decided to thank him.

"Sure. You want an aspirin?"

"Aspirin would be great."

"I'll see if we can find you some," he said, and he went out again, leaving the pad and a pen behind on the table along with his coffee.

I waited and drank coffee and waited some more, and it seemed another long time before he returned. He had a paper cup of water this time, and aspirin, and Hoffman, too. She'd brought a file with her, and held it with one hand as she took a position leaning against the wall, where she could keep an eye on both of us. Marcus took the seat opposite me, and slid over the water and the aspirin.

I took them both, draining the cup, then thanked him again.

"Not what you're used to, I'd guess, huh?"

"What?"

He indicated the empty water cup. "Tap water."

"No, it's ... it's great," I said.

He smiled and leaned back.

"Am I under arrest?" I asked.

"Do you want to be?"

"No."

"Well, let's see if you can help us out here, and then you won't have to worry about that."

"It's just that I have a lawyer," I said. "I'm thinking I should probably call him."

"If you want to, sure, but it seems like a waste of his time and your money to me. We've just got a couple questions."

I looked over at Hoffman, idly tapping the end of her file against the cinder block wall. The look she returned was utterly flat, like she was looking through me, almost like I wasn't there at all. Her hair was light brown, and she wore it full but short, and it ended about the middle of her neck. She had navy slacks and a black blouse and a black jacket. Like her partner, she seemed fit, but unlike him, she seemed long, rather than compact. I'd seen enough lately of how costumers dressed women to know that Hoffman knew she was attractive, and didn't mind letting others see that, too. She wasn't wearing any makeup, and I didn't see any jewelry on her, either.

I looked back at Marcus, who sat waiting patiently.

"I guess it's okay," I said.

"Yeah, I'm sure it will be," he agreed, and he uncapped his pen. "So why don't we start with you finding your brother, okay?"

I told him how I'd found Mikel, what I'd seen. He didn't interrupt, scribbling on the pad, and when I glanced at Hoffman, she was still looking through me. It was making me uncomfortable.

When I finished, he asked me to tell it to him again, just to make sure he'd gotten it all down right, and after I'd told it all a second time, he nodded and smiled and leaned back in his chair.

"So why were you in such a hurry to see your brother?"

I shook my head.

"Oh, c'mon, Mim. This has been easy so far, why make it hard now?"

"I really would rather not."

"Was it to score? Is that why you went to see him?"

"Oh, God, no," I said. "No. Jesus."

"You know your brother dealt?"

I shrugged.

"But he didn't deal for you?"

"No. I'm fine with alcohol. Anything stronger, I retain water."

He grinned. "No sign of that."

"He never gave me drugs, I never bought drugs from him. That's not what happened, anyway, this isn't a drug thing. It's Tommy."

"So you said. Why do you think that?"

"Isn't it obvious?"

"Well, it may be, but I'm asking you."

"Look," I said, trying to be patient. "Tommy's a drunk, okay? It runs in the family. When I was eleven he got loaded and ran over our mother with his pickup, and he did it on purpose, and that's the worst example of what he did drunk, but not the only one by a long shot. He got out of OSP a little while ago, he was staying with Mikel. Tommy got loaded and angry and shot Mikel."

"Not the other way around?" Hoffman asked. "Not Mikel got loaded and angry and your father just defended himself?"

"Mikel didn't drink. He didn't use, either. He just sold the stuff."

"Yeah, that makes it so much better," Hoffman muttered, and went back to tapping her folder.

"Did Mikel own a gun?" Marcus asked.

"Not that I know of."

"Did Tommy?"

"Well, he must have, because he shot Mikel."

Marcus nodded, as if my logic was unimpeachable.

"Was Mikel violent?" Hoffman asked.

I glared at her. "No."

"What about your father? Tommy?"

"Of course he's fucking violent, I just told you, he murdered our mother!"

Hoffman's expression curled, got a little tighter, and I finally realized what I was seeing. She didn't like me. Maybe it was principle, maybe she was one of those fuck-you-rock-star types. Whatever. It was fine. I didn't think I liked her much, either.

"When was the last time you saw your brother alive?" Marcus asked.

"Yesterday morning. He came over to my house."

"So you saw him the day he died."

"That's what I just said."

"What'd you talk about?"

I shook my head. "I really can't say."

"You can't or you won't?" Hoffman sounded snotty about it.

"I don't want to, how about that?"

She turned her attention to her partner. "This is a waste of time. Let's get this over and book her."

"Tracy, calm down," Marcus said.

"No, she's pulling this bitch rock-princess act, she doesn't give a damn her own brother was murdered, she's holding out on us, the only reason to do that is guilt, far as I'm concerned."

Marcus appealed to me. "Mim, you've got to help us out, here."

I looked at him, then at Hoffman, then back to him, then figured it out.

"Good-cop, bad-cop, right? That's what you're doing now?"

"Actually, we're both good cops. My partner's just a little annoyed that you're holding out on us."

I considered, then asked, "Have you found Tommy?"

"We're not talking about Tommy, we're talking about you," Hoffman said.

"Why won't you answer my question?"

"Why did we find blood in your bathroom?" she asked.

The question threw me, coming unexpectedly. "You searched my house?"

"We had a warrant."

I showed her my right palm. "I cut my fucking hand. I bleed when that happens."

"Have you disposed of any clothes?"

"Disposed? What, you mean like thrown out?"

"Yes, I mean like thrown out."

"No."

"We only found blood on one shirt, not much. Most of it seems to be on the towels and a pillow and its case."

"That's because most of my bleeding was on the towels and the pillowcase," I snapped.

"Lot of blood," Hoffman said. "I'd think it'd have gotten on some clothes."

"It didn't."

"Why not?"

"Because I was naked when I cut myself," I told her.

If she had a mental image, it didn't impress her.

"What about Tommy?" Marcus asked. "When was the last time you saw him?"

"Thursday morning. First time I'd seen him in fifteen years was Thursday morning."

"Did your father say anything about Mikel when he came over? Did he indicate that he and your brother weren't getting along?"

"We didn't talk about that."

"What did you talk about?"

I glared at Hoffman again. She took it the way she'd taken everything else so far. "He told me he'd heard my music and that he wanted to be my dad again."

Marcus asked, "Did he ask you for money?"

"No."

"Did you *give* him money?"

"No."

"I'm asking because you seemed uncertain there, for a second," Marcus said.

"I offered him money. He didn't take it."

"I get the impression you don't like your father. Tommy."

I bit off a laugh. "No, I don't."

"So why offer him money? Did you want him to leave you alone?"

I shook my head a little, then nodded a little. "Yeah. No. I wanted him to leave me alone, but that's not why I offered him money. I thought that maybe that was what *he* wanted, but he didn't take it, he just left."

Hoffman sighed. "So you offered him money to leave you alone? Is that what you're saying?"

"No, I offered him money to admit that he had meant to kill my mother, that it wasn't an accident."

"You said it was murder," Marcus said.

"I say it's murder, he says he was too drunk to remember. He pled to manslaughter."

"Why don't you tell us what you and your brother talked about?"

I shook my head. "If my lawyer says it's okay, I'll tell you, but I really have to talk to him first."

Marcus shrugged. "It's your choice, like I said, but—"

"Yeah, I know, but I really want to talk to my lawyer," I said. "Right now."

Marcus's smile melted, and he capped his pen and flipped the pages of his legal pad, then got to his feet with a little sigh. Hoffman shoved off from the wall, went to the door, and leaned out to call to someone. A uniformed officer appeared in the doorway, and Hoffman told him that I wanted to use the phone. The officer nodded, glancing at me, then did a double take.

"You go with him," Marcus said. "He'll take you to a phone."

"Thank you."

"Oh, it's the least we can do," Hoffman said. "After all, you've been so helpful."

CHAPTER SEVENTEEN

They let me use the phone at one of the detective desks, and I dialed Chapel while my guardian officer stood by, just far enough to stay out of earshot if I kept my voice low, but close enough to stop me if I decided to make a break for it. There were other cops around, too, other people I assumed were detectives, and they each took their turn staring at me.

The clock on the wall said it was twenty-seven past six, and the lightening gray out the windows confirmed that it was in the morning. I had to call Chapel's office, because that was the only number I could find, and I got an answering service, and the guy who took the call asked if he could take a message.

"No, actually, you can't," I said. "You need to call him and say that Miriam Bracca's been arrested."

The answering-service guy told me he would do just that, and I hung up, thinking that it wouldn't be long before Chapel called back. The officer moved me from the desk to a cheap plastic bench on the other side of the room to wait. Hoffman and Marcus went to their desks and proceeded to ignore me.

The clock read three minutes to seven when Chapel walked through the door. His hair was wet, either from his morning shower or the still falling rain, and he was wearing a suit today, and it fit him perfectly. He made straight for me, and he didn't look happy at all, and Hoffman and Marcus saw him enter, and moved to join us, but he beat them to it.

"How long have you been here?" Chapel asked me.

"I'm not sure, maybe six, seven hours."

"Dammit, Mim, why didn't you call me sooner?"

"She couldn't," Hoffman told him. "She was drunk off her ass."

"Repeat that outside of this room, it's slander," Chapel told her.

"Actually, Mr. Chapel, it isn't," Marcus said. "I'll swear out an affidavit to that effect, if you like."

"I'll let you know if it's necessary," he said. "Is she under arrest?"

Hoffman shook her head.

"Splendid. Now I'd like to speak to Miss Bracca alone, if you don't mind."

"Be our guest," Hoffman said.

Chapel and I talked for most of an hour, with me laying out every damn thing, including my reason for storming over to Mikel's and the large quantity of Jack Daniel's I'd consumed on getting home. I fumbled some of it, and he made me go over those parts again, and when I had to describe finding Mikel, it made me want to start crying, because it was finally sinking in.

"I didn't tell them about the pictures," I said. "I don't suppose it matters now, but I didn't."

"No, it really doesn't," Chapel said. "I'm going to have to tell them about that."

I nodded.

"All right, I'll talk to them now. You just sit tight."

I nodded again, feeling my exhaustion.

It took another fifteen minutes, at the end of which all three of them came back.

"Let's go," Chapel told me.

"We're done?"

"For now," Marcus said. "We know how to reach you if we need you."

We were in the elevator going down to the garage when Chapel said, "You can't go home."

"But—"

"Mim, the media's going to climb on this like nobody's business. They'll be camping outside of your place, they'll be dogging you everywhere you go. Unless you want that, and my read on your personality is that you really don't, you can't go home."

"I could stay with Joan."

"Joan's your lover?"

"God, what is it with you? Joan's my foster mother!"

He shook his head. "The press can find her, it won't be secure enough. I want to check you into a hotel."

"I don't want to go to a hotel."

"It's either that or meet the press."

The elevator stopped, and we were in the garage. Chapel led the way to his TT, popping the locks with his remote. He put me in the passenger seat and told me to buckle up, then went around to his door.

"What hotel?" I asked.

"The Heathman."

At least it was a nice hotel.

"Duck," he said.

We were on the exit ramp, about to hit the street, and I didn't get it, just looked at him blankly.

"Duck, dammit," Chapel said again, and he reached over with his free hand and took my head and shoved me down, and then I got it.

"You're shitting me," I said, more to the floorboard than to him.

"Wish I was. All local affiliates have vans, and I'm seeing multiple photographers. Stay down."

"I don't have anything," I said, feeling miserable. "I don't have clothes or anything for a hotel."

"Don't worry about it."

"I need to change clothes."

"Give me your sizes, I'll have someone pick you up some things."

"But my guitars are at home."

"You can buy a new guitar, Mim." He checked his mirrors. "Okay, you can come up for air, now."

I sat up, craned around in my seat. We were already a block away, but I could see the vans. He hadn't been exaggerating. I also saw that we weren't headed for the Heathman, but instead for the Hawthorne Bridge.

"You're going the wrong way."

"I'm making certain we're not followed."

That seemed to me to be overly paranoid, and I said as much.

"You really have no idea, do you?" Chapel said, reaching over to the mobile phone that was sitting in a cradle on the dash.

"I have idea, I have plenty idea," I said.

"Barry," Chapel told his phone, and the speaker came on and the tones of the number began to fill the car. While it was dialing, Chapel said, "No, I don't think you do. I think you left on tour a year ago and you were a musician, and sometime during the past year, you became a celebrity, and nobody sent you the memo. You keep on pretending your life is normal, all you're going to do is keep getting into trouble, Miriam.

"You are no longer normal, and it would serve you well to remember that."

There was a click from the speakers, and a man's voice came on. "Yes?"

"Barry, it's Fred. We've got a situation, you'll hear about it as soon as you turn on the news. I need you to get a couple things together for me and take them over to the Heathman for a guest, name of Lee.

"I need your sizes," Chapel said to me.

I gave him my sizes.

"Anything in particular?" Barry asked.

"She likes jeans and T-shirts. She'll need underwear, toiletries, all those good things. Shoes, too. What size are your feet?"

"Seven."

"You hear that, Barry?"

"Got it. Anything else?"

"That's it."

"I'll have it by eleven," Barry said, and hung up.

We crossed the river back to the east side, then turned north and up to Burnside, then west again and back across the river. Chapel drove calmly, eyeing his mirrors. I didn't say anything for a while, lost in my thoughts.

It occurred to me that I didn't know how to be a grown-up.

With my mother, there hadn't even been a memorial, and the body had eventually been disposed of by the State of Oregon in some way or another that to this day remains a mystery. Once they had put her in the ambulance, I never saw her again. I didn't even know where she'd ended up, if she'd been buried someplace, or cremated, or what.

"I can't go to a hotel," I said suddenly. "I can't go to a hotel, I have to plan the funeral. That's what I'm supposed to do, isn't it? He has to be buried, and I have to plan that, and I have to call his friends and tell them he's dead and I have to call the paper and do the obituary and all of it. That's what happens now, doesn't it? I have to do all that."

"Don't worry about it right now," Chapel said.

"But I have to do it, Tommy won't do it, God, they don't even know where Tommy is—"

"Your father's being held right now, it looks like they're going to charge him."

"They've got him?" I asked, stunned. "They had him the whole time, that's what you're saying?"

"He's under arrest, they picked him up early last night at your brother's place."

I digested that, and it seemed good, but then it didn't, because in a way it only made things worse.

"Then I have to go to the condo," I said. "Mikel's condo, I have to go there and get his things and . . . and what do I do with his things? I mean, he doesn't have a will, I'm sure he doesn't even have a will, why would he, twenty-nine years old and shot dead, how could he see that one coming, huh?"

"Mim, just relax."

"I have to handle his estate. No, settle his estate, that's what it's called, right? You're an attorney, you know. It's called settling the estate, right?"

We'd stopped in front of the Heathman, and I wasn't certain how long we'd been parked. The engine was silent, and the uniformed doorman was coming to help me out of the car.

Chapel put a hand on my arm.

"Mim, you've got to calm down. Just wait here. Don't get out of the car."

He waited until I nodded, then his hand slid from my arm, and I heard him take his keys from the ignition and get out of the car. The doorman was portly, black coat, black hat, red stripes, with a bushy beard and mustache, and after Chapel entered the hotel he turned back to me, curious. I looked away hastily, up the street, to the Portland Center for the Performing Arts and the Schnitz and the movie theater on the corner, its marquee listing all the films currently being shown.

The Black Tarot topped the bill.

Then my door opened, and I gasped, relaxed when I saw it was Chapel. He helped me out of the car, into the hotel, to the elevator, and then down the hall and into the suite.

It was a Van-quality room, nicer than I was used to. There was a sitting area with a couple of armchairs and a desk and a couch, and nice abstract paintings on the walls. A sliding partition at one side was open, leading to a raised king bed. The furnishings were wood and looked expensive, and there was an electric kettle on a table, and a miniature French press coffeemaker, and two tins of ground coffee. There was a minibar with a basket of treats and three bottles of Oregon wines, and two televisions, and three telephones, and two bathrooms, and flowers in a vase on a nightstand.

Chapel went to the closet and pulled it open, taking down one of the complimentary robes for me and draping it over the back of a chair. I looked at it and at him.

"You should shower and get some sleep," he said. "You're going to need your health and your rest."

I nodded, dropped into a chair, thinking to hell with my health, what I wanted was a drink and a smoke.

It was like he was reading my mind. "How drunk were you when the cops picked you up?"

"Drunk," I admitted.

"Blackout drunk?"

"Not that drunk."

"I couldn't ask you this at the station, so I'm asking you now. Did you kill Mikel?"

I came out of my chair and tried to punch him. He blocked it easily, pushing my arm away, and I tried to swing at him again, calling him a list of names, beginning with the basic profanities and working up to the multitiered ones. He was shouting back at me to calm down, and he blocked again and then gave me a shove, sending me back into the chair. I had to flail for the armrest to keep from falling.

"You motherfucker—"

"Did you?"

"No! Jesus fucking Christ, what *are* you? How can you even ask that?"

He drew his lips back, pinching them together, breathing through his nose.

"How can you even ask that?" I repeated.

He crossed to the window in the sitting room, looked out, then closed the blinds. The blinds, like the other furnishings, were wooden, too. Once he was satisfied that we couldn't be spied upon, he moved to the nearest easy chair.

"I had to ask."

"You didn't."

"I did, because the police are asking it, too. You're the one who said it could have been Mikel who was responsible for those cameras in your house. It's possible you went over there and confronted him and things turned violent."

I just shook my head, wouldn't look at him.

"You have to look at it from the cops' point of view."

It sunk in. "They don't really think it was Mikel selling those pictures of me?"

"They have to consider it."

"But he's the one who told me about them! That makes no sense!"

"It's the way they work, they have to consider it. They have to consider Tommy, too."

"It wasn't Tommy."

"Oh?" Chapel raised an eyebrow. "I'd think he'd have been at the top of your suspect list."

"I'm not saying he didn't kill Mikel. I'm saying he's not responsible for the pictures. Look, he came to my house Thursday, and just ... there's no way he could do that. He's too pathetic. Crime of passion, sure. But install cameras in my house? That's just not him, no way."

Chapel thought, barely nodded.

I asked, "How long do I stay here?"

"Next forty-eight hours, at least. This will get bad, Mim, and I want you as far out of it as possible. The media's going to go nuts, if they haven't already. Your brother dealt drugs, your father's a convict, you're a celebrity ... reporters wait their whole lives for this kind of thing. Throw in that you're the subject of someone's commercial voyeurism, and we have what we refer to in the legal profession as a fucked-up mess. I don't want you leaving these rooms. I don't even want you calling for room service. Don't use the phone at all, unless it's to call me. If someone comes to the door, you hide in the bath-room. I don't want anyone knowing where to find you."

"The police—"

"They want you, they'll come to me," he said.

"Where are you going?"

"Time for me to earn what Graham and the label and you have been paying me for. I'll handle the press, the police. I'll arrange for your brother's funeral. You leave all that to me."

"I should be doing something."

"You stay sober. Can you stay sober, Miriam?"

I nodded.

"Really? Or should I get the wine out of the room?"

"You going to remove the minibar, too?"

"I'll be keeping the key."

I twisted on the chair, uncomfortable, and wanting him to shut up. "I'm out of cigarettes."

"I'll have Barry get you a carton."

"I don't want to be alone." It sounded more plaintive than I wanted it to.

He nodded. "Who do you want to stay with you?"

"Joan."

He took a different mobile from his pocket, matte black and no bigger than a credit card, and asked me for her number. I gave it to him, and he dialed. It seemed to ring several times before anyone answered, and then Chapel started speaking, introducing himself. He didn't hand over the phone, just saying that he represented me, that my brother had been murdered, and that for the sake of my privacy he had moved me from my home to a hotel. I couldn't hear Joan's half of the conversation, not even when Chapel told her about Mikel. He asked her if she would mind joining me, staying with me for a day or so, and there was no appreciable pause for her to answer, and then he was saying I was at the Heathman, under the name Jennifer Lee, and that the sooner she got here, the better.

Then he hung up and said, "She's on her way over."

"I wanted to talk to her. You should have let me talk to her. She knew Mikel."

He slid his phone back into his jacket, exhaling, and his face changed, smoothing. I realized that he'd been as worked up as I was, that he was as worried as I was, though maybe not for all the same reasons.

"I should have," Chapel said. "I apologize."

I thought about saying that I accepted it. Thought about offering him an apology of my own, too, for whatever good it would do. Maybe to bank against future transgressions.

Instead, I got up and grabbed the robe off the back of the chair, then went into the bedroom to change, slamming the partition behind me.

CHAPTER EIGHTEEN

Barry had dropped off clothes and smokes before Joan arrived, and Chapel left almost immediately after she got there. I had showered and eaten a room-service sandwich—ordered by Chapel—and was feeling so sleepy I was having trouble keeping my eyes open.

Joan gave me energy, though, along with unconditional comfort. I took it greedily, trying not to remember that I hadn't been around to give her the same when Steven died.

Chapel returned Saturday night, about an hour after I woke up, with a long list of accomplishments. He'd arranged the funeral for Monday afternoon, at a parlor called Colby's in Southeast. He'd picked Colby's, he told me, because they could be discreet, and that was going to be even more important, because Van and Click and Graham all intended to be at the service. He'd spoken to Graham, and passed along concern and condolences from all involved. Apparently even Oliver Clay had expressed sympathy for my loss. Big of him.

It was the mundane questions that threw me. What kind of casket did I want for Mikel? What kind of flowers? Should there be music at the service? Choral, or organ, or something else? Was there a song he liked? Did I, perhaps, want to play? Did Mikel want to be cremated, or buried, and if buried, where? Who of his friends did I want invited to the funeral?

"I don't know his friends," I admitted.

"If it's all right with you, I can go through his things, see if I can find an address book. Did he keep an address book?"

"He had a PDA, one of those pocket things," I said. "Should be at his house."

"Then I'll bring that back here, and you can put together a list of guests.

"You remember a car on your street, a gray Chevy?" Chapel asked me. "It was parked down the block from your house."

"The beater?"

"Burchett's people figured that's where the signal from your house was going, that the receiver was in the car."

"So Burchett found the tapes?"

"He couldn't get into the vehicle. But he told the police about it, and they've moved it to their lot. Their people are going over it."

"But that means that the police will have the tapes," I said. "If there are tapes, then they'll have them."

"Yes, but as evidence. Their existence might be leaked, but not their contents, not until they've got the people responsible."

That didn't actually reassure me very much at all.

Chapel went on, telling us that Tommy was still in custody, but that he hadn't been charged.

I asked him why.

"A guess? The police don't have the evidence and they're trying to get it."

"What about Miriam?" Joan asked. "Is she a suspect?"

"For about six hours, she was the prime suspect," Chapel told her.

Joan was almost incredulous. "For heaven's sake, why?"

"The search they executed at her home turned up a lot of blood, they thought it might have been her brother's."

"It wasn't," I said. "It was mine."

"They know that now." Chapel shook his head. "No, she's in the clear for the time being. Even if she wasn't, the D.A. would want to be damn certain before he took the publicity of charging her."

Joan was looking at me. "Why did they find blood in your house?"

"My hand," I said.

"You said you cut it on tour."

"I lied."

"Why would you ..." And Joan trailed off, because she figured out the answer to that one, and it led to another question. "That's why you're home? Because you couldn't stay sober on tour?"

Chapel wasn't speaking, and from his expression, he looked like he wasn't listening, either. I knew he was, but he did a good job of pretending not to.

I tried to make a joke, I said, "It's just the way Steven told it, Joan. It's just part of the job."

"He never said that."

"He sure did." I was indignant. "Before I left for the *Scandal* tour, we went to dinner, and you and he talked about the wild life on the road. About the way you two used to party when you were touring."

Joan's expression shifted, moved away from her anger to an almost curiosity, as if she was seeing me for the first time. "When was this?"

"When we went to Ringside for dinner, just before I left."

She glanced over at Chapel, then back to me, and now the curiosity had become concern. "That never happened, Miriam."

"It did!"

"We didn't eat at Ringside. We had dinner at our place before you left, sweetie, and you left early, because you had to get home and pack."

I tried to remember, and the thing was, now that she'd said it, I knew she was right. But I really thought we *had* gone to dinner at Ringside, I was certain I could remember the sound of Steven's voice, the way he kept laughing as he told his anecdotes about life on the road.

But it hadn't happened, and I withdrew to silence, feeling foolish and confused, and a little scared. If I was making that up, then what else was I creating in my mind? What else was I lying about?

CHAPTER NINETEEN

Sunday was broken only by Chapel's arrival with Mikel's PDA. I composed a list of fifteen names I thought I recognized, people that Mikel had actually liked, or at least, that I thought he'd liked, and I looked around for an entry for Jessica and didn't find one, but there was one for a girl named Avery Sanger, so I put her on the list, too.

Chapel told me he'd make calls, letting them know the when and where of the service, and then he left us alone again, and that was the most exciting thing that happened on Sunday.

We left the hotel in the darkness before dawn the next morning, Chapel guiding me out much the way he'd guided me in, straight to his waiting Audi. We were followed by the guy Burchett had sent over, and it was the first time I'd seen him, though Chapel assured me there'd been someone on duty outside my room the whole time.

As we were getting into the car, Burchett called Chapel and confirmed that it was safe for me to return home, that the press had finally gotten bored with waiting for my return. I was grateful for the news. I wanted to get home and get changed, to have some time by myself before the funeral.

Joan stayed behind on the curb, waiting for the valet to bring her Volvo, promising she'd pick me up for the service that afternoon.

In the car, Chapel gave me the latest.

"Now they're onto the pictures," he said. "The story has been on the networks, MTV and the like. NME and Dotmusic are covering it. *Rolling Stone*'s guy arrived in town yesterday. There's a good chance reporters will show up at the service since they know you'll be there, and if that happens I want you to keep your mouth shut. Don't answer any questions. Nothing, Miriam. Just keep your head down."

"I will."

"Van, Click, and Graham got in last night. They released a statement through the label about how they needed to be with you, to support you, and they've canceled the next week of dates to be here."

"Van must have bled over that," I said.

Chapel ignored the comment, turning us onto the Broadway Bridge. "Not as relevant, but it may interest you to know that as of Saturday night *Nothing for Free* had jumped twelve spots on *Billboard*'s Top Fifty, to eleven. We're expecting to hear it's in the Top Ten sometime today. *Scandal* reentered at sixty-seven. 'Queen of Swords' is in heavy rotation in just about every major outlet, and it's been the most requested video on MTV for the last two nights. You can interpret that however you like."

"My interpretation is that this is one fucked-up world," I said.

"I'm not sure I disagree. The third single off *Scandal,* what was that one called?"

" 'Lie Life.' "

"Was that written about Tommy?"

"I was riffing off 'Lush Life' by Billy Strayhorn. Van had this idea for a song about this asshole she'd been seeing, he was also a musician in town. So she wanted a breakup song where she could get angry and kick and growl, and I wanted to play with an old standard. That's all it is."

"There's a lot of death imagery in the song. It's getting play now, too."

"It's about how this relationship was bleeding her dry," I said. "The single didn't do very well."

"That may be, but it's getting play now."

"If you tell me the label's released a Greatest Hits compilation, I may have to kill myself."

"Don't do that."

"It was a joke."

"It wasn't funny."

The way he said it told me I should just shut up now.

There was no sign of the police, or the press, or even of Burchett's people. The lawn beneath the trees had been chewed by footprints, and pockets of mud slopped over the sides of the path. Copies of the last couple issues of the *Oregonian* were still on my porch, too, but those were the only real indications that I'd been gone. I unlocked the door and switched off the alarm, and Chapel told me he'd talk to me if he had more news later.

"You'll be at the funeral?" I asked.

"I wasn't planning on it," he said. "You don't need me there."

That disappointed me for a moment, and then I realized that he'd never known Mikel, and that he really didn't know me. I wasn't his friend. I was his client.

He got back in his Audi and pulled away, and I locked up and looked at the clock, and it wasn't even a quarter past six. I put on a pot of coffee, cleared my voice mail while it brewed, and drank a cup while smoking a cigarette, feeling oddly empty inside. The sun came up, and from the backyard it looked like the day would be clear and cold. At least it would be beautiful at the cemetery.

I fixed a bowl of shredded wheat and opened the copy of today's paper, heading for the funnies. When I finished the comics, I searched out the obituaries, finding them paradoxically at the back of the "Living" section. Chapel must have gotten something to the paper, because there was a notice about Mikel's passing. It was short, and didn't really say much about who he had been. There were no details included about where the service would be, or when, and the only connection between my brother and my celebrity was in our last name. I was simply his surviving sister, Miriam.

I decided I'd read the rest of the paper, too, mostly to see exactly how bad things were looking for me, personally. The story was still on the front page, but now below the fold for only two paragraphs before jumping to the end of the section.

That's how I learned that Tommy had been released.

I wasn't sure what I could conclude from that, if it meant that the cops didn't think he'd done it, or they did and just didn't have enough evidence to charge him. If Chapel had known, he hadn't bothered to tell me for some reason. If he didn't know, then calling him would be pointless.

I could call the cops and ask them, but that seemed to me to be asking for trouble.

Tommy had been released.

I realized, with some alarm, that I was relieved. When I looked at the feeling harder, I realized why.

Tommy hadn't killed Mikel. It had to have been someone else.

Fuck if I knew who.

Upstairs, I went through my closet, looking for something to wear to the funeral. Everything I had in black was inappropriate. Even my dresses, all of them too formal or too ratty or too sexy. There'd been a phase of Tailhook where we'd all gone for the Man in Black look, Van and I in short black skirts and black nylons—Van had gone with garters—and black suit coats and blindingly white blouses, and Click in the complementary suit. I had black jeans, black tanks, black tees, black shoes, black boots, black undies.

Nothing I could wear to my brother's funeral.

So I took my car to the Nordstrom at the Lloyd Center, the mall that got dropped in the Northeast by mistake. It's an indoor mall, with an ice skating rink at its heart, and I got there just as they were opening the doors, making straight to the east end for my shopping, dodging mall walkers and professional consumers. Fifteen minutes got me three outfits that looked like they would fit, and I thought about trying them on, but shoppers and salespeople had begun to recognize me, and the thought of getting trapped in a dressing room made me want to spit. I got out as fast as I could, was back home only forty-nine minutes after I'd left, and felt that at least I'd managed the shopping successfully.

I laid out my outfits on my bed, but the silence of the house started to grate on my nerves, so I hit the remote and switched on the television. I was picking out shoes and stockings with no holes when MTV News came on the screen, and Gideon Yago ran down the bullet points, and then he hit the tragedy in Portland.

I stopped what I was doing and turned to watch him. He said my brother's name, and my own, and the band's. He talked about how Tommy had been questioned and then released. A picture of me that I had never seen before came up on the screen behind his head, somewhere sunny, me smiling broadly at the camera.

He offered me MTV's deepest condolences.

I turned the television off, threw the remote across the room.

The last drink I'd taken had been in the wee hours Friday morning, just before I'd earned myself handcuffs. I'd been dry for over two days.

This seemed as good a reason as any to break the fast.

CHAPTER TWENTY

The service was well attended, if small. Van and Click and Graham were there, and Joan. A handful of other people who had known my brother, including a couple women, one of whom I took to be Avery, his newest. Marcus and Hoffman were there, too, but stayed clear of the crowd, at the back.

Tommy stayed in the back, wearing a suit that must have come from Goodwill or St. Vincent de Paul. He was there when I arrived, and he tried to speak to me, but I moved away before he could. I had Joan on one arm and Van on the other, and they provided insulation. After that, he kept his distance.

But not out of sight, and at the grave, when we were finished and moving to the cars, I looked back to see him standing beside where the marker would go. He looked hunched, and I realized he was sobbing.

Maybe if I hadn't been so drunk, I'd have gone to him.

Joan had found Van at my door when she came to get me for the service, and they came in together to discover me upstairs, in a corner of my bedroom, crying hysterically. I'd finished the bottle of Jack when I'd told myself I was only going to have one drink, and I was really worked up because I couldn't decide which of the three outfits I was going to wear. Van got the shower running and Joan got me undressed, and the two of them cleaned me up under the ice-cold water, washing vomit off my chin and out of my hair. I fought them a little, spitting and yelling.

"Knock it the fuck off!" Van finally snarled at me. She was in black, not too expensive, not too flashy, and she'd only put on a little bit of makeup. I thought she looked jet-lagged and she was certainly angry. She'd taken the coat off to keep it from getting wet. "Jesus Christ, Mim, it's your goddamn *brother*! Couldn't you just give it a fucking rest?"

"I hate you," I told her.

Together, they got me sober enough to stand, and dressed me. I was back in my head enough to exert some will, and that made it easier on them when I was willing to do what they said, and harder on them when I wasn't. Once they finally had my clothes in place, Joan sat me on the edge of the bed and held me while Van got my shoes on me, then went back into the bathroom for some makeup. She did my eyes and my lips, and when she was finished, they helped me down the stairs. Van put me in Joan's car, got me buckled in, and then went to her Beemer to follow us.

Joan didn't look at me once as she drove to the funeral home.

The service was blurry and went by fast, and there was a guy named Damien who was about Mikel's age and who gave the eulogy. Mikel had brought him along to a couple of the shows we'd played in town, and he was nice, and he spoke nicely, and he said all of the nice things, and I wondered if maybe he knew about pinhole video cameras and wireless broadband transmission.

I sat with Joan, and Van, Click, and Graham filled out the rest of our pew. I spent most of the time biting my tongue, trying to keep the drunk from making me soggy. The coffin was open, and Mr. Colby of the Colby Funeral Home had done a good job, because Mikel didn't look like he had when I'd found him, hurting and scared. He looked like he was faking sleep, that was all.

When the service finished, Click and Graham joined the pallbearers, and the rest of us followed them out. I walked between Joan and Van, following the coffin, and once it was loaded in the hearse we turned to our vehicles and got a face full of flashbulbs and hot spots mounted on television cameras.

It must have been every local affiliate, all of them out to catch the show, and there were even a couple out-of-towners trying to make their own coverage. Faces I recognized from television screens and studio interviews dimly remembered, all of them nonetheless strangers.

Most kept their distance, due in part to the six Portland police officers positioned around the entrance and on the curb. But there was one bitch who launched herself forward with microphone leading, cameraman over her shoulder, looking for the kill.

"Mim! Mim! Did you know that the Portland PD hasn't ruled you out as a suspect?"

I kept my head down, remembering Chapel's warning, but mostly because I was afraid I'd throw up again.

The Bitch pressed, "Is it possible your brother's murder is related to your own drug problems? Or to the pornography of you that's been released on the Net?"

Van let go of me, moving to block. "Hey, bugfuck, leave her be or we'll be planting two bodies at the cemetery."

"Excuse me, I'm talking to Mi—"

Van grabbed the mike from her hand, then used it to hit the end of the cameraman's rig. There was shouting. The police officers started trying to separate Van and the woman, and Hoffman waded in and put herself between the camera and us.

"Trouble with that?" Van was shouting. "My friend has no goddamn comment, okay?"

She threw the microphone overhand into the street, where it bounced off the side of a parked news van. Then she seized my arm so hard it hurt, and helped me again into the Colby Funeral Home's complimentary limousine, and I was on my way to the cemetery.

Joan had insisted on holding the reception at her house, and I skirted the fringes, not wanting to mingle with the other mourners. Damien tried to corner me twice, and I retreated farther into the house, trying to find a quiet space to be alone.

I ended up finding Click, Van, and Graham in Steven's old music room. Click and Graham had both worn sensible, somber suits, and neither of them looked comfortable or even correct in them. Graham looked like his tie was going to choke him to death, and there was just no way Click could sell mainstream with his tattoos and piercings.

Steven had collected instruments, a lot of them drums. Most were busted, ones he'd intended to repair. Before we'd signed with the label, he'd even worked over Click's kit a few times. He had two Ghanaian tribal drums resting next to a mismatched collection of snares, even a steel drum he'd made himself.

"No Clay, huh?" I asked.

"He thought it'd be presumptuous," Click said. "Considering how you barely know him. Offers his deepest sympathies."

I nodded, and there was a beat that threatened to become an awkward pause, and then Graham asked, "How you holding up, Mimser? You good? Given the circumstances?"

"Not so good. I'm sorry about all this press."

"Ink is ink. You just got to ride it out. Really sorry about that craptroll at the funeral home." Graham's face twisted alarmingly with sudden hatred. "Fucking *E!*, I hate them, I fucking hate them."

"Van shut that down."

"I spoke to Fred. He says things don't look that bad for you."

"Depends from where you're looking."

"He's good at his job, Mimser, he'll do his best for you. You've got to give the man some credit, he's managed to keep things pretty level on this end."

It sounded like he was talking as much about the pictures as Mikel's murder, but I wasn't certain. So far, none of them had told me they'd as much as heard about the images, and it added yet another tension, because now I wasn't certain if I should be embarrassed, or just should anticipate embarrassment.

"He seems more interested in the fact that *Nothing for Free* might break the Top Ten," I said.

"Ink is ink, like I said. Not to be a total dickwad, but that's kind of an upside, maybe, for a darkness, huh?"

I just stared at him. Every sale was more money in the pocket, and if Mikel was now serving to further promote Tailhook, well, there was really no way that Graham or the label could see his death as an entirely bad thing. It was the way it was, and there was nothing to be done about it. For that instant, though, I hated them all so much I wanted to scream their dead hearts to life.

"That was the first time I'd ever seen your dad," Van said. "At the service."

"Tommy," I said. "Call him Tommy."

"I didn't know about your mom."

"Now everyone does."

"I thought I knew just about every one of your dark secrets."

"I don't write about that one."

"You will," she said.

"No I won't. I can't."

She shook her head. "Clay's temp, I'd have you back in a heartbeat. But you've got to deal with this thing."

I held up my glass. "Mineral water."

"Not this morning it wasn't."

I tried to change the subject. "How long you guys back?"

Van looked annoyed, but Click cut her off. "Couple more days, time to see family and pay bills. Graham figured if we were going to have to cancel one date, might as well cancel three."

"Where to next?"

"Glasgow, then Dublin."

"It'll be cold," I said. "Bundle up."

"Our shit is squared away," Van said, pointedly. "Look after your own, Miriam."

The reception, such as it was, started breaking up before five, and I wandered upstairs as people began to leave, to get away from the platitudes, eventually reaching my old bedroom. Tommy was sitting at my desk, looking out the window. The room faced west, and the sunset was starting to fade, and that was the only light in there.

He caught me staring at him, got up hastily from the desk, trying to straighten his awful suit. Maybe it was the shadows, but he looked a lot worse for wear, and he hadn't looked all that good when I'd seen him on Thursday morning.

The silence got awkward fast, so I spoke, told him the first thing that came to mind.

"I used to live here."

He nodded. "I spoke to Mrs. Beckerman when I arrived. She told me ... she told me where your room was."

"How long you been here?"

"Only a half hour. I didn't ... I didn't know if I should come or not."

"Tell me you didn't do it."

He grimaced, slowly, as if feeling heartburn. "I didn't, Miriam. You've got to believe me."

"Do you know how it happened?"

He shook his head. "I'd been drinking...."

"You said you'd stopped."

"I had."

"You know about these pictures? About this fucker who was taping me in my own home?"

He flinched, nodded as if hoping he could get by with only the barest of confirmations.

"Do you know who did that? Was it one of Mikel's buddies? Damien?"

"I don't know anything about that." Tommy ran his hand over the top of the old stereo, disturbing the light dust. "You were drunk at the service."

"It would be you who could tell."

"I wasn't the only one who could tell." When I didn't say anything, he added, "You need to stop doing that. Need to stop drinking like that."

"I don't need this kind of advice from you."

Tommy took a step forward suddenly, grabbing my arm. I felt his grip tightening on me. My insides fell to liquid, seemed to foam up and fill my lungs, flooding them and forcing away my breath. I was eleven again, small and scared.

"Listen." He hit both syllables evenly, equally. "Listen to me, Miriam. You don't know how dangerous this is. You don't know what could happen."

I tried to pull away, to back away, but his grip just tightened. I suppose I could have kicked or punched or screamed, but I didn't think of it, I didn't even consider those actions as options.

He was my father. His anger, his power, all over again, inescapable.

It froze me in place, and it terrified me.

All I could manage was, "Please."

The word was enough, the effect was enormous. Tommy dropped my arm like I was a hot wire, backing away, and his expression changed from anger to alarm, and then to something else. He seemed confused, as if he'd lost his bearings.

"Oh, God," Tommy said. "Oh, Mim. I'm so sorry."

Then he pushed his way past me, going for the stairs, taking them quickly, double, triple steps at a time.

When I got downstairs, he had gone, and the party was over.

CHAPTER TWENTY-ONE

The caterers were out of the house within minutes of the last guest's departure.

Even though Click and Graham had departed, Van had lingered, offering to help with the cleanup. I could hear her and Joan talking in the kitchen, and just from the tenor of their voices, I knew they were talking about me, trying to stay quiet. I stood just outside the arch which opens into the kitchen, listening.

"... bad it was," Joan was saying.

"She took a fall in Tokyo," Van said. "End of the third set, just went right off the stage. Didn't even know she'd done it."

"She's not made for it."

"She's brilliant."

"She's a musician, Vanessa. Not a performer, not like you."

"She's great onstage."

There was a rustle, the sound of a cabinet opening and closing. "My husband knew."

"About the drinking?"

"Not that, not specifically. But he knew what she was in for, knew where you were all headed. He tried to warn her. He wanted her to understand how isolating it would be, how lonely. But mostly, I think, he wanted her to understand that she shouldn't trust it, not any of it, not anyone."

"You mean me, too?"

Another cabinet opened, closed. I heard a sigh. "Sending her home proved him wrong about you. But even now he'd say that for everyone else—and he really did mean everyone—it's about money. How much of it they can make off her, off the band. Those people, they don't care about art or entertainment. They just want to keep getting richer."

"There's nothing wrong with being rich."

"Depends how you get there, Vanessa. There was this thing, I heard it on the news this morning, about how the albums have shot up the charts."

"You think it's someone close to her?" Van asked. "Someone who put the cameras in her house and killed Mikel?"

"She doesn't want to think that her brother could have done a thing like that."

"Would you?"

I'd heard more than enough, retreated, back to the living room. Their voices faded, leaving me with my own.

We'd been with the Larkins for just under two weeks when the same Gresham detective, Wagner, came to talk to us again. He came in the afternoon, after school, and he got lucky, because Mikel was actually at the house, along with me. Mrs. Larkin invited him in and offered him a soda, then went to fetch us.

Mikel and I had been sitting together, in the room he shared with the eldest Larkin boy. I'd been trying to do homework, taking comfort in having him close. When Mrs. Larkin stuck her head in to tell us that Detective Wagner was here, Mikel put his magazine down and told her we'd be right there.

"What does he want?" I asked him as soon as she was gone.

"He wants to know what we saw." He said it all flat, trying to be bored by the horror of it all. "Dad's going to be on trial and stuff, and he wants to make sure that he really killed Mom."

"But he already asked. We already told him."

"He wants to check it."

"I didn't really see," I said, after a moment. "I was going back to the porch."

"You saw enough."

"But I didn't really see it, Mikel."

"I did."

"He just ran her over?"

He nodded, slowly, as if leery of the memory, then got off the bed. "We should go down."

I followed reluctantly, trailing after him down the stairs. The detective scared me, the thought of talking to him again, remembering again, disconcerting. I was still having nightmares, and having to listen to questions that would force me to see things I hadn't, make me recall things I was trying so hard to forget, filled my feet with lead.

But Mikel, he was tougher, and if he was scared, it didn't show, and that made it easier when I followed him into the kitchen. Wagner was at the dining table, with a smile this time, and Mrs. Larkin guided us to him, put us in chairs.

"I just want to check some things, all right?" he told us.

"Sure," Mikel said.

He started by asking where we were when it happened, what we were doing. Wanted to know how long Mom and I had been working on the pumpkin in the driveway, wanted to know how she'd been acting. If she was upset with me, perhaps, or maybe just upset about something else entirely. My answers were sullen, one-word, a string of nos.

"He picked me up on the corner," Mikel told Wagner.

"Where were you going?"

"Meet some friends."

"And your father saw you?"

"He stopped the truck. He was mad. He doesn't like my friends. Told me I had to come home."

Wagner asked some questions about Mikel's friends, and my brother confirmed that they sometimes got into trouble. Sometimes they broke things, sometimes they took things, but it wasn't like it was ever anything someone would miss, it wasn't ever anything important, Mikel said. Wagner asked him if he was still getting into trouble, and after glancing to Mrs. Larkin, Mikel confirmed that, too. Not embarrassed, almost defiant.

"What about you, Miriam? You staying out of trouble?"

"Trying," I said.

"That's good."

I looked at Mikel, longing to be tough like he was, to be strong and act like I didn't care. Wagner made more scribbles on his pad, flipped pages, asked a couple more questions. He asked if Tommy ever hit our mother, if he ever hit us.

"He never hits Mim," Mikel told him, by way of an answer.

Joan was saying my name, and Van was standing at the door, ready to take me home, and I got off the couch, feeling caught by the memories.

Joan gave me a hug and a kiss, and I thanked her for everything.

"I mean everything," I said.

"You're worrying me, Miriam," she said, and then told me to call in the next day or so. She'd be back in school, teaching again, but she said she'd try to keep her evenings free.

The top was up on Van's convertible, and when she switched on the engine the stereo began blaring Radiohead, and she lunged for the button to turn it off. There wasn't much of a point to the silence; we didn't have anything to say to each other.

She drove me home, and I got out of the car, thanked her for the lift.

"I'm having a thing at my house," Van said. "Tomorrow night. If you want to come."

"You mean a party?"

"Just for fun. I'm keeping it small."

"I'll probably give it a miss," I said.

"Thought I'd offer."

"I don't really hate you, you know that, right?" I said.

"Sure you do," Van told me. "Just not for the reasons you think."

There was a new mess to clean up after I'd changed into comfortable clothes, and I went through my bedroom and bathroom, mopping up the spills and finding the top to the bottle of Jack, trying to ignore the smell. I brought it downstairs and poured a small shot before putting it in the pantry with its brothers-in-proof, then checked the phone for messages while I took the drink. The voice-mail lady told me there were two messages, which I took to mean that the press had found a new story to pursue for the time being.

The funeral home had a question about the bill, but said it could wait until tomorrow. The other one from Hoffman had been left only ten minutes before I'd gotten home. She said she had some questions for me, and would I please call when I got the message. She left her home number.

Chapel would throw a fit, but if Hoffman had questions for me, maybe I could ask some questions of her, maybe get an idea about what was going on with Tommy. That's what I told myself, anyway.

"This is Tracy."

"It's Miriam Bracca, I'm calling for Detective Hoffman."

"This is she." She sounded surprised. "Didn't think I'd be hearing from you."

"You left a message."

"I've got some questions I'd like you to answer."

"I don't know. I'm thinking I should probably talk to Chapel, first, or at least have him present."

"Look, you're not a suspect, and I'm not going to try to trick you into anything. I've got some questions, I'm hoping you can help me

find your brother's killer, that's all this is. Chapel would just compli-
cate it."

"Is my father still a suspect?"

"Are you willing to talk to me?"

"Yeah, if it's actually a conversation and not an interrogation."

"Are you at your home?"

"Why?"

"Could I come over there? I'm in Sabin, it'd take me about ten
minutes or so to get there."

"You're sure I'm not a suspect?"

"You're not a suspect," she assured me.

"Then why do you want to talk to me?"

"I'm hoping you can help me find a new one."

It made me laugh, I don't know why.

"Sure," I said. "Take your best shot."

CHAPTER TWENTY-TWO

'd left the porch light on, and it was her, and I shut off the alarm and let her in, saying, "Did you speed?"

"Why else become a cop?" Hoffman said. "For the perks."

"The perks?"

"I get to shoot people, too."

"Oh."

I peered past her at the street, not seeing much but Hoffman's car—it was a VW Passat, either black or blue or green, I couldn't tell—and my trees. I stepped back in and locked up once more, but didn't bother with the alarm, this time. After all, she had perks.

"We towed the Chevy, if that's what you're looking for," Hoffman told me.

"No. Just keeping an eye out for reporters. What'd you do with the car?"

"Evidence of a crime, we brought it in, had the lab go over it. It was the receiver base."

"So now you guys have voyeur video of me."

"We should be so lucky. All of the storage devices had been removed from the car. If you're on tape, you're on tape somewhere else."

"You know who owns it? The Chevy?"

"It was stolen out of Roseburg back in May."

I nodded as if this was significant information, and we went into the kitchen. I parked at the table with an empty cereal bowl for an ashtray. Hoffman had come over wearing a coat and hat, one of the black watch cap ones, and she removed them both before sitting down. She had on a Lewis & Clark sweatshirt, and a turtleneck beneath that, black. She was wearing faded Levi's, and short black boots, and she had that aura that some PNW women get, the very healthy ones who are fit and stay fit and spend summer weekends windsurfing in the Gorge and winter ones skiing or snowboarding Mount Hood.

"Bet you rock climb, too," I said.

"Do I have granola in my teeth?" She smiled at me, and I understood she was making an effort to get us started on good terms, both with her manner and her words.

"Call it a lucky guess."

I waited for her to take the seat opposite me, expecting her to get out a pad and a pen. She draped her coat over the back of the chair, after stuffing the cap in a pocket, then sat down.

"You're not going to take notes?"

She tapped her forehead. "Like a steel trap."

"You want a cigarette or some coffee or something?"

"No, I'm fine."

I shrugged and lit one for myself. She looked me over as if trying to find clues, then pushed the bowl a little closer to me, so I wouldn't have to reach. Her fingers were long, like Joan's. On her right thumb was a ring, a simple silver band with an inlaid and intertwined repeating symbol. I stared at it a second before recognizing the letter as Greek.

"Oh, my God," I said. "I get it now. You're a dyke."

She arched an eyebrow at me. "Sure. Aren't you?"

"What? No!"

Hoffman's head came back a little bit, and her expression plainly was asking me to give her a break.

"I'm not," I said.

"You speak queer."

"Passing queer. Pidgin queer. Not fluent queer."

"I'm not here to out you."

"I'm not gay. God, Chapel thinks I'm gay, too. I'm not, see, what I am is *single*. You're confusing images. I'm the Quiet One. Van's the Sexually Adventurous One, the Possibly Bi One, the Maybe a Confused Lesbian One."

"Van's not gay," Hoffman said, matter-of-factly. "Everyone who is knows she isn't. There are people in the Black Hills of South Dakota who haven't come out to themselves yet, they know Van in Tailhook is straight."

"So I'm the Gay One?"

"I know a lot of women who will be very disappointed if you're not." She looked me over, as if appraising. "Or see it as a challenge. Don't tell me this is news to you."

"It is news to me. You're telling me that I now not only have to fear that every man I meet has seen naked pictures of me, I've got to include women, too?"

"Not all women. One in ten to one in four, depending whose study you believe."

"That makes it so much better."

"You've got a huge lesbian following, you didn't know that? I thought you celebs tracked things like that, where you're getting coverage. You practically have a column devoted to you in *Curve*."

"Now you're just yanking my leg."

"Maybe a little. But you do know what *Curve* is."

"I know what *Soldier of Fortune* is, too, that doesn't make me a mercenary."

She smiled again, then said, "You still willing to answer some questions for me, Miss Bracca?"

"Mim. One dyke to another?"

"That had been my intent, but I'll settle for closeted dyke to out dyke, if you like."

I blew some smoke off to a side, shaking my head. "Go ahead."

"Do you have a drug problem, Mim?"

I was getting tired of having to answer that question, and maybe that was why I surprised the hell out of myself by saying, "Yeah, I drink too much."

"That's all?"

"Isn't that enough?"

"Alcohol is legal."

"If I tell you about the illegal stuff, you gonna slap cuffs on me?"

She shook her head. "You don't do coke or heroin or anything like that?"

"None of those things. Chapel asked me this stuff, too, when I went to see him about the pictures."

"He was asking for a different reason. He was asking to spare you embarrassment, maybe to anticipate possible blackmail. You're saying you've used?"

I held up a hand and ticked off controlled substances. "I've done coke, pot, X, shrooms, dropped acid, and even eaten opium. That was when we were in Hawaii." I brought the hand down. "Once each for all of it, and only ever on the tour. Look, I know what you're thinking, and I'll say it again. Mikel never sold me drugs, never gave me drugs. He hated the fact that I drank, and he didn't like me smoking."

"Both your parents drink, or just your father?"

It was like being in the Larkins' dining room all over again, except this time there was no Mikel, and Wagner was being played by a woman. I didn't answer, but she waited me out.

"Both," I said.

She leaned back in her chair, thinking. I finished my cigarette and crushed it out. Her eyes were on something past my shoulder, and I guessed this was what detectives looked like when they were trying to crack mysteries.

"Can I ask you something, Detective?" I said.

She came back. "Tracy."

I needed a second, and then another, before I started laughing. "Detective Tracy? *Dick* Tracy? A lesbian Dick Tracy?"

She smiled, more amused at me than at the joke. She'd probably heard it a lot before.

"Sorry," I said.

"What were you going to ask?"

"Is Tommy still a suspect?"

"Yes, he is."

"Are you looking at any of Mikel's friends?"

"We've talked to his friends. Their alibis check."

"If you think it's Tommy, why'd you let him go?"

"We didn't have enough to charge."

"So you don't have evidence that he did it, but you think he did."

"That's not what I'm saying, Mim. I'm saying he's still a suspect, that's all."

"Why?"

"Why? Because your father's got three hours he can't account for, roughly from the time your brother was murdered until the time he called in the nine-one-one."

This was news. "Tommy's the one who reported it?"

"He called from the condo to say his son had been shot. The first unit found him there, took him into custody. He was drunk, he blew a point one-nine on the Breathalyzer. To put it in perspective, you blew a point one-three when we picked you up."

"I told you he'd been drinking—"

"No, you told us you thought he had, because your brother didn't, and you'd seen bottles and cans throughout the condo."

"You're saying that my father shot my brother, then left long enough for me to come by and discover the body, and then he came back, got drunk, and called the police?"

"If I thought you were lying about the bottles, yes. But I know you're not. That's where it falls apart."

"Only there?"

She ignored that. "We didn't find a weapon anywhere, we didn't find gloves, and Tommy's GSR test came back negative."

"GSR?"

"Gunshot residue."

I remembered that they had swabbed my hands after they'd brought me in, too. Then I wondered how seriously they'd looked at me for my brother's murder.

She turned in the chair, showing me her profile and raising her right hand, as if shooting my microwave. With her other hand she made sprinkling motions over her right hand and forearm. "When you fire a gun, traces of the charge get absorbed into the skin. The test is very simple, very accurate. Both you and your father tested negative."

"And no gloves means what?"

"Either he ditched the gloves, along with the gun, or he didn't do it. We're still looking for the gun."

For a long time I didn't say anything, and it was like that morning, when I'd read in the paper that Tommy had been released. Surprise at what I was feeling, and relief, and more, and I didn't know why I even cared. It bothered me that Hoffman was sitting there, telling me that Tommy was still a suspect.

"Why would Tommy kill Mikel?" I asked. "Mikel had been nice to him, Mikel was taking care of him. If he was going to kill one of us, it would've been me."

"What if he learned that his son had been selling naked pictures of his daughter on the Internet?"

This time, I got really angry. "People keep saying that! Mikel didn't do it!"

"Fine, give me proof."

"I don't—"

"Mikel had access to your home the entire time you were away," Hoffman interrupted. "He knew enough about computers to set up the system here. He sold drugs, and apparently he did it only for the money, not for the product. Why not try to make a little extra off his sister?"

"There are so many things wrong with that, I don't know where to start! He was my brother, don't you get that? He would never do that to me, he was always trying to protect me. And as for money—Jesus, all he had to do was ask."

Hoffman didn't say anything for a moment, giving me time to calm down.

"It wasn't Mikel who took the pictures," I insisted. "And it wasn't my father who killed him."

And as soon as I'd said it aloud, I discovered that I believed it. Tommy had committed a great many sins, but he could never have taken a gun and shot his son. It didn't matter how drunk he might've been, it didn't matter how provoked he might have felt. It never would happen. And if he wasn't drunk, if he was sober when he did it, then we were talking about a level of premeditation that was beyond him. He wasn't a planner. He was like me; life happened to us, we didn't do things to life.

I sat there, and I thought about it and thought about it, and the only thing I discovered was that the more I thought about it, the more certain I became. Maybe it was utter bullshit, maybe there was no reason or logic to it.

But if the cops pinned the murder on Tommy, either because he was a drunk or a bastard or had one murder to his name already, it meant that the son of a bitch who *had* killed my brother would get away with it. I couldn't let that happen. If not for Tommy's sake but for Mikel's, there was no way in hell I could let that happen.

Hoffman gazed at me, and it was disconcertingly close to the looks she'd shot at me in the interrogation room three nights before.

After a second, I said, "Tommy knows what happened. He didn't do it, but he knows what happened. He says he doesn't remember, but I think he's lying."

"And you know this how, exactly?"

"Because I know how that works."

"That's not really something that'll stand up in court."

I fidgeted with my pack of smokes, trying to use my hands to keep my brain quiet. "My brother's been murdered, you're accusing him of pimping my image. You're saying my dead brother is responsible for some asshole in ass-crack Dakota beating off to my picture every night."

Hoffman considered, just watching me. I hated the look, because I had no idea what was going on behind it. I got out a new cigarette, lit it, blew smoke. It was like she was hardly breathing.

"What?" I finally demanded.

"I'm just trying to figure you. You go on stages around the world, and you play guitar, and you sing, and jump and run and sweat and dance, and you have thousands of people watching your every move when you do that."

"Van," I said. "Not me."

"Van more often, sure, but you, too. And television, you go on television, and millions—literally millions—of people watch what you do. Those people, they're watching your body as much as hearing the music, they're objectifying you just as much, they're sexualizing you just as much."

"You're saying that the pictures shouldn't bother me? Isn't that like telling me I was asking for it?"

Hoffman shook her head vigorously. "No, hell no. What's been done to you, it's a kind of rape, and I wouldn't dare diminish it."

I threw up my hands, frustrated, not getting it, not getting her.

"It's you," she said. "It's you, your body, and if it were me, I wouldn't be ashamed, even if I could afford to be. I'd sure as hell be angry, I'd be boiling, but I wouldn't be ashamed."

"Well, you weren't the one humiliated."

"It's only humiliating if you let it be, if you give it that power."

"You know what? I don't want to talk about this anymore."

"You've got to own it—"

"I don't want to talk about this anymore," I repeated, slower and clearer, to make sure she understood.

She did. "You're used to getting your own way, aren't you?"

"Ah, here we go. This is the part where you call me a bitch rock-princess again, is that it?"

Hoffman slid her chair back and rose, pulling her coat free. "No. You're a bitch because you're pretty blatantly miserable. The rock-princess part, that's just frosting."

"I've got a reason to be miserable."

"Sure. But maybe you just like it." She had the coat on, adjusting it. She took the cap from her pocket and set it on her head, tucking stray hair beneath it. "Hell, you're an *artist,* you've got to suffer, right?"

"And it was going so well," I said. "Yet here we are, back to the fuck-yous."

"Hey, gumdrop, if this was a date, you'd have known it. Don't get up. I can find my way out."

CHAPTER TWENTY-THREE

The ringing phone pulled me free from the nightmare.

Reporters and humiliations, of cameras on me at all the worst times. Flashes capturing me in bed in Montreal, not with a groupie but with a cop, and photographers pursuing me into bathrooms, finding me drunk and naked and lying in my own vomit and blood. Big Technicolor production, cast of thousands, everyone from the funeral, everyone from the press, everyone from the audience. Chapel taking notes on his legal pad, and Joan standing with dead Steven, each looking pained with disappointment. Damien asking me to sign something, even though I wasn't Van.

So the phone was really a lifesaver, as far as that went.

"Hello?" I said. It came out more as a slurry than a word.

"This is Scanalert operator one-four-seven; is this Miriam Bracca?" The voice was male, and young, and very efficient.

I sat up, felt around for the light. It had started raining again, and there was the sound of it pattering on the roof and running along the edges of the house. "Uh, yeah?"

"We've registered an alarm activation at this number."

"You have?"

"Are you alone?"

"Yeah," I said, and then thought maybe it was a reporter being cagey. "Why?"

"If you are not able to speak freely, say the word 'later,' now."

"I'm alone. There's no alarm going off here."

"May I have your password?"

"My what?"

"I need your password for a system reset."

"I don't know. Joan? Mikel? Tailhook? Telecaster?"

" 'Telecaster' is the password. I'm very sorry to have bothered you, ma'am."

"Wait, that's it?"

His efficient yap disappeared, and now he sounded slightly exasperated. "If there's no audible going off there must be a malfunction in the system. We'll run a diagnostic and send someone out later tomorrow to see if we can't isolate the problem. Once again, sorry for the inconvenience. Thank you for using Scanalert."

I rubbed my eyes and listened to the dial tone, then put the receiver back in the cradle and got out of bed. It was cold, and I put on my robe and my slippers. The cable box on the television was reading 3:48.

I went out to the top of the stairs and listened.

Nothing but rain.

The steps creaked when I descended, and I hadn't noticed how irritating that was until now. It was stupid, too, because that, more than anything else, made me feel nervous. Creaking stairs and rain on the roof, and a phone call in the dead of night. Maybe it had just been some reporter with a clever way of trying to find out if I was sleeping with someone. Hell, maybe it was a reporter who knew Dyke Tracy had paid me a visit, and was hoping she'd stayed. Clearly a chunk of my subconscious had done the same.

The alarm panel was showing red lights when I checked it, armed.

The LCD said that we were safely in "Stay" mode, with "all portals secure."

Not a bad title for a song, maybe. All portals secure. No way in. No way out.

I went back upstairs and found my notebook in the night-stand, wrote, "All Portals Secure!" in it, then underlined it. I left the book out, so that I'd see it in the morning. I probably wouldn't even remember why I thought the line was so intriguing when I woke up.

I took off my robe and my slippers and got back under the covers, clicking out the light. I listened to the rain overhead, to the layers of sound. One instrument, many notes, I thought.

When I fell asleep, I didn't have any more nightmares.

The next time the phone woke me it was day. The cable box said it was 10:12 , and the voice on the phone said it was Fred Chapel.

"I heard from Detective Marcus this morning," Chapel told me. "He informs me that the Portland police are not pursuing you as a suspect in your brother's murder."

"Oh, goody," I said.

"They're going to want your help. They'll most likely come by in the next few days for a follow-up interview, to see if they missed any-thing, and they'll have questions about the pictures as well as your brother. I'd still prefer it if I were with you should that come to pass, but for now, you're off the hook."

I didn't tell him he was a day late and a dollar short, and that I'd already tried being helpful to the cops, and it hadn't gone very well.

"Does that mean I can go back to the bottle?" I asked.

He didn't think it was a joke. "If that's your thing, go ahead."

*   *   *

Showered and dressed and with a fresh cup of Peet's blend in my hand, a cigarette cornered in my mouth, I went to shut off the alarm and get the morning paper. When I opened the door, a FedEx envelope fell inward, onto my bare feet. I picked it up and there wasn't an address tag on it, just the envelope. It didn't feel like there was anything inside.

I got the paper, brought it and the envelope back to the table. I pulled the tab and tore it open. The contents refused to dump out when I shook it, and I had to reach in to free them. There were two items, a piece of paper, and a thicker sheet, a little tacky on one side.

It took a moment for me to realize that the tacky sheet was a photograph. I'd never seen one like it. It was eight by ten, and it felt fresh, as if it had just come from some one-hour place. The image was in shades of red, popping out of a black background. People seen in red.

I was looking at my bedroom. I was looking at myself, asleep, in bed.

With a man, standing beside me, and holding a thing that wasn't as red as I was, or as he was, in his hand. Pointing it at my head.

A man pointing a gun at my head.

I dropped the coffee and the cigarette and the photograph all at once, felt the scald as the liquid splattered from the mug to my leg. The cigarette died with a sizzle in the spill.

The other piece, the paper, was a typed photocopy, with toner streaks across its face. It read:

GO ASK TOMMY WHY I'M HOLDING A GUN TO YOUR HEAD.

I dropped that one, too.

In my chest I could feel my heart beating so savagely and so hard, I imagined bruises rising on my skin.

I had to get out of this house. It wasn't a safe place, it wasn't my place, it had become someone else's. I picked up the photograph and the paper, each of them now stained with spilled coffee, and stuffed them back in the envelope, panicked trying to find my keys and my coat.

And I went.

All portals secure.

Bullshit.

CHAPTER TWENTY-FOUR

Maybe there's a lower brain, or a higher one, or something, a part that understands before the conscious kicks in.

Maybe I was just so worked up, I didn't even realize that I was thinking.

I was racing in the Jeep, and I wasn't trying to think at all, but I was realizing shit left and right. By the time I'd hit Broadway I understood my nightmare on a whole different level, knew that at least one of the cameras had been literal.

The man with the gun, he was alone, I was sure he was alone, because the angle, it was from the bureau, and that was where he had set the camera holding his fancy film. Working in the dark, without the light, and he had set the auto feature or whatever it was, and gone and posed with his gun and my head, and the camera had snapped, and in my dream last night, that was the noise that had registered.

I was crossing the Broadway bridge, passing people illegally, and I had to brake hard at the curve, where the road turns unexpectedly north-south. I passed the post office, turned west again, heading up Flanders. I ran the lights at Eighteenth and Nineteenth, over the freeway, not even realizing I had done it until the sound of horns penetrated my shell. I didn't slow down, climbing the hill, and I was sure that was where Tommy would be. He didn't have anywhere else to go.

Mikel's.

Parked on the street, out of the car holding the envelope so tight it hurt, bending the cardboard in my fist, and with my other fist, I pounded on the door. Mikel's Land Rover was still in its spot, and there was another car in the berth next to it, an older Ford SUV, dingy and dinged. I was trying to remember if I had seen it before when I heard the door open.

I turned, starting to say "Tommy—" and then I didn't say anything else, because it wasn't Tommy I was looking at.

The man standing there was about six or seven inches taller than me, wide, but how wide I couldn't tell, because he was wearing a big black Columbia rain parka, the kind with flaps and pockets and an oversized hood, and it hid a lot of his shape. The hood was up, and in that frozen instant when the door opened and I took it all in, I remember thinking he didn't have a face inside that hood, that it was just darkness, nothing more.

Both of his hands came up, gloved in black leather, but in one of them was a gun, maybe the same gun from the photograph. I tried to react, to step back and shout and escape, but he grabbed me by the shirt and yanked me inside. I fell coming over the threshold, hitting the wall, and I dropped the envelope and brought my hands up to protect my face.

The door slammed, and I felt a hand against my back, felt the palm between my shoulder blades, and the Parka Man shoved me, and I twisted to keep from getting my nose smashed against the wall. He held me upright, pressed against the wall, and he put the gun against my neck. The emptiness in the hood leaned closer, and I saw his eyes and his mouth through narrow holes in the mask.

"You've sure grown up," the Parka Man said in my ear.

The hand on my back bunched into a fist, taking my coat, and he yanked hard, pulling me off my feet. He was probably twice as heavy as I was, and it seemed like he was twice as strong, and I felt like a straw doll when he forced me down the hall, the gun still biting into my neck. When we reached the entrance to the living room, his fist opened, and he shoved forward, hard, and I staggered, lost my balance, and went sprawling onto the carpet.

Tommy was on the floor in the center of the living room, not quite where Mikel had fallen only four days before. His knees were drawn up to his belly, and his arms were bent behind his back, and his face was bleeding a new stain into the carpet. His mouth and brow looked like a mess of torn skin, and I saw froth at his lips as he struggled to breathe. I saw something white shine in all of that red and pink, a broken tooth or an exposed bone.

Parka Man grabbed my arm, and I was twisted around, and I saw the gun coming up at me again, and he hit me with it. There was a gap, jarring like a bad edit, and then I was on my back, still on the floor, and pain was blossoming from my forehead, making the world tumble, making everything so very much brighter.

The Parka Man leaned down and reached for me again, and I tried to fend him off, screaming and kicking. He shoved his gun against my cheek and his other hand into my throat, forcing my head back down. The barrel of the gun on my skin was sharp and wet. I couldn't breathe.

"Scream again and I write this off here and now," Parka Man said softly. His mouth was close to mine, and his breath hit my lips and ran up my nose, and if I'd had the air, I would have gagged. "Scream, I do you both right here."

I couldn't move, and I couldn't even nod. The terror was so complete that it felt like I had no body, that I was just a form of fear, lying on my dead brother's floor. I tried to make some kind of noise of understanding or assent or surrender, but the flat pressure on my throat grew as Parka Man pushed the barrel of his gun a little harder into my skin, his gloved hand a little harder on my throat. Then both were suddenly gone, and he was backing away. I started coughing, rolled onto my side, trying to stop it, terrified that even that would be too much noise, and I saw Tommy again, and he hadn't moved.

"Get up," Parka Man said.

I tried, had turned onto all fours in an attempt to rise, but it still wasn't quick enough for him. He came back and grabbed me by my hair, and I started to shriek but stopped myself, even though I felt roots tearing. He shoved me at the easy chair by the foot of the couch, and I went into it headfirst, twisting. When I completed the turn, he was standing by Tommy, holding the gun on me.

"Sit. Still."

I felt blood running from my forehead, catching in my right eyebrow. It felt like it would start dripping into my eye. I didn't move.

Parka Man backed out of the room, into the entry hall, out of sight. There was a cordless phone on the wall by the stairs to the second floor, where Mikel's bedroom had been, but before I even thought about going for it, he came back. He was folding the FedEx envelope in both hands, forcing the cardboard to bend down, and as soon as he'd finished he put it in one of the parka pockets, then brought the gun out again from another.

"He's alive," Parka Man said, and he used the gun to indicate Tommy. "Remember that. Bad as he looks, he's alive."

I could see that Tommy's hands were cuffed together behind his back.

"You want him to stay that way, you'll listen to me," Parka Man said.

The blood that I'd feared would run into my eye turned right, flowing along the ridge of my brow, and I could feel it trickling along my hairline, down my jaw.

Parka Man came closer, holding the gun casually in his hand, pointed down. I waited for him to stop, but he didn't, kept coming, until he was standing over me in the chair. I stared at his middle, at his parka, at all the shiny metal of his zippers and buttons and clasps.

His free hand came up to my face, and I flinched, but kept silent. I felt a gloved thumb touch my brow, follow the line of blood, wiping it away. I could feel the stitching that surrounded his finger. When he reached the end of the blood trail, he dragged it across my cheek, toward my mouth. He touched my upper lip, pressed, then flicked his finger away.

It felt like something inside me would explode. Somewhere beneath the edge of the parka was his groin, and I thought about kicking, striking out hard.

Then I remembered the gun.

He made a noise, like he was happy with the way things looked, like he was satisfied. He backed away, toward Tommy, and used the toe of a black work boot to roll him onto his belly.

"Didn't want to have to do it this way," Parka Man said. "But he was being stubborn. I'd have settled for a hundred thousand, honestly, but he had to get a spine or soul or whatever you friggin' drunks discover in AA, so now we're doing it the hard way. So the price goes up, too."

I stared, confused, terrified, trying to make sense of the words. It was as if he wasn't really talking to me, more to himself. I told myself he was crazy, but he didn't sound crazy; he sounded like someone who enjoyed having power, enjoyed using it.

"Straight to the source this time," the Parka Man said, and his black-toed boot kicked Tommy in the gut. It wasn't savage, almost absent, and I thought I heard Tommy groan. "No middleman."

He looked up from where Tommy sprawled, the emptiness inside his hood settling on me.

"A million dollars. Not too much, not for you. You've got until noon Friday to get it, in cash. Soon as you have it, you go home, turn on your porch light. Leave it on. I see the light, I know you're ready, and I'll tell you where to bring it. I don't see it on, the next time you see your daddy is when the Detective Division comes and asks you to identify the body. You understand me?"

Tommy made a cracked sound that died in the carpet.

"Yes," I heard myself say.

Parka Man slid his gun back in his pocket, crouching. He grabbed Tommy with both hands, one on the cuffs, the other on his upper arm, hoisting him to standing. Tommy's legs seemed like they were hollow, like they were crazy straws beneath his torso, and they bent with his weight, unable to support him.

"Believe me when I say this," Parka Man told me. "I'll know if you talk to the cops. I will know if you even whisper to them. If that happens, I'll kill Tommy, here. I'll take my time about it. Then I'll come and kill you, too. You understand that?"

"Yes."

"That's good. Who says celebrities are unreasonable, right?"

"Right."

"You just sit there and catch your breath, think sweet thoughts for a couple minutes after I'm gone. You're in no hurry. You've got until noon on Friday, like I said."

He grunted, turning Tommy and then hoisting him onto his shoulder in a fireman's carry. They went down the hall, out of sight, and I heard the front door open. A couple seconds later I heard it close. An engine started outside, and I supposed it was the Parka Man's SUV, and it sounded like it was coming closer, and then it was moving away, and then it was gone.

The shaking started in my hands. It ran up my arms, it slid into my legs. My stomach went wild. It felt like stage fright, and it felt nothing like that, because this was terror, and it was different.

I was certain I was going to vomit, steeled myself for it, but it didn't happen. Then the shakes went away, just as they had come, and I thought about getting up, but didn't. My stomach settled, and I started to feel heavy and strangely euphoric, almost postorgasmic. All of the adrenaline, I guess, leaving me high.

The room had huge windows on the east side, to allow the view of the city. The room had been tidied after Mikel's death, and the fresh bloodstains on the carpet looked grotesque next to the ones that had refused to come out.

There wasn't really any doubt, anymore.

It didn't matter if Tommy was everything he had claimed when he'd come and asked to be my father again. It didn't matter if he was as sorry as he said, as sad as he seemed. Maybe he wasn't. It didn't matter.

I couldn't be the reason he died.

He was all I had left.

Outside, I heard a siren coming closer, and I didn't think it was coming here, and I didn't know what I would do if it did. The wail climbed, fell, climbed, and then receded, passing by.

I made my way into the bathroom, turned on the light over the sink. There was a gash on my forehead, not very deep, but long. The skin was torn, and in the opening I could see red flesh, still seeping. The blood that the Parka Man had smeared was already dry, tight on my skin. There was some bleeding on my scalp, too, showing through the curls where the Parka Man had torn hair.

I splashed water on my face, and the cut stung, but in its way that made me feel a little better, made me focus a little more.

A million dollars, that was a lot of money, but I had more than that. It couldn't be that hard to get the cash, and Parka Man had given me most of four days to do it.

I'd get the cash.

Explaining the cut, that would be something else. It looked like I imagined a gash from the edge of a piece of furniture might look, if for example someone had tripped and not caught themselves in time. Something a drunk might not even remember doing to herself if she had gotten really hammered after her brother's funeral.

I can do this, I told myself. I can do what needs to be done.

I didn't think I was lying this time.

CHAPTER TWENTY-FIVE

I t was stupid, but it was the only disguise I could think of, so I wore a ball cap and sunglasses when I went to the bank. I'd bought both of them at a Walgreen's down the block from my branch, and maybe it was the cut, or maybe I just didn't matter that much anymore, but no one seemed to recognize me when I made the purchase.

There was a small group waiting in the teller lines when I got to the bank, the last of the lunch crowd, and I stayed out of their way, trying to be inconspicuous, and it totally backfired and people stared. Maybe sunglasses and a ball cap would do it at the movies, but in a bank, it just made me stick out a little more. I got a withdrawal slip from the stand and filled it out precisely, and waited until the line died down before attaching myself to the end. That didn't work, either, because another three people came in right after I'd done it, and assembled behind me. They were all women, professionally dressed, and none of them looked much older than I.

Four people in front of me, and the line had just shortened to three, when I heard one of the women say, "You know who she looks like? She looks like the girl from Tailhook."

"That's not her. She's too short to be her."

"Not Van, not that one, the *other* one, the one whose brother just got killed."

"That's not Mim."

"I don't know, it looks like Mim."

"It could be."

"No it couldn't, she doesn't live in town, she lives out in Lake Oswego."

"That's Van, Van lives in Oswego. She has that big house they showed on television that time."

The line had shortened to one, and I really wanted the women behind me to shut up.

"Did you hear about the photos? There was this bit on the news about these photos."

"Oh, God, I know! My boyfriend showed them to me, can you imagine letting someone do that to you?"

"You could ask her, you could ask if that's her."

"I wouldn't want to be rude."

There was a teller open, and I moved to his station. He was middle-aged, balding, and he smiled at me when he took my withdrawal slip, then looked at it and laughed and handed it back to me.

"I think you need to fill out a new one," he said with a very amused smile.

I checked it, shook my head, slid it back. "No, it's correct."

"I think you wanted those zeros after the decimal point, not before."

"No, it's correct."

He stopped being amused. "Young lady, you're not very funny."

"I'm not trying to be funny. I need it in cash, please."

The teller took the slip once more, went over it again, then frowned at me with suspicion. He asked me to wait a moment, then began tapping on the terminal to the left of his cash drawer. He scowled at the figures on his screen, and I figured he was just making certain that the money was there. Then his posture changed, and he leaned forward on the shelf, gesturing for me to come closer.

"I'm terribly sorry, Miss Bracca," the teller said. "I'll get the manager."

I started to protest, but he was already out of the station and heading down the row of fellow tellers. I told myself not to worry, that he probably needed the manager's permission to access that much cash. I was a little surprised he hadn't already asked to see some identification.

Along the line of tellers, one of the women was finishing her transaction. I caught her staring at me, and when I caught her, she blushed and turned away hastily.

My teller came back, flanked by an older woman. The woman wore glasses, and had red hair, and it was obviously dyed.

"Miss Bracca," the woman said. "I'm Catherine Lumley, why don't you come with me?"

"Fine," I said, and got out of line. Catherine waited for me at the end of the counter, and she pulled the short door back, allowing me through. With her free hand, she pointed to her office, past the vault door, and I headed inside. She followed close behind me.

The office was carpeted, and then had an Oriental rug on it, to add to the plush. There were four filing cabinets and a big desk and three leather chairs. The cabinets and the desk were some dark wood, like the rosewood used in fretboards, and all of the handles for all of the drawers were brass and shiny. I could almost feel the money.

"Please have a seat," Catherine Lumley said. "Would you like something to drink? Coffee? Water or anything?"

I took one of the chairs facing the desk, and she surprised me by staying on my side and taking one of the seats beside me.

"I'm fine," I said. Even knowing the balance in my account, I was starting to feel like an imposter.

"You should have come to me right away. As a valued client, if you ever have any trouble with any of our personal bankers, you should never hesitate to speak to the manager."

I looked at her blankly. Then I took off my sunglasses and repeated the look.

"If you'd like, I can call Mr. Rodriguez in here." She added it in the same apologetic tone that the teller had used.

"You mean the teller? No, I mean, he was fine, everything's fine."

"He should have recognized you, of course. But I can call Mr. Rodriguez right now."

"Okay," I said. "I give up. Who is Mr. Rodriguez?"

Lumley chuckled, then stopped when she realized I wasn't kidding. "Oh, I'm so sorry, I thought you knew. He's your banker."

"I don't have a banker. I have a bank, this bank. This is the bank I've been using since high school."

"Yes, and we do appreciate your continued patronage, Miss Bracca. But in cases of accounts in excess of one million dollars, we always provide our clients with personal banking facilities. Alexander Rodriguez has been handling your account since February."

"Doing what?"

"Ideally, whatever you require."

"I see," I said. "Well, I require withdrawing a million dollars in cash, if that's all right."

She hesitated, and I was afraid she was going to ask what I needed it for, and I realized with a little feeling of panic that I didn't have a good lie ready. "I hope this doesn't mean you're closing the account?" she asked.

"No, not at all."

"I'm glad to hear that."

"So . . . it won't be a problem?"

"No." She smiled at me, then got up and went around to her side of the desk, to her computer. She clacked keys for a couple of seconds, and the smile remained, even seemed to grow a fraction. "Will hundreds do? Or smaller bills?"

The Parka Man hadn't specified. "I think hundreds will be fine."

Lumley straightened, beaming at me. "Then I'll have Mr. Rodriguez call you Monday, as soon as the cash is together."

"Monday?"

"Yes, it'll take until then for us to get that much cash."

Someone living in my belly inflated a balloon, painted the word "panic" on it, then let it go to ride the currents up to my head.

"I need it sooner," I told Lumley.

Lumley began to look concerned again. "I'm afraid there's no way we can do that."

"Who can? There must be someone who can, right? I have the money, I have more than enough money."

"Your combined balance currently stands at four million, six hundred and eighty-seven thousand, nine hundred and eleven dollars," Lumley said. "That's not the problem, Miss Bracca. We're a bank, not the Federal Reserve. We simply don't have that much currency here, in fact, we never do unless we know there will be a need for it."

"Can I open an account at another bank?" I asked, trying to keep the balloon from going higher. "Do a wire transfer?"

"You misunderstand me, I'm afraid. It's not *us*, it's the amount. Any bank in the region will have the same problem. What you're asking to withdraw is a very large amount of currency."

It was Tuesday afternoon. If I believed Lumley, and I didn't have a reason not to, then it wouldn't matter where I went. I suddenly realized I'd have the same problem no matter who I banked with. Which meant that come Friday noon, I wouldn't have the money, and I didn't believe Parka Man would give me a reprieve. Clearly, he'd anticipated this problem, but not how long it would take; that was why he had given me the time. If four days later I still didn't have the money, he wasn't going to be happy, and his unhappiness would probably manifest itself by inflicting a lot of pain, and probably death, on Tommy.

The beating had looked so painful, the damage so much, and sitting in Catherine Lumley's office, I saw Tommy again in my mind's eye. All the times I'd wished him to suffer, and now that he was suffering, I felt sick.

Lumley was waiting for me.

"How much can you get me by Friday?" I asked.

"I'd say five hundred, perhaps six hundred thousand dollars."

"Which?"

"Six hundred thousand," Lumley said. "Yes, I should think that wouldn't be a problem."

"Then I'd like you to do that, please."

"We'd be happy to. I'll have Mr. Rodriguez call you as soon as your cash is ready."

"Thanks," I said.

"No," said Lumley. "Thank *you* for banking with Four Rivers."

Graham's apartment was in the Pearl, and that's where I headed next. During the last few months I'd been with the tour, he'd made a habit of traveling with cash, upward of fifty thousand dollars at a time on some legs. He'd kept it in his briefcase, used it to pay for incidentals and emergencies and shopping sprees, but mostly it was for travel. Cash was the best way to get around the paparazzi and their penchant for digging through credit card receipts.

There was no way he was carting four hundred grand around in his briefcase, but he'd know where I could get it.

I took Burnside across the river, back into downtown, then up toward Powell's. The Heineken Brewery used to be on Burnside, this huge old brick building that had stood since the bad old days, when Portland was renowned by sailors the world over as "the worst port in the world." But Heineken sold the property a couple years ago, and some developers bought it and promptly tore the whole thing down. Now there were expensive condos and yuppie health food stores.

Graham's apartment was in an earlier iteration of the process, a twenty-odd-story collection of new apartments with an Art Deco feel. He'd bought it after *Scandal*, when it had become clear that Tailhook was staying together, and that he was part of the package. Prior to that, he'd lived exclusively in L.A., and he still kept a home there. He'd bought in the Pearl because it was considered the trendiest damn section of town, full to the popping with young urban professionals, all of them beautiful, all of them eager, and most of them looking for a date. Click had his place just a little farther north from Graham's.

I parked the Jeep and hopped out, and there was a security guy at the desk in the lobby, and he wanted to know who I was visiting. I told him I was Miriam Bracca to see Graham Havers, and the guard got all flustered and begged my pardon and told me he hadn't recognized me.

"It's okay," I said.

"Mr. Havers has some company there already, I don't think it'll be a problem if you head on up without me calling first," the security guy said.

"If it is, I'll tell him I snuck past you."

Security Guy grinned like we'd just become the best buds in the world. "Cool. And if anyone asks, I'll say I've never seen you."

I laughed and he grinned even bigger, and then I got in the elevator and went up to eighteen. There was no one in the car and no one in the hall, and I rang the bell beside Graham's door, and waited. There was no music coming from inside, which was strange, because normally when Graham was home, he was playing something, usually a new band, usually someone none of us had ever heard before.

Graham answered the door, looking like he'd had some rest and wasn't planning on any company coming by. He was in purple Adidas workout pants and a white V-necked silk shirt, and he was barefoot.

"Mimserama!"

"Hey, can I come in?"

He threw a glance over his shoulder, into the main room, then reached a hand for my shoulder, to guide me inside. The gesture popped a sudden memory of the Parka Man's gloves on my arms and face, and I stepped back without thinking. Graham looked confused, but before he could voice it I went past him.

"Guy downstairs said you had company," I said. "I hope you don't mind."

"No, it's not a problem. You've met them, I think." Graham edged around me, leading down the hall and gesturing into the main room, where his lifestyle was plain for any and all to see. He had a wide-screen Philips monitor mounted on the wall, between two arched windows that looked out into downtown, and two huge Klipsch speakers at the far corners of the room. The stereo setup was NAD and multi-component, each piece seated gently in a chrome cabinet. The space was open, with low furniture, all modular, all vaguely Danish.

Detective Marcus had been standing at one of the three CD racks, examining the titles. Hoffman was on the couch. Both now directed their attention to me.

Graham continued past, saying, "You guys know Mim, of course, talked to her already. They just dropped by for a few questions."

He told the last to me, adding a little shrug, as if to say that it all seemed silly to him.

"Miss Bracca," Marcus said. "Pleasant surprise."

"You and me both."

Hoffman didn't say anything.

"I can come back," I told Graham.

"No, we're pretty much finished here," Marcus said, before Graham could answer. "We'll be going now. Thanks for your help, Mr. Havers."

"Hey, anything to assist, you know how that is."

"You'd be surprised what a minority you're in."

Graham made a comment about being grateful for the police in general, then headed back down the hall, to get the door. Marcus followed, wishing me a good day, and Hoffman came last, but she stopped as she was passing me.

"Rough night?" she asked.

It took me a second to realize she was talking about the cut on my head. I tried to fumble out my prepared lie, but I didn't need it, because she'd already continued on her way. I watched her and Marcus shake Graham's hand, and then they left, and he shut the door after them.

"No idea what the hell *that* was about," he told me cheerfully when he came back. "Just dropped by, wanted to know if I had any idea about anything about your brother or those pictures. Wanted a list of possible enemies, shit like that. I told them every unsigned guitarist. Then they asked for disgruntled employees. I told them I'd try to get them something, but the way Van is, that list would be fifty pages long."

"Just for the tour managers," I said.

He nodded, grinning, then focused on me, concerned. "What happened to your head? You take a spill?"

"A bad one."

"Were you loaded, Mimser?"

"No. I'm just a klutz."

He laughed. "I love it, an Oregonian using Yiddish. Klutz. You're not a klutz, kiddo. You want something, I've got stuff in the fridge, I've got some chai and some of those energy drinks that you and Van were chugging on the road. Bought a damn flat of the stuff, and I can't stand it. Taurine, what kind of fucking flavor is taurine?"

"It's kinda citrus," I said. "I don't need anything."

"God, I do. I've got an ounce and a half of coke in the bathroom, I was gonna wet myself when that Hoffman one asked if she could use my facilities. Don't think she noticed it, though."

"You left it out on the counter?"

"Hell, no, it's in my shaving kit."

Graham left me laughing and went into the kitchen, then came right back, opening a can of soda. He flopped on the couch, and waved at me to take any seat I wanted.

"You hear the latest?" he asked me. "*Nothing for Free* is at seven, and *Scandal* just hit forty-nine. Our illustrious sponsor called me this morning, offering to tack on another twenty-five dates."

"You going to take them?"

Graham chugged his soda like it was water, then lowered the can and began drumming one of his irregular beats on its side, staring at me. I wondered if he was actually on the coke he'd been talking about.

"Talked to Van about the albums, didn't talk to her about the dates yet, there's an issue, kind of, but maybe you should talk to her."

"There's an issue?"

"There's a request, it's not an issue, it's a *request* that if they *do* add the dates, they add them with you back on the stage, not with Clay."

"Oh."

Graham swept on, ignoring the awkwardness. "I got a call, there's a company down in L.A. called Muze Media, they put out videos, you know, the kind you see advertised on the cable outlets, late-night. *Sexy Coeds in New Orleans Show You Their Hooters* and shit like that, but they're asking if we have any home video, maybe from the tour, anything like that. They'll package and sell it, they're offering a sweet deal on that."

"We don't have anything like that."

"The Midwest stuff, this past summer, on the bus, Click had a camera, we were all passing it around, you remember, right? You and Van and Click all goofing around, making your home movie. You know who has that tape? Do you have it?"

"I'd think Click does."

"I'll have to call him." He drained his soda, then began working the can in one hand, making the aluminum pop and crinkle. He was staring out the window, or maybe at the window, and his expression went a little blank, as if he was totaling figures in the spreadsheet of his mind.

"Hey, Graham?" I said.

"What? Sorry, honey, just thinking, you know."

"Yeah, listen. I need some money."

"You have money. You have more than *some* money."

"Yeah, but I need cash," I said. "It's hard to explain, but there's a purchase I need to make, and I have to do it by the end of the week, and the bank, they can't get me the cash in time. But I was thinking, you've got cash, and you always said it was *our* cash."

"You mean the Mad Road Money? Yeah, that's Tailhook's, that's not mine. I've got a couple grand here, if that'll do it, but I'd think the bank could cover that. How much you need, baby?"

"Four hundred thousand," I said.

Graham stopped working the can and stared at me. "Come again?"

"I know it's a lot."

He continued to stare at me, and all of his nervous energy was gone. "Why do you need four hundred thousand dollars in cash, Mim?"

"Like I said, I'm buying this thing and—"

"What thing?"

"Property, it's in Lake Oswego, near the water. Secluded, but it's one of those private communities, you know, and they're nervous about me moving in, because of everything and all. But if I can pay this guy in ready cash, he's willing to sell to me."

"You're dumping your place?"

"It's just ... the cameras and everything, Graham, it's just been too much, you know?"

"But you put so much work into that place."

"I know, I know, but I can't ... I can't stay there. And Lake Oswego, you know, it's quiet, it's real secluded. If I pay this guy in cash, then maybe the press won't find out about it. I could use a place like that."

He was wavering, I could see it.

"Be a good place for me to dry out."

That was the push, and it took. "I can see that. But four hundred, Mimser, I've never carried a quarter that much. I can free up about a hundred, hundred fifty thousand."

"I'll write you a check."

"Yeah, and you should talk to Van, too. She watches the money and she'll want to know why I'm spraying cash like a stuck cow. Pig. Whatever it is that sprays when it's stuck."

"Normally a pig," I said.

"You need it when?"

"By Friday. I have to meet this guy Friday noon, so if I can get it no later than Friday morning, that'd be great."

"Yeah, I can do that," Graham said, after a second. "We're leaving tomorrow evening, but I should be able to get it to you before then."

I got up and went and gave him a kiss on the lips, just a thanks. "You're a saint."

"You're gonna have to talk to Van, you know. You should ask her at the party tonight."

"I'm not going."

"I know it's soon after the funeral, but it could cheer you up."

"I don't think I'd be comfortable."

"Mim, you're part of the *band,* honey. Van loves you, she's just being a hard-ass because she cares. That thing in Sydney, that's not what this is about, that's just the symptom, you know. Van's got voice and she's got presence, and even she knows that it's worth shit if she doesn't have you giving her a way to use them. We all want you back, we all want you healthy and happy, not ... you know."

"The way I am now?"

He crinkled the can again. "You should go, baby, at least stop by."

"I'll think about it."

"I'll be there. Click'll be there. Be a chance to talk about these new dates, too. You tell Van what you told me, about this place, this Oswego lakeside-rehab-hideaway you're buying, she might think that's a big step, might lift her anti-Bracca embargo."

"You think?"

"It's what she says, it's about the band. Getting you onstage, that'd be good for the band," Graham said. "You should go."

I told him I'd think about it, and let him hug me before I went out the door. Graham's hugs are small things, as if he's afraid that pushing his body against yours would be too sexual, would somehow corrupt the manager-talent relationship. But he gave me a good squeeze this time, as if to say that he knew I was fighting the good fight, that he was in my corner.

I headed out, back to the car, thinking that all I needed now was a quarter of a million dollars in cash, and that either Van or Click could easily provide it. Click was probably the safer bet. But Graham would talk to Van, tell her what I was doing, and if I didn't then go to her, she could shut the whole thing down, at least for the time being. So Click wasn't going to be an option.

The clock said it was almost four-thirty, and if I headed out to Lake Oswego now, I'd get swamped by traffic, and it'd take an hour, at the least. Which meant I'd arrive as Van was preparing for her party, something I didn't want to do, because a party, to Van, was like a show. She wouldn't want to be distracted before the curtain went up.

So I headed home, thinking that what was best for the band wasn't always what was best for the performers, and wondering what I should wear.

CHAPTER TWENTY-SIX

Van's place was custom all the way, built in the hills of Lake Oswego, about twenty minutes southeast of Portland when the traffic was behaving. Lake Oswego once upon a very long time ago was big with loggers and cowboys and pioneers who wandered west on the Oregon Trail. Now it was big with money, fringed with upper middle class, an exceptionally white neighborhood in an already very white state, where urban professionals moved their families because the thought of raising those same families in the city made their bowels go loose. The Big Wealth surrounded the actual Oswego Lake, in houses shrouded in trees, with boat docks and views without neighbors.

Van's house was still experiencing growing pains; like me, Van had been dumping money into her home ever since the tour began. Unlike me, though, Van had started from scratch, buying the property, then leveling the structure that stood on it. She'd had all sorts of headaches from the local homeowners and the county—Lake Oswego is in Clackamas County, unlike Portland, which is in Multnomah—but in the end, being Van, she'd won out. Her lawyers shouted louder, perhaps. Or maybe she just crooned at them with the mike.

Whatever the case, when I pulled up, I could see that the majority of the work had been completed. The house was bilevel, built onto the slope, so that the entry floor was actually the second, with another below, closer to the water. The drive down from the road dipped sharply before winding through the trees, and it provided a nice curtain of anonymity. But when I hit the bottom of the drive I could see the lights on, and over the Jeep's engine, I could hear the music. There were already two dozen cars parked all around and along the driveway, and I could see some late-arriving guests making last-minute adjustments in rearview mirrors.

I parked and got out, and the music was louder. Van was still on the Radiohead kick. The song was "You and Whose Army?"

Seemed a fair question, and I just stood by my Jeep for a couple minutes, smoking a cigarette and trying to screw up my courage as each new arrival pulled up. "Keeping it small" meant only about fifty to seventy-five people were expected. Van's really big parties drew more than two hundred. Sometimes it seemed like the only thing you needed to get invited was to be able to find the place on a map.

I didn't want to ask Van for money. I didn't want to be at a party. I didn't, especially, want to be at one of Van's parties. The last one I'd attended had been the night before we'd left on the most recent leg of the tour, and I'd spent almost the entire night getting drunk out on the balcony, throwing things into the lake.

"Mim?"

It was Click, and he'd come up behind me, and the surprise had my heart checking the exits. If he'd bothered to dress up for the party, I couldn't tell. Maybe he'd changed to his really good Winterhawks jersey. The Chuckies were still mismatched.

"Just me," he said mildly.

"You."

"I said your name twice, nothing."

"Lost in thought."

He came up beside me with a chuckle, looking at the house and pulling his rolling kit from his back pocket. "You've got a lot of those to be lost in at the best of times."

"Goes with being The Brains."

"I'm just the central nervous system, I wouldn't know about that." Click rolled himself a cigarette, and I lit it for him, and he thanked me and blew out a plume. "Surprised you came."

"I need to talk to Van."

"You're not going to change her mind. I already tried."

"It's not about the band."

"No? Then you better get to her early. She's gonna be busy tonight."

"Fleet week already?"

Click made a grunting noise, like I'd socked him. "Rose Festival's not until summer, you know that. Might want to check your claws at the door."

I dropped my butt and stomped it out. He was right; if I was already this defensive and Van wasn't even present, things weren't likely to go well once we got face to face. I was going to have to get that under control, and fast.

"Heard about the album?" Click asked.

"Graham says it's at seven."

"Must feel strange to you. Feels fucking strange to me."

"It does," I agreed.

He was still watching the house, smoking his hand-rolled. "Don't change the fact that it's a good album."

"Guess not."

"Might want to keep that in mind, that's what I mean." He flicked his cigarette down the driveway, toward the house, and it sizzled out in a puddle. Then he offered me his arm. "Let's wow the little people, what do you say?"

"How can I refuse?"

"Oh, hey, so it turns out we're sleeping together," he told me when we were halfway down the walk.

"No shit?"

"Turns out that's why you're on hiatus. We had a messy breakup, you and me. Apparently I'm seeking solace with Van."

"Brutal."

"Tell me about it."

A haze of smoke was leaking out of the house as we reached the door, a mix of cigarette and pot, and the music was louder, almost to the point of distortion. We stepped into a crowd of men and women, most of them in our age group, and I instantly realized the small-party estimate had been off, and that there must have been more cars parked outside than I had noticed.

There were hip-hopsters and punkers and retro grungers and people like me and Click, who'd decided that what we wore would be what we wore. I'd defaulted to my band outfit, just cargo pants and a black long-sleeved T-shirt, but only because it was too cold to wear the tank.

A couple of people shouted at us when we entered, waving hands or bottles, but their voices were swamped by the music, and Click and I just smiled and waved back. He dropped my arm and shouted in my ear.

"I'm gonna get a liquid. Catch you later?"

"I'll be around," I shouted back.

Click headed in the most likely direction of the kitchen. I worked my way past the entry crowds, down the stairs to the main room on the lower floor. Several people broke their conversations to watch me pass, and most even said hello. What they were actually thinking as I passed was anyone's guess.

The living room space was a cavern, two stories high and long, and most of the party had moved there, doing nothing to defeat the size of the room. Another stereo was going down here, fighting with the music playing above, blasting dance remixes. A cluster near the far wall writhed, shimmied, and ground to the beat. On a big-screen television, one of the guests was playing a video game. The volume on that was cranked up, and the explosions on the screen seemed to keep fairly good time with the surrounding music.

Graham was with the dance contingent, grooving away, and he saw me come off the stairs and raised a hand, and I raised one back, then did a double take. My eyes were playing tricks. I looked hard, saw it again, and this time I was certain.

Dyke Tracy was dancing with him, her hair slicked back, working up a sweat. The outfit was new, not the work clothes and not what she'd worn when she'd grilled me in my kitchen the previous night, very casual, this time, just the jeans and the tee and the sneakers. Graham said something to her, and she shot a look my way and grinned.

I didn't know if I should panic or laugh. Both seemed reasonable options.

Marcus wasn't on the floor, and I cast around for him, trying to find him in the corners or on the stairs, but he wasn't there, either. I took that to mean Hoffman was here on her own accord, not on the job, but that didn't raise my comfort level.

Time to do what I came to do and get the hell out.

I stopped and listened at Van's bedroom door, and didn't hear anything like sex going on, so I figured it was safe to knock.

"Who?"

"Mim."

There was a pause, and then the door swung open and Van stood there. I'd interrupted her halfway through makeup, and she'd done her eyes, but everything below the nose was still untouched. She didn't look surprised or thrilled to see me, just turned and went back to her makeup table.

"Would you close it?" she asked.

I shut the door and took a moment to appreciate the room. It was large and white and functional. A big bed, good for sleeping or play-

ing, a big television in the corner, and the makeup table. Doors led to
the bathroom and the closets. One wall had a beautiful oil painting, a
field of trees in what looked like a pretty fierce autumn storm, and
when I moved my head, the light on the painting seemed to change,
pulling the background into relief.

Van finished with her lips, capped the stick, and then turned to
give me some attention. She was wearing another of her tees, this one
gray and with the sleeves cut off. On it was a fifties-style woman's
face, neatly coiffed, eyes beneath sleepy lids, her mouth open, wiping
at her chin with the back of her hand. Beneath it all was the slug GOT
CREAM?

It was the kind of shirt she wore simply to get a response, and for
that reason alone, I ignored it.

"You have a detective on your dance floor," I told her.

"Only one? I invited two."

"Did you?"

"Two came by today, Portland PD, Graham sent them over. About
what happened to your brother and the pictures and all of it. I was doing party prep at the time."

"I know them."

"Right, of course you do." Vanessa turned back to the mirror on her
table, picked up the hairbrush. "Anyway, I invited them. As guests, not
cops."

"You live dangerously," I said.

She laughed at my reflection. "You're one to talk."

"Not kidding, Van. There are at least fifteen people smoking joints
upstairs, and God knows what's going on in the bathrooms."

"Nothing's going to happen." She began pulling the brush through
her hair, still watching me in the mirror. "Graham told me you'd be by."

"Did he tell you why?"

"He said you needed to get together some cash for a purchase, and
you couldn't get the bank to hand it over in time."

"I'm not after a loan, Van. I need to cash a very large check, and
the bank can't cover it in time."

She finished fixing her hair, then got up and went to the closet. There was another mirror hanging from the inside of the closet door, a double full-length one, and she checked herself very carefully in it. I didn't see anything wrong, but Van apparently did, and she spent a couple seconds adjusting the waist of her jeans, making sure they hugged low on her hips.

"So tell me about this place you're buying."

I'd refined the lie in the intervening hours, and I thought it flowed easily, not too smooth, but honest. "It's on the other side of the lake, smaller than this place, but it's really nice. Four bedrooms, two full baths, and there's a really good space for a music room. And there's a deck, you know, with a hot tub. The whole thing's right on the water, really quiet. But you know how they are out here, they're all worried about the publicity and noise and shit, and if I can get them a big lump sum down, that'll make me look good."

"Graham said it'd help you dry out."

"I think it would."

She nodded slightly, then checked herself again. She indicated her shirt. "You haven't commented."

"You wouldn't like what I had to say."

"Please, go ahead."

I sighed. "All right, I think it's sexist, gross, and that it pretty much declares that you'll give a blow job to any guy who wants one."

Van examined herself in the mirror again. "You get all that from the shirt?"

"You asked."

"Shit." Van pulled the shirt off, tossing it on the closet floor, then disappeared inside, rummaging around. "How much you need?"

"Two hundred and fifty thousand in cash. But I need it by Friday."

"Three days? And how much is this place?"

"Seller'll let me have it for a million." I managed to say it like the number wasn't significant, like we all were used to dealing with seven figures as a matter of course.

Van emerged, pulling on a green silk shirt. It clung to her shape, and she fixed the middle two buttons, leaving the others open. Her belly, flat and toned, and her cleavage, not flat but also toned, were deftly exposed. The hoop in her navel glinted.

"Better?"

"You look hot."

She made a noise of agreement, then checked herself in the mirror a final time. Satisfied, she closed the closet door, then addressed me.

"What's really going on?" Van asked. She didn't sound angry or annoyed, just very matter-of-fact, as if she was used to all of my lies, and this was merely another of the legion.

"Nothing. Look, Van. I'm just trying to buy this place and this guy already has another buyer. He said if I paid him in cash, he'd sell to me. But he's only giving me until Friday."

"I had that company you used, the one Chapel called, come by. They went through this whole house, did a complete search. I figured it was prudent, especially with what happened at your place. They didn't find anything."

"This isn't about the pictures."

"Mim, I'm not an idiot, okay? Please, please, please stop treating me like one."

"I don't treat you like an idiot—"

"Then why do you keep lying to me?"

"I'm not—"

"Is whoever took those shots blackmailing you? Are there more pictures?"

"It's not blackmail."

"Paying isn't going to stop it. You pay, whoever he is, he's just going to come back for more. You can't do this." Van came closer, lowering her voice. "You can't do this, Mim."

"That's not what this is. That's just not what this is, Van."

"Who hit you?" Van asked. "Your father? Did Tommy hit you?"

"No. No, it's—"

"You've got a bruise on your throat, you know that? Right under your chin, it's hard to see, but when you move your head and the shadow's gone, it's visible, and it's a bruise." Her face suddenly went blank, and her highlighted eyes widened. "Oh God, Mim, did someone choke you?"

She reached a hand for my chin, and I evaded it by stepping back and looking away.

"Please, Van," I said. "I need the money, and I need it in cash, and if I could get it myself I wouldn't be here, I wouldn't ask. My bank can't get it to me until Monday. I'm good for it, you know I can write you a check or make a wire transfer or whatever you want, but I've got to have the money, and I've got to have it by Friday."

The way she was looking at me, it made me think of Joan.

"Mim." Van said my name softly. "I just want to help you—"

"The way you sent me home?" It burst out as a shout, and I felt like shit the second after I heard myself say it, but I followed it up anyway. "You mean the way you helped me like that? You want to help me, Van, just give me the cash!"

It hurt her, and it showed in the anger that flared in her eyes, and I had to look away from her again.

"All right, Mim. You write me the check and I'll call my banker tomorrow, have him get the cash together. You can pick it up from Graham when it's ready."

I had my checkbook in one of my cargo pockets, and a ballpoint, and I went to the makeup table and wrote it out. After I signed my name I looked up at the reflection, and Van wasn't even watching me anymore, but was sitting on the edge of the bed and looking at the door. I tore the check free and put the book and the pen back in my pocket, then brought it over to her.

She looked at it in my extended hand, and I felt sick because I thought she was going to tell me she had changed her mind, but she took it. She folded the paper perfectly in half.

"Thank you," I said.

"It's funny," Van said quietly. "I never figured out of the three of us, that you'd be the cliché."

"And what does *that* mean?"

"It means you're the one angling to live fast, die young, and leave the good-looking corpse." She got up and tucked the check into her jeans pocket. "You're going to self-destruct or something. It's becoming pretty obvious that I can't stop it, either, any more than I can stop you drinking."

"Would it make you happy to know I haven't had a drink since my brother's funeral?"

"You think that's a fucking achievement? Sober for twenty-four hours? Call me in a month, tell me the same thing."

"I will."

"I don't think you will. I don't think you'll be able to."

She went to the door, ready to leave and join her guests. I followed her out, into the hallway. The party noise rushed at us, loud voices and the thunder of music. We walked back to the main room together, but just before we hit it, Van put her hand on my arm and stopped me.

"Whoever it is, whatever they have on you, they're never going to stop," she said. "They'll bleed you until you're dead, and then they'll pick over your corpse. Think about that."

Then she waded into the room, taking hugs and laughter, pulling admirers into her wake exactly like what they were—groupies following a rock star.

CHAPTER TWENTY-SEVEN

I was out the door and halfway to my car when Hoffman caught up with me, saying, "Hey, wait a minute."

"No," I threw over my shoulder, and kept going. I heard her sneakers slapping in puddles as she accelerated, long strides, coming alongside. She reached the Jeep ahead of me, put herself between me and the driver's door. It was cold enough that her breath made clouds with each exhale.

"Please get out of my way," I said.

"Look, you're not a suspect, it's okay to talk to me."

"I don't want to talk to you. Hell, I don't want to see you. You weren't even supposed to be here tonight."

"I was invited."

"Well, that was Van's mistake, and I shouldn't have to suffer for it."

Hoffman gave a half-laugh. "You really have no idea how to deal with me, do you? Your gaydar went off and you went straight to the bunker."

"If that's what you want to believe."

"I think we both know it's the truth. I think we both know you've been waiting for a nice butch to come along and take care of you for a while now."

"I think we both know you're full of shit," I said, or at least started to say, but everything after "think" was lost in her mouth, because she started kissing me.

She was fierce about it, and a flicker ran through me, urging me to resist, but there was another one, stronger and hotter, and that was the one I went with, feeling the cool of her sweat and the heat of her skin and the warmth of her body against the chill of the air. I pressed myself into her, and she put her hands on my hips and pulled me with her as she stepped back, and we moved, me pushing up on tiptoe to keep my lips to hers, as she got me around to the back of the Jeep and out of the light.

Her fingers came up, touched my neck, light on my collarbone, and I tried to touch her back, but she wouldn't have any, batting my hand away and pinning me to the back of the car with a thigh between my own. The pressure transferred to muscles, my knees shaking, and she put her mouth on my neck, and it felt wonderful and strange, that softness against the bruise there. I let my head rest against the Jeep, feeling the cold metal and glass on my back, and I pulled air loud, pulled it again louder when her hands went under my shirt.

There were stars visible through the trees, and the music was still whispering in the background, and I heard her breathing, quick and sure, and my own, more ragged, louder. She growled from her throat, her hands shifted, my breathing caught, resumed, faster. Her mouth brushed my ear.

"Jesus God, I want you," she murmured.

And it was so nice to be wanted, and she rocked against me, and I thought I would dissolve, and there was no panic and no fear, and for a euphoric moment, there wasn't even me.

Then she was pulling away, catching her breath as I tried to catch my own. She gave me another kiss, the ferocity gone.

"You've got my number," Hoffman said. "Give me a call."

CHAPTER TWENTY-EIGHT

t was just eleven when I got home, and I locked up and set the alarm, thinking that whatever had just happened, I was happy for it. That lasted until I saw the "all portals secure" message on the LCD.

Like the alarm had done me a damn bit of good thus far. Like I was going to be able to sleep in my bed tonight feeling anything close to secure.

I took a long shower, realized that I wasn't ready to sleep just yet, and pulled on some clothes. There was a last, lonely beer in the fridge, and I opened it, lit a smoke, and went down to the music room.

He waited until I'd set the bottle down and was reaching for the Les Paul, and I heard the sliding of nylon on nylon, and then he grabbed me from behind, easily, like he did this sort of thing all the time. I started to scream, first in surprise, though terror was next on the list, but there was leather suddenly covering my mouth and nose, fingers strong and hard pressing with the one hand while he wrapped his other arm around my middle, pulling me back, pinning me to him.

I struggled, just blind panic, my feet lashing out in the air. My right toe hit the stand for the Les Paul, and it toppled and took one of the Strats and the Godin LG with it, sending them all into my Marshal half-stack with a crash. His grip stayed tight on my face, and he was pinching my nose, and I was suffocating. I got my hands up on his arms, trying to break the grip that was killing me, and I realized I'd never had the strength to do that kind of thing, and I never would.

There was sound in my ears, feedback, high-pitched and ascending, but with a fuzz beneath it, like white noise. I tried biting the hand over my face, but my teeth touched nothing but leather. It felt like I was drunk, and I could feel my hold on his fingers and hand slipping.

A voice broke through all the noise in my head, hanging in my left ear, terrifying because of its lack of feeling.

"Thing about a soundproof room," the Parka Man said. "You can scream all you want."

Then he pitched me forward, letting go of my face, and I felt the concrete beneath the padding on the floor, and I slammed into the guitar stands. The headstock of the fallen Strat caught me in the right side, in the ribs, and it hurt and made me cry out with what little air I had remaining. I tried righting myself, gasping, and he came at me again, pulling me up by my shirt. Threads popped in his grip.

"Go ahead, scream." The voice came from beneath the hood, behind the mask, and I saw his lips for a second in the cutout, thin and curling. From the corner of my eye, I caught the movement of his free hand, and it disappeared, and then my belly was crushed.

I couldn't breathe, and I couldn't see, the world swimming. He must have dropped me then, but I don't remember it. I was still choking for air, but now I couldn't inhale, it was as if my diaphragm had frozen, locked in a sustain. Nothing coming in, nothing coming out, and I was going to die without making a sound.

Parka Man dropped a knee beside my head, grabbed my hair again in one gloved hand. He lifted my face, twisting, making sure I could see him, making sure that I couldn't see anything.

"Cops," he said. "Talking to you, you talking to them."

New shame cascaded through me, the knowledge that he'd been

watching me at Van's, had seen Hoffman and me. I tried shaking my head, to tell him that he was wrong, that I hadn't told anyone anything, that the thing between Hoffman and me was just a stupid kiss, nothing more. His grip was so tight that when I tried the movement, I felt my hair tearing.

"You better not," he told me. "Nothing about me, about you, about Tommy. They ask whatever they want, you don't answer. Lie to your heart's content, they expect that, but you don't ever mention me. I'll know."

The shake hadn't worked, so I tried a nod, still pushing for a breath. Everything below my ribs felt like it had just stopped working, like it wasn't even attached any longer.

"I'll know," he repeated.

He shoved my face down again, into the floor, letting go of my hair. I saw the edge of a boot, and then my diaphragm unlocked with a spasm, and I gasped in a breath. He made the same noise he had in Mikel's condo, the one that sounded like he was happy, but he wasn't moving, and I could feel him looking at me.

"Roll over."

I couldn't even manage a plea.

"Roll. Over."

I closed my eyes and pushed my palms against the carpet, rolling onto my back. I brought my arms around, I suppose it was a strange, instinctive kind of modesty, trying to protect my chest, and I thought he would at least let me keep that, but I felt his gloves on my arms, and he pulled them away.

"Open your eyes," he told me.

It might have been the hardest thing I'd ever been asked to do, and for what felt like minutes, I couldn't, I just couldn't. I thought about his threat, about screaming, calling for help, but even if I had lungs like Van, no one would come. In my music room, soundproofed and cocooned, I had no way out.

Nothing looked back at me, just the mask inside the hood, dark on darker, empty. I couldn't even find his eyes, but I could feel the stare creeping down me. Everything Hoffman had said rushed back at me. I'd felt the eyes of tens of thousands watching me live, I'd known millions more had done the same on screens and pages. Pictures taped to walls and downloaded onto desktops, the gaze of men and women, boys and girls, and I'd had to accept it without too much thought, because it was the kind of thing you couldn't think about for too long, and even now, with the new pictures, they paled next to this.

This was new humiliation, and I wanted to wail. I wanted to beg him to release me, to leave me alone, because I didn't deserve this.

Some songs end the way they want to end, you can't do anything about it, and when you fight it, you end with junk. It was his song now, I realized: he'd pick the ending.

The Parka Man put the heel of his boot on the fingers of my left hand, my fretting hand, and let the promise of more weight rest there, pressing just a little. His head hadn't moved, the dark, vacant holes still watching me. I bit into my tongue, not wanting to give him a sound.

"I'll know," he said.

Then he dropped the rest of the weight, and I tasted blood in my mouth as he ground his heel on my fingers. In my knuckles, I felt bone grinding on cartilage. My eyes filled with tears, hot ones, spilling down the sides of my face, dripping into my ears.

It hurt so bad that when he stopped, I didn't know it.

"I own you," the Parka Man said, and I heard his boots climbing the stairs. Then only silence.

I rolled onto my side, holding my fingers in my right hand, and I wept.

CHAPTER TWENTY-NINE

t took two rapid-fire shots of Jack to make the pain in my hand subside a little, and even then, the sickness in my head remained. I broke ice into a dishtowel, wrapped my fingers with it, praying they weren't broken. The ache was constant, and felt deep in the bone.

I checked the whole house, trying to make certain he was gone, looking in all the closets, in all the hiding places. It was when I was checking the pantry that I saw how he'd done the alarm, and that was the final straw, maybe.

The control box was high on the wall, above my stock of canned goods, and the door to it was open. I had to take a chair from the kitchen table to get a good look, and when I did I saw that all of the fuses had been pulled, except for the one to the control panel. It could tell me that all portals were secure to the day I died, it would always be lying.

He could come and go as he pleased. He'd done it twice already, maybe more than that. He certainly had been waiting for me in the basement even before I got home.

It was what Van had said, too. He wouldn't ever stop. Even if he was sincere now in his promise to return Tommy to me in exchange for cash, that would change, that would change as soon as he saw how easily he could control me.

Which is what made me remember the other thing Van had said, about how I was going to end up. But Van was wrong about one thing: I was doubting that the corpse I left behind would be all that nice on the eyes.

He owned me.

He would kill Tommy. Then he would kill me.

The only way I could stop it was if I found him first.

It took me until dawn to find a place to start, and it seemed weak, even by my desperate standards, but I didn't have anything else. Thinking about everything he'd said, how he'd said it, the one thing I kept coming back to were the words he'd used in Mikel's condo.

You've sure grown up.

It could mean a lot of things, I told myself. It could mean all kinds of things.

But maybe it means foster care.

There were forty-nine Larkins in the Qwest White Pages, and another twenty-three when I used the iMac in my office to do a Google search. Since I couldn't remember the first name of either of the parents or most of the kids, I almost panicked. I couldn't remember the name of any of the four sons.

Of the two daughters, I knew one of them was called Sheila, and I remembered that because I had been so mean to her. Another Google search, this time specifically for Sheila Larkin in Portland, Oregon, kicked back several hits, and by the time I'd sorted all of them it was already past nine, but I'd narrowed it down to three. One of them was thirteen, and had a page devoted to her favorite television shows, movies, and musicians.

She wasn't a fan.

The second one was just a faculty listing at OHSU, in the Pediatric Care Unit.

The third was attached to a Web site for "Cuddle Group Daycare," and that was the one I went with, because at the top of the Web page for the site there was a spinning Jesus fish. A phone number and e-mail link were included at the bottom of the page.

I called, and it was answered after four rings. Children were hollering in the background.

"Cuddle Group Daycare."

"I'm trying to reach Sheila Larkin," I said. "Is she there?"

"This is she. Who is this, please?"

"My name's Miriam Bracca. I don't know if you remember me."

There was the barest of pauses. "Of course I remember you. What can I do for you, Miss Bracca?"

"It's actually a little awkward, I was wondering if I could come and talk to you."

Another pause. I heard a child's shriek, but I couldn't tell if it was delight or outrage.

"When?" Sheila Larkin asked.

"Sooner the better, actually."

"If you don't mind some dirty diapers, you can come over now." She gave me an address in the southeast part of town, near Reed College, and I told her I thought it would be about an hour before I got there, and she said that would be fine.

I changed into day clothes, then gave myself a status report in the mirror. My fingers hurt, and the knuckles were swollen, but I could move them, and there was no visible bruising. The gash on my forehead looked calmer, too, less angry. But now I had a golf-ball-sized bruise on the side of my chest from the collision with the Strat, and the marks on my throat were clearly visible, if somewhat faint.

I used makeup to cover what I could, and was headed downstairs when the doorbell rang.

It was Hoffman and Marcus. He was wearing a duplicate of his work suit, and she was going with another slacks-blouse-blazer combo, and when I opened the door she shot me a grin, and when I didn't return it, it crumpled like rice paper.

"I was on my way out," I said.

"This won't take long," Marcus said. "Could we come in?"

I tried to look past them without being obvious about it, tried to determine if the Parka Man was watching. Leaving them to linger on the porch was only going to make matters worse, but letting them inside might get Tommy killed.

"What's this about?"

"Let's go inside, we can talk."

My hesitation was growing obvious, and I caved, letting them through and then closing the door fast behind them. I had to hope Parka Man wasn't watching, that he was confident in the scare he'd thrown into me the night before.

They waited, followed me down the hall to the kitchen. Hoffman held up just inside the archway, watching me with her cop look, the one that made it impossible to read her emotions. Marcus went to the table and took a seat.

"What's this about?" I asked again.

"Have you seen your father in the last twenty-four hours?" Hoffman asked.

"Nope," I said, and I sounded convincing to me.

"He was staying at your brother's place, did you know that?"

"I'm not surprised. I don't think he had anywhere else to go."

"But you haven't been to see him there?"

"Why would I?"

"You haven't been there?" Hoffman asked again.

"No, I haven't seen him since the funeral."

"He's not at your brother's," Marcus said. "We went by to talk to him this morning, early, and he wasn't there."

Hoffman's expression faltered, her brow creasing, and I knew she was trying to figure out why I'd gone cold on her, and I only hoped she took it the wrong way.

She said, "Normally, someone doesn't answer the door, we don't make a thing out of it. They're out or they're asleep."

"Both possible," I said.

"That's what we'd be thinking, too, except that Allan, here, he saw something that got us a little worried. He saw some blood, dried blood, on the front step of the condo."

She paused, waiting for me to react. I didn't say anything.

Marcus picked it up. "Blood at a crime scene, that's not unusual, you know. And your brother's place, that's a crime scene. So I'm all fired up to go in, hey, it's blood, maybe there's trouble. But Tracy here, she's cooler than me, she says wait a sec, she pulls out her phone, gets one of the state techs on the line, one of the guys who processed your brother's murder. And she asks them if they pulled any blood evidence from outside of the house. You know what the answer to that is?"

I shrugged, shaking a cigarette loose from my pack on the counter. It was easier to look at the yellow box of smokes than at either of them.

"The answer was no, there was no blood pulled from outside. So we effected an entry, because that's probable cause, you see."

"Your father's missing," Hoffman said. "There's a large amount of blood—and it's new, it's not your brother's—in the living room there. Your father's clothes are still in the guest room. How'd you cut your forehead, Miss Bracca?"

It was the refusal to use my first name that did it, made me see where they were going.

"I took a spill," I said.

"Looks nasty."

"I was pretty loaded."

There was silence. Marcus and Hoffman waited. I tried to think of something to say, and it occurred to me that any lie I gave them now was only going to make things worse. If they knew it was Tommy's blood on the carpet, then they had probably found some of mine, too; if they had, then they'd be able to match it to the samples they'd taken from my towels and sheets and so on when they'd searched my own home.

Which meant they'd know I had been there. It was only a matter of time.

Marcus asked, "We're wondering if you'd be willing to come downtown with us and answer some more questions."

"I really can't," I said. "I have an appointment I need to keep."

"It won't take long," Marcus said.

"I'm thinking I should call my lawyer."

"As always, that's your prerogative."

Hoffman didn't say anything.

I found Chapel's number and called his office as they watched me. When the receptionist answered, I gave her my name and said I needed to speak to Mr. Chapel.

"I'm sorry, Miss Bracca, but he's busy at the moment," the receptionist said.

"It's Joy, right?" I asked.

She seemed pleased that I'd remembered. "Yes, it is."

"Joy, could you tell him that there are two detectives in my kitchen asking me to go downtown with them?"

"Just a second," she said.

The hold music, appallingly enough, was Rosie 105 FM, and they were halfway through the second verse of "Lie Life." I thought about singing along, and decided against it.

As the third chorus was ending, Chapel came on the line. He was brusque.

"It's Hoffman and Marcus?"

"Yeah."

"Put one of them on," Chapel said.

I extended the phone to Hoffman. "He wants to talk to you."

She took the phone out of my hand, meeting my eyes. There was anger, and there was hurt, and I tried to give her nothing in return. She put the phone to her ear and said her name, and then for most of a minute, didn't say anything else.

Then she said, "No, you've made that perfectly clear," and offered the phone back to me.

"They're leaving," Chapel told me. "I've told them that they are under no circumstances to question you about anything without me present, and that if they want to take you downtown, they're going to need a warrant. I'm going to stay on the phone. You follow them out, make sure they leave your property. I'll wait."

"Gotcha."

I set the phone down on the counter, and Marcus was already half-way to the front door, Hoffman following. I went after them. Marcus exited first, but Hoffman stopped on the porch to pick up the morning paper and hand it over.

"Don't make last night a mistake," she said. "Let me help you."

I shook my head, said, "I don't need help."

And I shut the door on her.

"**W**hy were they there?" Chapel demanded.

I relayed everything the detectives had told me, without embellishment.

"Do you know where your father is?"

"No idea."

"And you haven't been to your brother's condo?"

"Not since I found his body," I said. "Can I ask you, that bit about a warrant? Are they liable to come back with one?"

"Not unless they've got some damn compelling evidence and the D.A. is willing to charge you. It's the same situation as before. And with the pictures in the media, and so soon after your brother's murder? Unless the D.A. knows you did something wrong, unless he can prove it, he'd look like a complete asshole. If what you're telling me is right, they don't even have a crime."

"They said there was blood."

"That doesn't mean anything. Suppose your father went on a bender, cut his wrists, and then thought better of it? Maybe he's in a bed at Legacy Emanuel or Providence as a John Doe. Until they know what's happened to him, they've got nothing. And if they think there's a murder, they need a body, or a head, or some heart or brain matter. Otherwise, they've got nothing."

"So I don't have to worry about them?"

"Not unless there's something you haven't told me," Chapel said.

I was finding it easier and easier to lie without pause. "No, nothing. They just made me nervous, that's all."

"They're detectives, they do it on purpose. Call me if they come back."

I told him I would, hung up, and headed for my appointment with Cuddle Group Daycare.

CHAPTER THIRTY

t was Sheila Larkin's business, and she ran it out of her home eight blocks south of the Reed campus. I drove past the grounds and its falling leaves, onto the slender streets with the slightly upscale housing dedicated to the campus faculty. Pumpkins perched on porches and walks, waiting to be lit up as soon as night fell, and a couple of the homes had more prominent Halloween decorations, paper skeletons hanging from awnings. One home had an elm in its front yard with half of a broomstick jutting from its trunk on the one side, a witch splayed against the tree on the other, as if she'd crashed her flight.

The decorations at Cuddle Group Daycare were bright and nothing as sinister, construction-paper pumpkins of orange and black smiling brightly from where they'd been taped to the windows. There were eleven kids under care, and three other providers aside from Sheila, all of them women her age or younger. The kids ranged from a towheaded toddler who careened around the playroom, head-butting all of the adults in their legs, to a four-month-old little girl, who sobbed hysterically in one woman's lap.

Sheila Larkin looked nothing like I remembered, and when she answered the door, I didn't recognize her at all. She seemed to have
stopped growing upward shortly after I'd come out from beneath her
parents' roof, then made up for the lack of progress by expanding
horizontally, instead. Her hair was long and worn in a ponytail, and it
made her seem shorter and fatter.

She smiled at me, though, and offered me her hand, and I followed
her into the din of children. We negotiated the playroom, stepping
over toys and tots. The other women were all careful to not look at
me, or at least, to not look at me when they thought I could see them
doing it, and I wondered what Sheila had told them. There were small
gates up in every doorway, and Sheila had to open and close three of
them before we were done. The kitchen was clean, but cluttered, and
smelled of last night's fried chicken and baby poop. Sheila offered me
a seat at the table and a glass of something to drink, and I took the
seat and passed on the glass, and after some more mild fussing about,
she joined me.

"I was surprised to hear from you," Sheila said. "I didn't think
you'd even remember us."

"I wish I could say I'm surprised that you remembered me," I said.
"But I think I made a lasting impression."

Sheila smiled, and seemed to relax a little. "You know, it was
Donny who told us first, that you were a big rock star, now. We were
all so impressed, I had to call Daddy and tell him, and he sounded so
happy that you had grown up well. He said that all those prayers we
were making for you, some of them must have gotten through."

"I guess some of them did."

Her face fell. "I'm so sorry about your brother. I barely remembered
him, but then I saw it on the news last week, and all I could think was
that it didn't seem fair at all. And they say your daddy did it?"

"He's a suspect," I said. "But they don't know who did it."

Sheila adjusted herself in her seat. "I don't expect this is why you
called, though, is it? To talk about that?"

"No. I'm actually wondering if you can tell me about your family.

After Mikel's funeral, I started thinking about all the people who had taken us into their homes, and about how...how rotten I was, at least. And I wanted to say I was sorry. I was hoping to start with you, sort of work my way through the tree, so to speak."

"I'm not sure that's necessary. You had been through some awful things, we all understood." Sheila looked embarrassingly touched, for a moment.

"It doesn't really excuse the behavior."

"Well, if it matters, I forgave you long ago. I know my parents did, too."

"How about your brothers?"

Sheila grinned. "Oh, you don't have to worry about them."

"No? They're well?"

She laughed. "They're crazy, that's what they are! Moved up to Alaska about two years ago, the lot of them. Donny's teaching Eskimo boys and girls out in the bush, I think that's the word for it, and William, Ben, and Bobby, they're entrepreneurs. They've got a couple planes, they all learned how to fly, you see, and they sell tours."

Scratch the Larkin boys, I thought, and she saw disappointment on my face and misread it as something else.

"Oh, I know," Sheila said. "I think it's crazy, too, but they love it. Only problem they're having, according to what Mom says, is that they can't find any women. Not enough single girls in Alaska, I guess."

I made a sympathetic noise, and asked her a few more questions, mostly to round out the conversation. She told me that she'd been married for six years, now, and that she had three kids of her own, only one of them part of the quorum in the next room. Her husband was an investor-broker for Prudential here in town, and they were very happy. Before she'd had her first child, she didn't know what it was she wanted to do with her life. But when the first baby was born, she had discovered that she had a knack for child care, and she'd gone to school to get certified, and opened the business on her own. She said the work fulfilled her.

"That must be what making music is like for you," Sheila said.

*   *   *

I started feeling the foreboding as soon as I was back behind the wheel of the Jeep. The Larkins had been a long shot in the sea of long shots, and if I'd been honest with myself, I wouldn't have gone with them first.

The Quicks should have been number one.

My dashboard clock said it was coming up on noon, and it adjusted my priorities.

I had to get over to Graham's before he left town, to pick up the cash.

The guard in the lobby was the same one from the day before, and he grinned at me when I came in, saying, "Hey there, Miss Bracca."

"Hi," I said. "I'm sorry, I didn't catch your name yesterday."

He looked almost embarrassed. "Oh, yeah. I'm Lee."

"Nice to meet you, Lee. I'm Mim." I shook his hand.

He laughed. "You can go on up, Mim."

Graham answered his door within seconds of my knocking. He was dressed in his travel suit, which was one of the nicest he owned. I'd asked him once why he always wore a three-piece for an airplane, and he'd hemmed and hawed, then admitted that he was scared to death of flying. When I'd said that wasn't really an answer, he'd gone into a lengthy explanation about how many rock stars die in plane crashes, and the reason for that being that musicians travel a lot, always going from gig to gig, and with odds like that, he figured he should be ready.

"It's my good-luck charm," he'd said. "I figure the one day I don't bother to get dressed up, that'll be the day the plane goes down."

He had all but one of the three pieces in place, the jacket draped over the arm of the couch, and he ushered me in and then presented me with the bag of cash as if he was introducing a deb at a ball. The duffel was bright yellow, with black trim, and had a Nike swoosh on the side. He pulled open the top flap, and revealed a mass of bills, hundreds, strapped together in bunches with paper bands.

"Got Van's donation to the fund this morning. You want to count it?" Graham asked, leaning over my shoulder and nudging me. "Make sure it's all there, huh?"

"That is a fucking lot of money," I said.

"That is, indeed, a fucking lot of money. It has its own smell; you smell that?" He took a deep and audible inhale through his nose. "Paper and ink and something else, you know what I mean? You got to get it out of here, it's making me horny as hell, and I've got a strict hands-off policy with the talent."

I zipped the duffel shut and hoisted it onto my shoulder, and was surprised at how much it weighed. Not as much as my Tele, but close, and I wondered what another six hundred thousand dollars would do to the weight.

"Off to Glasgow?" I asked.

"Yeah, flight's in just over three hours. I've got to hustle. I'll walk down with you."

He pulled on his jacket and got his travel bag from where it was waiting by the door, and we rode the elevator together. Lee wished us both a safe and good trip, and I didn't challenge his assumption that I was back to gigging. I suppose it was the duffel on my shoulder that did it, made him think that I was hitting the road again.

"Can I drop you anywhere?" I asked Graham.

"You can put me on the MAX line, if you would, that'd be nice," he told me.

"No cab?"

"Hey, I can get out to the airport hassle free for a buck fifty, why should I pay for a cab?"

"Because Van hires a limo."

"Van's the star. I'm management."

We climbed into the Jeep, and I dropped him at one of the many MAX stops on Yamhill, so he could catch the train. I wished him a safe trip.

"What happened to your hand?" he asked as he was climbing out.

"Nothing."

"Mim, your knuckles are all bashed up. That's not good, that'll screw your playing."

"I'll get it checked out."

"You had damn well better. I never did take out that policy from Lloyds."

"Did Van get her shrine?"

"Still working on that, too."

I grinned and kept it in place until he'd slammed the door and turned away, and then I popped into gear, and headed for the main branch of the Multnomah County Library.

He'd never been anyone but "Mr. Quick" to me, so the first thing I looked for was his Christian name. The government employee listings did the trick, though I had to search back three years before finding Gareth Quick, in the Office of the State Treasurer. Either he'd retired or been laid off or quit, but he hadn't appeared to have died, because there was a listing in the Salem White Pages for a Gareth and Anne Quick, and the address given rang true in my memory, and I figured it was the same place, the same house. There were no listings for either Chris or Brian Quick, though, so I'd have to talk to the parents to find them.

It was late afternoon when I was finished, and I was getting anxious to get back to my house and get the money out of my car. Lugging it around in the library had made me feel odd, and I'd kept expecting someone to ask me to open the bag. Even though the money itself wasn't illegally acquired, the thought of having to explain it made me nervous.

Trick-or-treaters were already out and moving along the sidewalks, jack-o'-lanterns on every residential block glowing a warm orange. I didn't have anything to give any visitors who might stop by, so I stopped at the Safeway near my house on the way home and dumped forty dollars on bags of assorted sweets.

Inside, I made sure the porch and all of my front lights were off, then took the duffel bag down to the basement. I supposed there were safer places to store the money, but I hadn't been able to think of anything. In the end, I folded the bag up as small as I could get it, and then stuck it in the hollow back of my Fender blues amp, then pushed the amp so its back was against the wall. As long as I didn't switch the thing on, it shouldn't be a problem.

I filled a big bowl with candy, positioned it and a chair just inside my front door, then turned on the lights, trying to make the house as welcoming as possible. It was probably silly, but Halloween was the way I remembered my mother, because she always loved it. No matter what else was going on in my life right now, if I was going to have to wait until morning before I went to see the Quicks, I'd damn well honor her memory tonight.

While I was waiting for the first trick-or-treater to arrive, I checked my messages. There were five of them, and only four from people I didn't want to talk to. A guy calling himself Peter Bergman who said he was from *Rolling Stone* had called, wanting to talk about my brother for the story he was writing, and he left a callback number; two of the local television outlets and one radio had called, asking if I'd be willing to do an interview; and Click, who chastised me for ditching him the night before, and wished me well, and said that he'd call to check in from the road.

The doorbell rang just after I'd finished, and I went to answer it, ready with the bowl of candy.

It was Joan, bundled in the same old coat she'd worn every winter for the last decade, carrying a pizza box.

She saw the look on my face and said, "You didn't think I'd forget?"

"I almost forgot myself," I admitted. I let her get the box on the kitchen counter and herself out of her coat before giving her a hug. "You are too nice to me."

"If it's true, then you shouldn't be pointing it out."

I got down plates and cans of soda, and we pulled slices of pizza and sat in the front hall, making small talk and eating. She told me about her day, about the trouble with the music program, the ever-present budget cuts.

She waited until I was done eating and had taken our plates to the kitchen before she asked me what happened to my forehead.

"It's nothing," I said. "Accident-prone."

"It looks painful."

"It's not too bad. Only hurts when I think." I furrowed my brow, to prove the point.

There was a brief, but very awkward pause, and her eyes seemed to get a little dimmer. She tried to hide it, but I knew what she'd concluded, that she had gone to my lie without needing any direction, because it was the logical place to go. I wanted to tell her she was wrong, that I hadn't been drunk, that I hadn't been drunk since before the funeral, but I knew she wouldn't believe me.

We were spared by the doorbell, a group of two Harry Potters, a Hermione, and a very traditional bedsheet ghost. One of the Harrys was actually a girl, and after they'd stated their demands, I went after her.

"So what's the trick?" I asked.

She didn't miss a beat. "Turn you into a newt."

"That's a good one; think I better pay up." To Harry Number Two, I asked, "And you?"

"Newt?"

"Taken."

He adjusted his plastic glasses. "I'll give you warts. Warts all over your face, they'll be totally gross and stuff."

"Ew. All right, a handful, that'll keep my skin clear?"

"For now."

"Oh, a tough guy. Okay. Next?"

The ghost told me he'd haunt me until I was so scared I'd wet my pants. Both of the Harrys and the Hermione thought that was funny, and giggled. Joan, listening in the hall behind me, nearly bust a gut. The ghost got a really big handful.

Hermione told me that she'd make me rich.

"I am rich," I told her.

"I'll make you richer."

"Not sure I want that."

She frowned, gnawed on her lip, adjusted her pillowcase full of swag. "Nobody else does this, everyone else just gives us candy."

"Hey, you want candy, you got to do it right."

Hermione smiled with an idea, said, "Okay, see, I know who you are, and if you give me candy, I'll bring your brother back from the dead."

It threw me for a second.

"You can do that?" I asked.

"Not yet," she admitted.

I dumped two handfuls into her bag. "Let me know when you've worked that out, okay?"

Joan pulled another chair from the kitchen and joined me, and we had fun with it, and for a while again, I forgot to be afraid. It had been Joan who made Halloween a pleasure for me again, she who had explained that it was trick *or* treat, and that you had to play along with the extortion.

Given where I was, this kind of blackmail was a hell of a lot more enjoyable.

It was when I was dumping candy into the bags of unidentifiable monsters, soldiers, and two teenagers too old for it, but in good costumes—both were Star Wars Jedi Knights—that I registered what I'd been seeing on the street the whole time.

A car, parked just inside the view from my door, across the street. That alone wasn't alarming, but there was someone inside of it, and that gave me pause.

I told myself it wasn't the Parka Man, that even if my porch light was on, he had to know it was for Halloween. Since there'd been no return visit after the two cops had descended that morning, I had to assume he had faith that the terror he'd put in me would stay, that I'd pay up on time, without causing him trouble.

Couldn't be him.

It wasn't something I could concentrate on, either, with Joan beside me and kids parading to and from my doorstep. Each time I looked out, I tried to keep it subtle, and, once, I saw whoever was in the car move, but I didn't see any features.

The last trick-or-treater came by just before nine, and that was good, because I'd almost run out of candy. I'm very generous on Halloween, I give handfuls, not just one or two pieces, and some years I've been reduced to giving away whatever is suitable in the kitchen, bags of pretzels or chips. I never give fruit or vegetables or things like that. What kid in their right mind wants an apple when they can have a Snickers bar?

Joan left around nine-thirty, giving me a kiss and saying that she had to get to bed. I told her I'd call that weekend, and that we could finally go out to the dinner I'd promised her.

She liked that.

Once she was gone, I checked the street again, and again there was motion from the car, and I suddenly knew who it was. There were a couple candy bars left in the bowl, and some Shock Tarts. I picked it up and went down the walk and across the street. The car was a Ford, blue, one of the newer ones. As I was crossing the street, the driver's window purred down, and I could see both of the occupants.

Marcus was behind the wheel, on my side.

"Trick or treat," I told him.

He grinned. "That for us?"

"Sure."

He reached into the bowl, picking out both the remaining pieces of chocolate, then handed one to Hoffman. Neither of them looked particularly upset that I'd seen them.

"Have a good Halloween?" Marcus asked me.

"Pretty good. I like the holiday."

"You seemed to enjoy talking to the kids."

"Why are you guys watching my house?"

Marcus looked over at Hoffman. Without looking up from the chocolate bar she was unwrapping, she said, "Why don't you stop hiding behind Chapel and just answer our questions, Miss Bracca?"

"Because I don't like the questions. Because I don't have any idea where my father is, and I don't know what's happened to him."

"That's why we're watching your house," Marcus explained.

"Isn't this harassment?"

"No, actually," Hoffman said, and she finally looked at me. "It's called investigating. Harassment would mean we didn't have a reason to watch you. But you've given us that. This is what we call keeping a suspect under surveillance. You could help yourself and us if you just stepped out from behind your lawyer for a little while."

"I like it behind my lawyer," I said. "He blocks the wind. Why am I a suspect?"

"We figure you were at your brother's place yesterday," Hoffman said.

"I told you I wasn't."

"We figure you're lying to us."

"If I call Mr. Chapel and tell him you're out here—"

"There's not a damn thing he can do about it," Marcus said.

"And exactly what am I suspected of doing this time?"

"Murdering Tommy Bracca," Hoffman said.

It was cold on the street, and I hadn't bothered to put my jacket on before I came out. It made me want to shiver, and I had to fight it.

"Still don't want to talk to us?" Hoffman asked.

I went back into my house without answering her.

CHAPTER THIRTY-ONE

I t all looked worse for the fourteen years since I'd last seen it. The lawn, once perfectly mown grass, was now marked with bare spots of mud, dotted with tangled weeds. The house needed a paint job. Even the station wagon in the driveway looked the same, just older, more beat-up.

I got out of the Jeep and checked down the street, and the Ford was there, a couple houses down at the curb. It was sunny, bright autumn, and painful to my eyes. The sunglasses I wore today were on out of necessity, not anonymity. Marcus and Hoffman were wearing sunglasses, too. I wondered if they'd gotten any sleep, or at least, any more than I had. They'd still been parked outside when I'd gone to bed.

It was ten past nine, Thursday morning, when I walked up to the door of the home of Gareth and Anne Quick.

Wrapped in precisely the same heavy dread that had surrounded me the last time I'd reached this door.

* * *

Anne answered, and she, too, looked like the years hadn't been easy on her. The last time I'd seen her was when she'd handed me over to the Children's Services woman, to take me to the Beckermans. We'd spent two nights in a Best Western prior to that, and Anne Quick hadn't talked a lot. It had been hard for her to accept what her sons had tried to do, what they had been trying to do for so long. I'm sure it was only because her husband had seen it that Anne even believed the boys had done something wrong.

The whole time we were at the motel, I got the feeling that she believed what happened had been, somehow, my fault.

Fourteen years later she looked smaller and harder, with wrinkles that wouldn't stay concealed with Oil of Olay. Her hair was still black, but dyed; there was gray creeping in at the roots, like a tide that had come just a little farther than anticipated onto a shore. She was dressed for garden work.

"Can I help you?" she asked.

"Mrs. Quick," I said, and I took off my sunglasses and dropped them in a pocket, sheepish. "I'm Miriam Bracca, I don't know if you remember me."

The wrinkles around her eyes bunched, as if in committee. She looked me over, and her mouth got tighter, more sour. She had one hand on the door, and from her grip, I thought she might be about to slam it on me.

"Yes, I remember you."

"I was wondering if I might come in, speak to you and your husband? Is Mr. Quick here?"

"Of course he's here." She said it strangely, as if I should have known the answer already. "What do you want to talk to us about?"

"May I come in?"

She adjusted her hold on the door, and then she pulled it back, opening it wider, puffing a disgusted sigh. She waved me in as if it was easier than refusing me entry, then shut the door and came around, leading the way to the den. The interior, unlike the exterior, had gone through some changes. The architecture was early seventies, with a sunken den, and the carpet had been replaced, thicker than the old, blue instead of the tan I remembered. The couch had been replaced, was now a multisection modular monstrosity, the kind where segments can turn into recliners. Through the glass doors into the backyard, I could see the signs of gardening, preparing for the winter, torn-up plants, a wheelbarrow.

Gareth Quick was outside, on his knees, working with a trowel in the flower bed.

"The boys don't live here anymore?" I asked.

"No." Anne said it flatly. She pulled the sliding door open, adding, "Well, come on."

I stepped onto the back patio. Gareth Quick looked up from his work, and his eyes went from me to his wife, and there was nothing in them but confusion. He settled the look back on me and smiled.

"You're very pretty," he said. "What happened to your head?"

"This is Miriam, honey," Anne told him. "You remember Miriam, don't you?"

"Miriam?"

"Yes, she lived with us for a while, when the boys were in high school."

The smile stayed in place. He looked, unlike his wife, as if the years hadn't had a physical effect on him. Even the haircut was the same, reminiscent of the military, close and neat. Like Anne, he was dressed for gardening, but unlike his wife, the clothes didn't seem to settle correctly, a little baggy where they should have held tight, a little loose where they should have been snug.

Physically, he could have been the Parka Man, but I already knew it wasn't him. It was his voice, it just wasn't the same.

And there was absolutely no recognition of me in his eyes.

"The boys?"

"Brian and Christopher, honey. Our sons."

Alarm crept laboriously across his face.

"What did they do?" Gareth Quick asked, and his voice dropped and wobbled, just the way it had when he'd found them dragging me through the hallway. "What did those little shits do to you, Miriam?"

"Nothing," I assured him. "I'm fine, sir. It's all right."

There were tears in his eyes, and his chin had dropped onto his chest; he wasn't even looking at us, now. He began to sob.

"What did we do?" he was saying. "God, what did we do that was so wrong, Annie? What did we do so wrong?"

"It's all right, hon," Anne said, and she dropped to her knees and put a hand on his shoulder. "It's okay. You're at home, and I'm here, and there's nothing to worry about."

He pushed her hand away, his sobs racking his thin body.

"Could you wait inside?" Anne asked, without looking at me, without taking her eyes off him. "In the kitchen, maybe?"

I nodded and backed off, retreating to the kitchen. It had changed, the cabinets and counters replaced, even the table. I took a chair and waited, and the déjà vu stampeded, and for a moment, it was as if I had never left, all of the wounds raw and open.

It was almost twenty minutes before Anne came back, and she was leading Gareth by the hand. An open archway past the table had another view of the den, and she brought him past me, that way, and got him settled on the couch. He seemed perfectly fine with that, and she put the remote control in his hand, turned on the television, and the soft noise of morning talk bubbled into the space.

"I'll be in the kitchen," Anne told her husband.

He nodded, focused on the screen.

She joined me at the table. "Alzheimer's."

"I didn't know," I said, and started to add that I was terribly sorry, but she cut me off.

"How could you?" She checked over her shoulder, to make certain Gareth was still where she'd left him. He hadn't moved. "Almost three years, now. He's not going to be with me much longer."

"You're caring for him by yourself?"

"A nurse comes during the afternoons, when I have to go to work. I'm part-time, real estate."

"I'm a musician," I told her.

"Is that what you call it?" Her mouth got smaller, even more bitter. "I'd have thought 'entertainer' might be a better word."

"I suppose you could call it that, too."

"What did you want to talk to us about?"

I thought about spinning a lie, like I had with Sheila Larkin, but it was clear Anne Quick had very little patience, and what amount of it was left she needed for her husband.

"I'm trying to find Brian and Chris," I told her.

"Why?" This time there was no mistaking the hostility.

"I need to speak to them," I said.

"You going to sue them? Have them arrested? You looking for some sort of revenge?"

"No, ma'am, I just—"

"They were perfectly nice boys, you know, they were wonderful boys, until you came into our house. They were just wonderful young men, their father loved them so much, he worked so hard for them, to give them everything they needed. Then we took you in, and you destroyed it."

I stared at her. Someone's memory was playing tricks, and it wasn't mine.

"The way you led them on," Anne Quick continued, her voice like acid. "The way you teased them, they were *boys,* what were they supposed to think? And now you make a living doing just that, don't you? Selling a whiff of sex, a little promise here and there, strutting around with a guitar and your drug-addict friends."

My mouth had gone dry. Behind Anne, her husband was still watching television, head cocked to one side, eyes bright with fascination, oblivious.

"I never led them on, ma'am," I said. "I never did anything to encourage them."

"You believe what you want to, that's fine. I'm sure you don't think of yourself as a slut now. But you sure as hell were one then."

I tried again, trying to ignore the hostility. "I didn't come here to make any trouble, Mrs. Quick. I'm just looking to contact Chris or Brian, that's all."

"Why? To get them locked up again? To accuse them of attempted rape, to make a big story? Do you need more headlines?"

"They were arrested?"

"Don't act like you don't know." She spat it at me. "Don't act like you don't know."

"Are they in prison?"

That made her more defensive, as if she'd thought I'd expected that. "No, they're not, thank you. They've been just fine and they've stayed out of trouble, so they don't need you making it worse."

"Because if they've been in prison," I said, "I'd hate to think that was my fault."

Anne Quick gave me a suspicious appraisal. "What does *that* mean?"

"If it was my fault, I mean. If something I did got them in trouble. I'm ... well, I was hoping I could make it up to them."

"And how would you do that?"

"I'm rich," I said.

The hard little eyes seemed to brighten momentarily. Green-eyed monster, I thought. Not jealousy, but greed.

"You're going to give my *sons* money?"

"I didn't want to insult them," I said. "Didn't want them to think it was charity. I was thinking of it as a gift."

She needed a couple of seconds to chew on that. On the couch, Gareth had started flipping channels.

"I can't imagine it's easy taking care of Gareth like this," I told her. "You must be working very hard."

"All the time."

"If you'd let me, maybe I could help you out with that, too."

"I don't want charity, either."

"Of course not. But you and Gareth, you opened your home to me, and I owe you for that. I'd really like to make it up to you."

"Would you, really? Or is it just that you think you can buy what you want?"

I gambled, then, pushing my chair back and getting to my feet. "I'm sorry to have insulted you this way, Mrs. Quick. I'll go."

She didn't move and she didn't speak, so I headed out of the kitchen, had gotten all the way to my hand on the doorknob before she called after me to stop. I heard her coming, hurrying to catch up to me.

"I apologize," she said, and it looked like she was choking down rotten meat. "It's just … it's been very hard, you can imagine."

"I understand."

"If you'd be willing to help … ?"

"The medical bills," I said. "Would you let me cover those?"

"You'd … you would do that?"

"I don't want to see Gareth suffering," I told her, and it was the honest-to-God truth. "I'll have my attorney contact you, he'll arrange to have the bills come to me."

She didn't speak for a few seconds, possibly because she couldn't. She finally had to nod.

"And the boys," I said. "Where can I find them?"

"They're outside of Junction City, that's near Eugene."

"Do you have an address?"

"I'm sure I do around here somewhere."

"If you can get that for me," I said. "And if you don't mind me using your phone, I'll call my attorney, see if we can't get this bill thing handled right now."

Anne Quick, my new best friend, offered to dial for me.

CHAPTER THIRTY-TWO

Junction City was about another fifty miles or so south of Salem, still heading along Interstate 5. I left Anne Quick talking to Chapel on the phone, and was back on the road before ten, with the Ford following as I went. Once again they weren't trying to be hidden. They knew I saw them there, and they didn't care.

The weather was holding, and the drive wasn't too bad, except for the part passing Albany, when the stink of the paper mill fell over the road like a shadow of death. When Tailhook first started getting gigs outside of Portland and we'd drive down to perform in Eugene, we'd try to see who could hold their breath the longest going through the zone. Van always won.

Junction City is a big name for a little community, mostly farming, just northwest of Eugene, in the peppermint fields. I reached it just past eleven. It's rural, with the slightest of downtowns, and the bare essential of amenities, and I stopped at a mom-and-pop convenience store on the side of the road. I parked on gravel and hopped out, feeling the bruise on my side tighten as I moved. Inside, I bought myself a bottle of Arrowhead and got directions from the middle-aged man behind the counter to the address Anne Quick had provided. He was wearing coveralls and a flannel, and he eyed me and my earrings with some suspicion before determining that I wasn't here to undermine his way of life. I didn't correct his assumption.

The Ford pulled up while I was getting the directions, and Marcus and Hoffman got out. Marcus made straight for me at the counter, then asked the man if there was a bathroom he could use. I almost laughed aloud.

"Don't leave without me," Marcus threw over his shoulder at me, then went to use the facilities.

Hoffman was stretching by the car when I came outside, arching her back with her arms extended over her head. When she stretched, I could see the gun in the holster on her waist. I unlocked my door and was about to get into the Jeep when she said, "Christopher Quick."

I closed the door again, looking at her over the hood, waiting.

"Son of Anne and Gareth." She dropped her arms, put the weight of her gaze on me. She still had her sunglasses on, hiding her eyes, but I felt it just the same. "Brother Brian. Both recent guests at OSP."

"You gonna tell me what they went in for?"

"Aggravated assault and attempted rape, the both of them. Why are you talking to the Quicks?"

"You're not supposed to be asking me questions," I told her.

"Yeah, but here, out in these peppermint fields, you can't really hide behind your counsel, can you? Why the Quicks?"

"I stayed with them for a few months when I was a kid. They were one of the foster families I was placed with."

"Thought that was Beckerman."

"The Beckermans were the last family I was placed with. Before the Beckermans, there were the Quicks. Before Quick, there was Larkin. And in the beginning, there was Bracca, Thomas and Diana."

She took it in, then glanced in the direction of the store. Inside, Marcus was at the counter, picking out a piece of beef jerky.

"I was going to call you," I said.

Hoffman turned her sunglasses back to me. "If I'd known you'd become a suspect again, it never would have happened."

Marcus came out of the store, then, before I could respond. He handed a bottle of Arizona green tea to Hoffman, opened an RC cola for himself, then settled on the hood of his car, grinning at me.

"Lot of commuting just to dispose of a body," he told me.

He so obviously didn't believe that was what I was doing, I almost laughed.

"You tell us why you want to talk to the Quicks, we'll do it for you," Hoffman said. "We're detectives, we could detect. We could determine you're not a suspect, but instead the kind of person who wants to help us."

"You don't know I'm going to talk to the Quicks."

"You're not in Junction City to enjoy the air." Marcus took a deep inhale. "God, I fucking *hate* peppermint."

"At least it's not Albany," I said.

"You don't want to talk to these guys without us there, Miss Bracca," Hoffman said.

"Why not?"

"These are not nice boys," Marcus said. "Christopher and Brian, they take drugs and they get violent and they have impressive records for such young men. Christopher and Brian have ties to God's Army."

"They're a band?"

"They're a militia," Hoffman said.

"White racists, fighting for God's People against the Forces of Darkness," Marcus added. "That would be people like my lesbo partner here, and me, a government patsy, and you, you drug-taking promiscuous rock star, you. Declared war on the false government of the USA when abortion was legalized. Don't like blacks, Jews, Catholics, the whole rigmarole. And they probably won't like you very much, at all, come to think of it, since you've got miscegenation of the races going on, what with a black man playing drums."

"They used their time inside to get in good with some of the more passionate racists," Hoffman said. "Yet another success of the penal system."

No wonder Anne had been so hostile, I thought.

"So you see why we're kind of concerned with you going to talk to these guys alone," Hoffman added.

"Did your father maybe know Chris or Brian while at OSP?" Marcus asked.

"Not that I know of."

"Pity. See, if he had, we'd call that a lead. And if you could confirm something like that, well, it would make our job easier."

"I don't know who Tommy knew in prison."

"Then why do you want to see these two?"

"That's none of your business, and I see a pay phone over there, I can call my lawyer."

"Where's your father?" Hoffman asked.

"I don't know."

"And you're not looking for him? That's not what this is?"

"No, it's not." I pulled my car door open again, climbed back into the Jeep. "Now, sing along with the chorus, you know the words: If you have any further questions, you can talk to my attorney."

The Quick brothers lived down a dirt track off Prairie Road, behind an expanse of peppermint field, in a house just outside a line of pine trees.

I say house, but I'm being generous, because what I really thought when I first saw it was shack. There were power lines coming to it through the trees, electricity and telephone, perhaps, and maybe there was running water, too, but none of those things changed my assessment. The road went from paved to dirt on the way in, a long straight line that wasn't dusty only because there'd been recent rain.

More than the out-in-the-middle-of-nowhere feeling that came from the sprawling fields and the distant hills was making me nervous as I pulled up. If Chris and Brian had both been at OSP, that tied all of us together, them, Tommy, me, maybe even Mikel. While I had no idea what prison was actually like, it didn't seem impossible that Chris or Brian or both had learned who Tommy Bracca was, that it had come out in some conversation or some interaction that the Miriam Bracca they knew as boys was his famous daughter.

It didn't take much imagination to see them hatching a plan, then, trying to find a way to use the information to make some money. If they'd gotten out around the time Tommy had, then all either would have needed to do was wait until I came home, and then they could get the whole thing rolling. Pictures and kidnapping and all of it, all wrapped together. Maybe the pictures had been one plan, and Mikel had learned about it somehow, so they'd killed him.

The more I thought about it, the more I thought that I was headed straight into a lot of trouble. If Chris or Brian was the Parka Man, then they'd already proved themselves dangerous, already proved they weren't afraid to kill. It meant they knew enough to plant cameras in my home, to get past my alarm, to take pictures of me while I slept.

The thoughts lingered, expanding with horror as I realized how bad things could have gotten. Whichever Quick had forced me into his truck at gunpoint, whichever Quick had been in my home, he'd had me alone and defenseless and, once, even completely unaware. Jesus, one of them had finally gotten me out of my clothes. If he'd wanted more than just a scare or a photograph, nothing would have stopped him from getting it.

The Jeep popped and slid along the ruts in the road. At the end of the drive there was a clearing, with a rusted hulk of a tractor and a stack of empty and perforated oil drums vaguely framing the front of the shack. I pulled in and parked and waited a few moments, and there was no motion from the door, no signs of movement beyond the two scum-stained windows.

I didn't see the Ford anywhere in my mirrors.

There was an odor in the air as I stepped out of the Jeep, foul and heavy and eliminating the scent of the mint all around, and I could see wisps of smoke rising from behind the house, farther in the trees. The only sound came from the Jeep as I shut my door, and then that died away, and there was nothing else.

I took a breath to steel myself, nearly gagged on the stink in the air, and started for the shack. It was bright and the sun was almost directly above me, but it wasn't doing much to warm me. When a blackbird bolted off a branch in one of the nearby pines, I nearly shrieked, expecting three dozen more to come and suddenly swarm on me. Shades of a Hitchcock movie—cold and still and menacing.

The door was wooden and loose on its hinges, and a red and white plastic sign ordered me to keep out, and another hung below it, warning me not to trespass. I knocked tentatively on the door, anyway.

The door swung open at my touch, then stopped inches into its swing. Through the parting I could see a corner of the shack opposite me, a metal bed frame with a sloppily dressed mattress. Shelves hung to the walls, with books and magazines.

I thought about calling out their names, or maybe identifying myself. Then I thought that I wasn't keeping out, that I was probably trespassing, and that maybe advertising that fact wasn't the smartest move I could make.

The door didn't budge when I gave it a little push, so I pushed it harder. This time it gave an inch, then seemed to push back, so I pushed it a last time and, before it tried to return, slid through the gap and let it fall shut behind me. The change in light was more dramatic than I'd anticipated, and it left me blind for several seconds, blinking away the autumn glare, trying to adjust to the dimness inside.

When my vision returned, the first thing I focused on was the light source, a computer monitor glowing on a workbench. It was a big screen, maybe nineteen inches, and running a screen saver, a parade of naked women, none of them obviously me. The PC was next to it, on the table, and flanking the other side of the monitor was a flatbed scanner. A set of cables ran from the back of the PC to the side of the table, unattached, waiting for attention.

Behind the monitor, on the wall of the shack, were clippings and papers. Most of them I couldn't make out, but there was a picture of Tailhook that I recognized, torn from some magazine. One of the publicity stills from the press kit that went out when *Nothing for Free* was released, the same one I had in boxes in my basement closet. Beside it was a printout, what looked like a copy of the tour schedule. Tacked to the wall, made out of nylon or maybe cloth, was a small red flag. A black swastika rode high in the center, and beneath it two stylized lightning bolts, in silver.

And there was a copy of Picture Three.

I took a step forward to get a closer look, and nearly tripped, and that's when I discovered why the door wouldn't open properly.

The body was on its side, facing the front of the shack, its legs crossed but extended, as if trying to run to the grave. Both hands were extended in the same direction, as if trying to clear the path. When the door had swung in, it had been blocked by the leg. A black puddle had spread out from the middle of the back, down to the boards that served as a floor, filling the seams between each plank. Flies buzzed over the puddle, sluggish and a little bored.

It wasn't Tommy, and it wasn't Mikel, but for that first awful instant it was both of them. Then I was certain it was Tommy, and I was sure it was my fault, I'd screwed up again, and I lurched forward and went to my knees, not thinking and not caring. My gorge rose, and it was the only thing that was keeping my voice from rising, too.

This man's head was shaven, his forearms tattooed, his face too young; he wasn't Tommy. There was enough in his death that I could remember him from life, could see him running away from me, down my street in the middle of the night. From fourteen years' distance, I could see Chris Quick, and he had died with the same fear on his face he'd worn when his father had caught him trying to rape me.

I'd come down in the puddle, felt the blood soaking through my jeans, and it wasn't Tommy and it wasn't Mikel, but maybe it was my mother, and I could smell the grass and the beer and the gutted pumpkins and the cigarettes and the truck. I could see my father, his look of horror; I could see Mikel, his look of despair.

The door knocked me as it was shoved open, pushing me and the body aside, and I toppled dumbly, wincing into the sunlight. Flooded with backlight, there was a new man in the doorway, and at first I thought he was wearing a parka, but there was no hood, only long hair flopping loose onto the shoulders of his jacket, and the sunlight licking around his legs showing a camouflage pattern, and his boots were black and high.

It was the same man who'd been in my bedroom the night I'd returned home.

I realized that at the same moment I realized he was holding a rifle in both hands, and that the rifle was pointed at me.

"Fucking cunt," Brian Quick told me, and he brought the gun up to his shoulder.

CHAPTER THIRTY-THREE

I could smell the pine and the mint in the air, crisp and clean odors suddenly revealed beneath the stench of blood and the chemicals brewing behind the shack. I could hear the sound of traffic on the Coburg Road out of Eugene, even though that had to be over a mile away.

I could see this man, maybe four years older than me, barely older than Mikel, the mass of metal in his hands, solid and unforgiving, pointed at me.

This isn't real, I thought. This cannot be real, this is another memory I've manufactured, another fiction created, but this cannot actually be happening to me. I am a musician, I play guitar in a band, I drink and I pass out and feel sorry for what a fucking good life I have.

I do not have guns pointed at me, I am not a detective, I am not a cop, I am not supposed to be here.

And the rifle was now at his shoulder and his mouth was opening to say something else, but the words I heard didn't come from him, they came from farther away, louder than before.

"Drop that weapon! Drop that weapon fucking now or I drop you! Drop it!"

"Mim! Mim, stay down!"

Brian Quick balked, staring at me on my knees in his brother's blood.

"Drop it NOW!" Marcus screamed.

The rifle came down, hit the floor without a clatter, like a brick.

"Back it up! Back it up, hands high!"

Brian was looking at me, I could feel it, but with the sunlight behind him, I couldn't make out his face, see if there was fear or excitement or anger in it. His hands had come down to drop the rifle, and he'd begun to step back, and Marcus was still yelling at him to reverse out of the shack, to do it slowly, to raise his hands. Brian started to follow the last order, but his right rose slower than his left, crossing inside his body as it came up instead of moving straight, and I gave it full-throat, everything I'd ever used onstage, everything Steven had ever taught me about using my diaphragm, and then some.

"Gun, he's got another gun!" I screamed, pulling myself out of the doorway, tumbling over Christopher Quick's corpse, and there was a shot that seemed so loud I figured the shack would fall down around me from the percussion.

To my side, behind where I'd knelt, a circle opened in the wooden wall, spitting splinters and showing green leaves beyond.

There were more shots, two or four or three, I couldn't count them they came so fast, and they didn't come from the same places. New circles opened in the wood around me and I cowered against the dead man, hiding my head and trying to breathe and not get killed. More shots came, but from a different direction, answered from the opposite, maybe behind me, now, but I didn't move, I didn't think I could.

It got quiet again. It stayed quiet.

I didn't move. My blood-soaked jeans were making me cold, my bruised side ached, but I didn't move.

I kept seeing Mikel and Tommy and my mother and the truck.

*　*　*

"Mim? Mim, where are you?"

I forced my arms apart, unwrapping my head. Hoffman was in the doorway, her gun in her hands, pointed at the ground. She saw the movement, focused on me.

"Oh, Jesus Christ," she said, like she'd been kicked and hadn't seen it coming.

I was starting to push myself up but she took a step forward, pushing me back down with one hand, putting her gun away with the other, shouting for her partner.

"Marcus, ambulance! We need an ambulance! Jesus, don't move, Mim. Goddamn you, where're you hit? Where'd you get hit?"

I kept pushing her hands away, and she kept batting them aside and trying again, and I flailed, finally managing my voice again. "Not! I didn't! Not me!"

She caught it at last, stopped, grabbed my wrists.

"Not me," I said. "Him, it's his blood. His blood. I didn't get hit."

Hoffman looked at me like this was another of my lies, too, like she couldn't believe I was this stubborn. I shook my head and indicated Chris's body, and she didn't let go of my wrists, just used them to pull me to my feet as she got to hers.

Marcus filled the doorway, breathless. "Sheriff's on his way, and an ambo ..."

Hoffman propelled me toward him, releasing her grip. "Cancel the ambo, add a coroner."

I stepped out, into the hot daylight again, Marcus guiding me by the shoulder. There was already the sound of a siren in the distance, maybe more than one. When I looked down at myself, I saw that the front of my jeans was soaked, and the bottom of my shirt.

Marcus led me back to the Ford, using his free hand to dial his mobile phone. When the call connected he spoke in fluent cop, using numbers and words like "homicide" and "medical examiner" and "fugitive" before he was through. Once we reached the car, he opened the rear door and had me sit on the backseat.

"Sure as hell looks like you got hit."

"Not me," I said, and pointed back to the shack. "Chris Quick."

"That makes the one who was shooting at us brother Brian?"

I nodded. "They did the cameras, you can tell, you just look in there you can tell they did the cameras on me. And they were at my house, it was Brian the first time, the one who put me in the truck, he must have a truck around here, a Ford truck. The first time, not the second time, the second time it was Chris. I should have recognized them, I should have known, but they looked different. It was them."

"You think Brian's got your father?"

I started to nod again, then heard the word "fugitive," just the way Marcus had said it on the phone, and I stopped myself before my chin came down, twisted my face so I wouldn't have to look him in the eyes.

"Brian got away?"

"He won't get far. You think he's got your dad?"

I swallowed, hard, mostly to put my stomach back where it belonged. "I don't know where Tommy is."

"That's not what I asked you."

"I know."

"You are fucking unbelievable—" he said, but then stopped, because the sirens had arrived. "Don't move, Miss Bracca. Stay right here."

I nodded, and the sirens cut off, and he went to speak to the new arrivals. I heard the frustration in his voice, could tell it was with me, and reaching its end.

But Brian had escaped, and unless Tommy was nearby, the cops weren't going to find him, either. Which meant that the only hope in hell I had of getting Tommy back alive was to stick to the original deal, and to pray that Brian meant to do the same thing.

Beyond the Ford, descending on the shack, were deputies in khaki, gesturing to one another, talking earnestly to Hoffman and Marcus. They gestured to me, to my Jeep, to me again. They gestured to the shack. A couple of deputies ran off into the woods. They seemed very busy.

Fugitive. The word resonated, sounded true. Brian had to keep our deal, he had nothing left, I realized. He was wanted now, known now. He could run poor, or he could run rich, and with a million dollars, he'd get a lot farther. He had to keep our deal.

And I needed him to, more than ever before.

Because I'd been wrong.

Tommy hadn't killed my mother.

CHAPTER THIRTY-FOUR

A deputy drove me in the back of his car into Eugene, to the sheriff's station near city hall. When I asked about my car, he told me it was part of a crime scene, and that it would be towed into town as soon as they were done with it. I didn't ask what that meant. At the station, he escorted me inside, and another deputy met us, this one female. She swabbed my hands, the same GSR test I was becoming way too familiar with, and I couldn't read her reaction when she saw the results. When that was over, the first deputy left, and the second one took my statement.

She asked why I'd gone to see Christopher and Brian Quick, and I gave her the story I'd given Anne, that I was trying to track down my old foster family, to pay them back for the kindness they'd done me.

The deputy recorded it without editorializing, and if she didn't believe me, she didn't act like she cared either way. When we were finished, she told me to get comfortable, that there'd be more people who wanted to talk to me. I asked her if I could get cleaned up first, and she told me that would have to wait.

"Can we keep this out of the papers?" I asked. "I mean, my part?"

"Your part?"

"I'm kind of well-known."

"Yeah, you kind of are. We'll see."

She went out, leaving me in the interview room by myself.

Nobody came to talk to me for another two hours, by which time I had just about gone crazy with the waiting. I'd started pacing the room, but that had very little entertainment value, and I was quickly exhausted. I sat at the table again, drumming my fingers, tapping my toes, and fighting the nagging that had begun in the car as I'd rode in from Junction City.

You fucking cunt.

You've sure grown up.

I don't have perfect pitch, but I have a brilliant memory for sound. I can pick up a melody fast, normally after only hearing it once if it's simple, two or three times if it's complex. It doesn't work for words, it doesn't work for speech, but for tone, for melody, for notes, I trust it.

Trying to conjure Brian's voice again, trying to see if it matched the one in my head, playing the two lines against one another, and they weren't fitting. I imagined Brian's curse spoken in a house, muffled behind a mask, softer, and all I got was that the octave was similar, if not the same, but that was it.

Which made me very nervous. Because it meant that Brian had someone else, someone besides his brother, that he was working with.

I'd begun to believe they'd forgotten about me when the door opened and Hoffman came in with a short Latino man, about her age, wearing a suit. He had a clipped mustache, and a thick neck, and the thickness seemed to run throughout him, along the shoulders and even down his arms to his hands. He had a stack of papers, and he pulled a chair and sat down, and Hoffman took another, on the end of the table, so she was almost between us.

"Miss Bracca, I'm Detective Munez. Thanks for your patience."

"Have you found him?"

Munez shook his head. "We will."

"You don't think he's going to go back to his place?"

"Not unless he's exceptionally stupid. Right now Brian Quick is the prime suspect in the murder of his brother, and he's wanted for the mass of charges he brought down upon himself when he opened fire on Detective Hoffman here and her partner. But it could happen. A lot of criminals are exceptionally stupid. This one seems a little brighter than most. Or at least more computer literate."

"I saw the computer."

He pressed his mustache down, as if it was in danger of coming loose. "It'll go to the State lab, they'll check the contents."

"The Quicks were the ones spying on me," I said. "They were the ones selling the pictures of me."

"It'll go to the State, like I said. They'll let us know for certain. Could you tell me why you'd gone out to see those two?"

"I told the deputy already."

"Yeah, I got that, but I'd like to hear it from you. Sometimes things get lost in these statements."

I put on my helpful face, and told him pretty much the same thing I'd told the deputy.

"You were bringing those two money?"

"Not cash," I said, as if the suggestion was ludicrous. "I was going to offer to help them out. I didn't know what they were up to at all, I mean, if I had known they were the ones spying on me, I'd have called you guys or Detective Hoffman or someone. I just ... I just thought they'd had a run of bad luck, you know? When I talked to their mother she didn't say what they'd done, just that they'd been down on their luck."

"Were they blackmailing you? About the pictures?"

"No, honest to God," I said. "Or if they were planning to, they hadn't started yet. They'd just been selling the pictures, I think. The only reason I came to see them was that I'd talked to Anne—their mother—earlier today. I found out that their father's got Alzheimer's. It's been really hard on the family, I just wanted to see if there was anything I could do to help out."

"Detective Hoffman here tells me that she advised you that both of the Quicks had a record, and that they were considered potentially dangerous individuals."

"She did, yeah, but... they were my foster brothers. I never thought they'd be like... *that,* you know? And when I saw Chris's body..."

"He was dead when you got there?"

I nodded.

"I imagine that was a surprise."

"What was that smell?" I asked. "There was this awful stink, what was that?"

Munez glanced at Hoffman, who kept her gaze planted on me. "The Quick boys were entrepreneurs, it seems," Munez said. "Aside from their cottage industry marketing dirty pictures of you, they were cooking crystal meth. Normally it gets brewed up in the high desert because the process stinks so bad. Setting up in a peppermint field, that's almost clever."

"If you say so. Next you'll tell me they were forging bonds or something like that."

Munez shook his head, chuckling, and made some notes. I risked a second glance at Hoffman. She was still watching me, no smile. She looked like she wanted to belt me, actually.

"Is there anything else?" I asked. "I'd kind of like to get home."

"A couple more things, but we can get through them pretty quickly if you're willing to cooperate."

"Of course," I said.

Hoffman snorted.

Munez said, "We've towed your Jeep in, but I'd like your consent to perform a search of the vehicle."

"Sure. Can I ask what you're looking for?"

"Methamphetamine. Chemicals or supplies used in the production of methamphetamine. Firearms. Large stacks of cash." He smiled at me. "I somehow don't think we'll find anything like that, but we need to be thorough."

"I understand. Do I just wait here?"

"It'll only take a few minutes," Munez told me, rising. "We're going to need your clothes, I'm afraid. I'll have a deputy bring you a change."

"You need my clothes?"

"Evidence. The deputy will take you to a washroom, you can get cleaned up and changed."

"Washroom would be great," I said, and gave him the same smile he'd been giving me.

When they left, the female deputy came back with a bundle under her arm, and she walked me to the ladies' room, stayed with me while I changed. I stripped off the jeans and shirt, then spent ten minutes getting the blood off my arms and hands before putting on the replacements. The jeans she gave me were blue and clean and enormous on me. I had to roll the cuffs up, and the waist kept slipping because she had to take my belt, too. The shirt was big, dark green, with the Lane County Sheriff logo on it, and comfortable. I wondered whose clothes I was wearing. When I saw myself in the mirror I looked silly as hell.

When I was finished, the deputy walked me back to the interview room without a word. Hoffman and Munez hadn't returned yet. I tried to think if I had anything embarrassing in my car, if I was going to need an explanation. If they went through absolutely everything, I figured the worst they would find would be some bad Euro Pop CDs.

It took close to another hour before they returned, around three-thirty when Munez came back, Hoffman still with him. He brought his papers again, and they took the same seats.

"We're finished with your vehicle, Miss Bracca," Munez said. "You'll be pleased to know we didn't find anything questionable, and we rotated your tires for you."

I laughed, and he grinned, pleased that I'd accepted his joke, then checked his notes once again. Hoffman shifted in her seat. He seemed to actively ignore her.

"So, what does this have to do with your father's disappearance?" he asked.

"I'm sorry?"

"Detective Hoffman tells me that this all has something to do with the fact that your father disappeared and your brother died and you being famous and like that and the pictures on the Net. She thinks maybe one or both of the Quicks knew your father at OSP. Your dad was an inmate there, wasn't he?"

I shook my head, doing my best to look bewildered. "I don't know anything about that. The first I knew that Chris and Brian had been at OSP was when Detective Hoffman told me."

"Hmm," Munez said, and scribbled some more notes, then took a moment to look over everything he'd written. Then he produced two typewritten pages and slid them to me. "Would you read these over, please?"

I read the pages. It was a typed statement about what had happened at the Quicks'. There was nothing I disagreed with.

When I looked up again, Munez slid me his pen. "If you agree with the statement, I'd like your signature and a date at the bottom."

I gave him both, slid the pages and the pen back.

Munez checked them again, then tapped the sheets together on the tabletop, squaring the edges. "Okay, you can go."

Hoffman snapped as if he'd lost his fucking mind. "What?"

He ignored her. "Thanks for your time, Miss Bracca. If we need to contact you, you'll be at your home?"

"Yes, I gave the number to the deputies."

"She's a material witness," Hoffman said. "Put her in a goddamn cell!"

Munez looked at her, and it was clear that no matter how much Hoffman had wanted to belt me before, I was maybe coming in second in the hostility department right now. It was clear, too, this wasn't the first time they'd had this fight.

"Well, Detective," Munez said. "If this was *your* case, then that would be your prerogative, wouldn't it? But it's not—what I've got is an officer-involved shooting with cops from way out of their jurisdiction, and an armed and dangerous fugitive rolling through mine. The Lane County D.A. isn't going to let me hold Miss Bracca here just because you think she's lying to you about something up in Multnomah, and I happen to think she's told us everything she knows about Mr. Quick."

"Then hold her for twenty-four." I had to give Hoffman credit for stubbornness. "Suspicion of murder for Christopher Quick."

"And risk a suit for harassment? C'mon, Detective. Even if her GSR hadn't come back negative, you and I both know she didn't cap him, the brother did. There's nothing in her vehicle or on her person tying her to the crime, and as far as I'm concerned, her story more than checks out."

"I've explained this. You've got the pictures, you've got the people who did it, you've got the fact that her brother was murdered last week, her father disappeared this past Tuesday—"

"Tuesday, huh?" Munez got his things together, then went and opened the door for me. I got up to join him.

"I just need you to sit on her for a couple of hours," Hoffman told him. "You can do that much."

Munez smiled tightly at me. "You get back to Portland, Miss Bracca, you might want to file a missing persons report about your father. Been gone since Tuesday, that's nearly forty-eight hours. We'll call if we have further questions, like I said. You can talk to the deputy at the desk about your vehicle, he'll tell you where you can retrieve it."

"Thank you," I said.

I heard Hoffman yelling at Munez through the door as I went down the hall.

*   *   *

The female deputy was at the desk, and she gave me my car keys and directions to where I could find it. I thanked her and made my way to the Jeep. Thursday late afternoon, Parka Man's deadline was Friday at noon. I'd make it back in plenty of time, but climbing behind the wheel, I knew how close a call it had been. Maybe Munez liked my smile, maybe Munez didn't like Hoffman, maybe Munez just couldn't be bothered; whatever the reason, I'd gotten out lucky.

I pulled out of the garage, onto the street, and Marcus was there, and he raised a hand to flag me down. I stopped but didn't get out of the car.

"Headed home?" he asked.

"Why? You gonna be back tonight?"

He made a slight, almost amused grunt, but there was a weight on him, now, a shadow, and he looked tired. "Somebody'll be there. We've got a mountain or three of paperwork that'll have to be filled out."

"About me?"

"We fired several rounds at Mr. Quick as he was departing. The whole incident has to be accounted for."

"Thank you," I said.

"For?"

"I'm pretty sure you guys saved my life."

"And here I was about to tell you how close you came to losing it."

"Trying not to think about that."

"You know, Miss Bracca, it wasn't just you who almost died. Quick was throwing those bullets our way when the shooting started."

"I'm glad he missed."

"Not as much as we are." There was no mirth in it. "Don't you think it's time you stopped dicking us around?"

The sky had gone to a late-afternoon blue, and there was purple rising to the west with the sunset, rain-heavy clouds. I hoped it would hold off until I was home.

"No, huh?" Marcus asked.

"You want to ask me anything else," I said, "you'll have to talk to my attorney."

Marcus stepped back from my door. "We will. See you tomorrow, Miss Bracca."

He went back inside, and I went for the interstate.

CHAPTER THIRTY-FIVE

First thing I did when I got home was get out of my new clothes and into a hot shower. I'd gotten stuck in traffic coming into town through the Curves, the winding portion of Five that descends through the South Hills before you hit the Marquam Bridge, and that's when the sky had really opened, and I'd begun to feel an itchiness along my legs, and I'd convinced myself it was Chris Quick's blood, dried and flaking on my skin.

When I was dry and dressed again I checked my voice mail, and among the garbage was a message from Chapel. He wanted to see me first thing tomorrow morning, and said that Hoffman and Marcus had been in touch.

I fixed myself dinner, a pot of Kraft macaroni and cheese, and I really wanted a drink or three, but kept myself to a couple of cigarettes and a diet Coke. I'd given things a lot of thought on the drive up from Eugene, and the only conclusions I'd come to were that I didn't really have any conclusion at all, and I was getting very scared, indeed.

If Brian Quick was the Parka Man, and if he was on the loose, then he now needed me as much as I needed him. But if he had another accomplice aside from his brother, then maybe I was getting ahead of myself. Why Brian had shot Chris, I didn't know, but greed seemed like a good motive for it. Remembering Anne's reaction to the scent of my money in the air, there was certainly a precedent for it in the family.

Maybe Brian had decided he didn't want to share a million dollars with his brother.

So the question really was, did I believe that Brian Quick and the Parka Man were the same person? And I just didn't know the answer to that. If I trusted my memory, the voices didn't match.

It was obvious that Brian and Chris were responsible for the pictures. They'd been at my home the night I'd returned from the tour, Chris inside, working on the cameras, Brian waiting outside. And when Brian had seen me, he'd seen all of their preparations for my return vanishing with my untimely arrival. He'd been so focused on keeping me out of the house, he'd panicked, and that's how I'd ended up in the truck without my clothes. It explained why he hadn't escalated; a rape would have sent me to the hospital, and maybe even more. All those cameras would have gone to waste.

Greed.

One or both of them had gotten into my home on several occasions, frequently enough to plant the cameras, to set up all the wiring and things that Burchett and his crew had discovered. If Brian could do that, then he could certainly bypass my alarm and take a fancy infrared photograph of me, then get out again without waking me up.

So there was evidence Brian could plan, he could do that. Yet he hadn't anticipated me showing up in Junction City, and when I had, his first instinct had been to open fire, a panic response, like the night I'd returned home. He'd reacted as if cornered.

That wasn't the Parka Man at all. The Parka Man had planned everything to the last detail, had predicted how I would react to the photograph, had been waiting for me at Mikel's place when I arrived.

Which brought me back to the accomplice angle, but now I was out of luck. There was no one left. "You've sure grown up," the Parka Man had told me, but everyone who knew that was accounted for. I'd seen Gareth Quick, and his Alzheimer's had seemed real enough, especially when coupled with Anne's hostility. Chris was in a Lane County morgue, and Brian was God Only Knew Where, intent on keeping the cops from sending him back to OSP. The Larkin brothers were supposedly in Alaska, and while I only had Sheila's word for that, hatching a plot from Nome that would be contingent on knowing when I was in Portland just didn't seem plausible.

What I needed to do was remember. Remember who it was I'd overlooked.

Who I'd forgotten.

The debate started around nine-thirty, while I was sitting in the living room with the Taylor, trying to rediscover what I'd wanted to play the night before. It wasn't going well, and the more I fought it, the worse it went. My fingers ached, and wouldn't take instruction right, gone sloppy, missing strings, too far from the frets. I was bearing down on the back of the neck too hard, and my left thumb started aching immediately, but instead of relaxing my hand, I fought it and gave myself more pain.

Then I lost my pick in the hole, and I had to shake it free of the chamber. When I finally got it out and tried again, I discovered I'd knocked the guitar out of tune, and almost every string had gone sharp, and the discord felt like it went straight up my spine.

Then I broke the high E on the Taylor.

I sat there with the silent guitar in my hands, feeling everything crashing over me. The smell of mint so strong I thought I would gag. Tommy, wherever he was, if he was still alive, and if he was, maybe that was worse, Steven, ashes, floating on the Pacific, and Mikel in his best suit in a box in the ground.

And I wanted a drink so bad, there didn't seem a point in staying sober.

I wanted to get the bottle of Jack out of the pantry and pour myself a glass and blast myself into oblivion, and I couldn't even do that, because once I had one, I knew I'd have another, and another, and another.

I'd never seen my father drinking liquor, only beer. It was my mother who had drunk Jack Daniel's, always on the rocks, always in a dark glass, so she could pretend it was iced tea.

I was a liar.

I was an alcoholic, just like my father, just like my mother.

Maybe it was just time to admit that I was my parents' daughter.

There was knocking on the door and I went to answer it, then stopped halfway down the hall. I checked from the window of the living room, pressing my face against the cold glass, and I could see a car parked across the street, and I could make out a woman on my porch, waiting at the door.

"Dyke Tracy," I said, when I opened up. "What a surprise."

"You drunk?"

It was a stupid question. I had the glass in my hand. "Go away."

"We need to talk."

"Oh?"

"Please."

It was the way she said it, nothing behind it or in it except fatigue. I knew the feeling.

"Yeah, come in," I said. "Fix yourself a drink. There's even beer in the fridge, untouched, pristine. Are you off duty? You can drink off duty, right?"

I went to my cigarettes and lit one, watched as she moved through my kitchen. She went to the fridge and looked inside, brought out a bottle of beer. I clapped one hand on the counter in approval, because I didn't want to spill my glass. She'd gone with the IPA.

"Click would approve," I told her.

"You're hammered."

"Nailed, baby."

She set the bottle on the counter. "That's not terribly smart, Mim."

"I'm not terribly smart, Tracy." I took a gulp of my drink, maintaining eye contact. "Bet you don't think I'm drinking iced tea, do you?"

She didn't answer.

"It's Jack rocks. It's a man's drink, but strong enough for a woman," I said. She didn't laugh. I finished what was in my glass, then went for the bottle to refill.

"They rushed the job on that computer they took from the Quicks' place," she told me.

"Shack. Not a place, a shack. I've been in places, they don't look like that."

"They found multiple files, images of you. They were in different stages of being doctored up like the ones that already went public."

"I look forward to seeing them."

"Thing is, according to Burchett and his people, there should be a couple gigabytes of video of you, just the raw video. There was no sign of it on the computer."

"Maybe it was boring, so they deleted it."

"They can check for that. It wasn't there."

I shrugged and sipped.

"I have a theory," Hoffman said, after a moment.

"I have one, too," I told her. "It goes, dinosaurs are thin at one end, thick in the middle, and thin at the other end."

"You quote Monty Python when you're drunk?"

"It's a theory." I sat at the table, a little heavier than I had wanted to.

"I think the person who killed your brother is the same person who took your father," Hoffman said. "And I'm beginning to think that's not the same person who took the pictures. Brian and Chris, they were planning on their little spy game back at OSP. Chris took computer courses in prison, Brian studied to be an electrician. I think they only planned to spy on you, maybe ultimately to blackmail you."

"They teach courses on kidnapping at OSP?"

"Not officially."

"So what the fuck is your point?"

"I don't think your father wanted to go with the person who took him. I think this person is the reason you've got a bruise on your throat and a cut on your forehead and swollen knuckles on your hand, and he's why you spent today running up and down the I-Five corridor. I think you've been trying to figure out on your own who that person is, and that for some reason you think it's someone from your days in foster care. That's why you went out to see the Quicks, and that's why you were trying to be so subtle about what we might have found at his place. Forging bonds. You were fishing."

I looked at the ash forming on the end of my cigarette. She seemed to have paused for a breath, so I took another drink from my glass.

"According to my theory, you're trying to get cash together, a lot of it, more than you can get easily by yourself. That's why you went to see Graham Havers. I thought you were surprised to see us there, but now that I think about it, I think it scared you.

"Which means you're coming up on the deadline, either expecting a call shortly, or maybe you've even received it, though given how shit-faced you are, I hope not the latter. Whatever, this call has instructions, telling you where to bring the money, where to find your father.

"Now, speaking personally, I like this theory, and, incidentally, so does my partner. We both like it a hell of a lot more than trying to fit you for a murder we're not even sure has been committed, and that, if it has, we're pretty damn certain you did not do. And this theory, it explains a lot of your behavior in such a way as to make it, if not excusable, at least explicable."

"That's a good word," I said, dropping ash onto the table. I drained my glass and got up, went for a refill. "Explicable."

"Any comment?"

"No." I emptied the last of the bottle into my glass.

"No, my theory is crap, or no, you have no comment?"

"If you have questions you want to ask me—"

"Talk to your attorney. We'll be doing that tomorrow. Right now, right here, I want to talk to you."

"You are talking to me."

"It's a little one-sided."

I got indignant. "I'm participating."

"I almost got killed today," Hoffman said. "Never had someone shoot at me before. But I almost got killed today. My partner, too. You could have died, too."

"These things you say, they are all true." I grinned. "Dyke Tracy."

"Goddammit, Mim!" Her cheeks looked flushed. "Being lied to, it's part of the job. But I have never encountered someone as stupid as you about helping herself. If I'm right, if you *tell* me that I'm right, I can get the FBI in on this, we can get a wiretap set. This kidnapper calls, we'll be all over him. But if you keep this up ... you keep this up, people are going to die."

"I don't know what you're talking about," I said, and I didn't even try to make it sound like I was telling the truth.

"Why won't you let me help you?" She was almost pleading. "Why won't you tell me what's going on? What could this guy have over you that's keeping you so scared and so silent?"

"You keep coming over to talk to me at night," I said. "Even when you're being Dyke Tracy, you come over here at night. Why is that?"

"I'm trying to solve your brother's murder. I'm trying to find your father!"

I shrugged. "I thought maybe it was because of the thing you have for me."

"That 'thing' is rapidly disappearing."

"Really?" I put my glass on the stove, by the empty bottle, and took a couple steps toward her. She was standing in the corner, where the counter turned, the microwave behind her. The clock read seventeen minutes past eleven. "I mean, really? Because at Van's party, it seemed like a very serious thing to me."

"Knock it off, Miss Bracca."

"Oh, Miss Bracca, huh? No *thing,* but I'm Miss Bracca, now?" I stopped right in front of her, looking up. "I thought you wanted me."

The muscles in her jaw flexed as she closed her mouth. I liked her lips, decided to taste them again. When I tried to put my hands on her hips, she caught my wrists, pushing my arms down.

"C'mon, now you're just playing hard to get," I told her.

Hoffman tried moving me back, to get out of the corner. I let my weight come forward and my arms spread out. She had my arms extended out like I was playing airplane pretty fast, but I just kept falling forward, giggling, and she had to let go of my wrists to catch me when I pitched into her. I tried to get my mouth on a breast, through her shirt, and she shoved me back and then I was upside down, and looking at her ass. That was really funny, especially when my head started banging against it as she took me up the stairs.

She dumped me on the bed, and I tried to stop laughing and say something more, but then I started to not feel too good, and I had to close my eyes and hold my breath. That seemed to help for an eternity, and then, in the sudden dark, I realized what it was I'd just done, and then it wasn't just my stomach that felt like it was going to erupt.

I tried getting up and slipped out of the bed, onto the floor on my side. My shoes were off, and my socks, and my feet were cold. The room was dark, and I realized my eyes were open, and that the lights were off.

"Tracy?" I called.

There was no answer.

I hoisted myself using the side of the bed, lurched for the bathroom. On my way in, I caught sight of the cable box, and the time.

It was twenty-two minutes past three.

When I made my way back to bed, it was a quarter to five.

I buried my head in my pillows, and fell asleep, waiting for the next bad thing to happen.

*   *   *

In daylight, I spent most of an hour worshipping the Porcelain God and regretting everything, every goddamn thing, I'd ever done, before I could begin to function properly. When I was finished I saw that I was still in my clothes from the night before, and my head was pounding, and I could feel my pulse beating in my thumbs. Undressing took time, and I nearly nodded off again in the shower, and when I realized that, I panicked and fell in the hurry to get out and get dry.

By the time I was dressed and ready to move, the clock was reading 10:48 A.M. I was heading out the back door when the telephone started ringing.

I hesitated, trying to figure who it was, and the thought that it was maybe the Parka Man was what finally got me to answer it.

It was Joan.

"Mim? I didn't wake you?"

"No, I was on my way out, actually."

"I can call back...."

"I've only got a couple minutes," I said.

She didn't seem to have heard me. "It's about Steven, I wanted to talk to you about...I was going through his things this morning. I haven't touched them since he died and I was thinking that I should ... I was really thinking that tomorrow I should start cleaning things out."

I felt the pressure of the clock, the absurdity of having this conversation at this moment. Over the line, I heard voices, not kids but adults, and wondered if she was calling me from school.

"If you would come over?" Joan asked. "Give me a hand? I'd ... I think I could use the support."

"I'll try," I said, knowing I wouldn't.

Her voice got harder. "It's not the same as a funeral, and I know he wasn't Mikel, but I'd think you could find the time if you wanted to."

"No, absolutely. I'll be there."

It wasn't that she heard insincerity; she heard the haste, and took that the wrong way, too.

"I suppose I'll see you then. If you remember."

She hung up, and I hung up, and felt the wound like an acid burn, lingering.

But there wasn't time.

I had to get to the bank.

CHAPTER THIRTY-SIX

Catherine Lumley moved to greet me with a big smile and an outstretched hand.

"Wonderful to see you again, Ms. Bracca."

I know it was just the hangover, but it hurt my eyes to look at the smile. "We'll be going upstairs, to Alex's office."

"Alex?"

"Rodriguez, your banker."

She took me off the floor quickly, through a doorway and up a carpeted flight of steps. "You have something to carry the cash?"

I patted the strap on my shoulder, for my backpack. "All set."

"Wonderful," Lumley murmured.

We came into a quiet hallway with doors along both sides, and at the third down on the right, she stopped and tapped gently, not with her knuckles, but with her lacquered fingernails. I didn't imagine anyone within could have heard the sound, but there was an answering voice immediately, telling us to come in.

Alexander Rodriguez was much younger than I expected, only thirty or so, and looking like he took his job very seriously. His tie was navy blue and boring, the knot at his throat so small, I wondered if it was actually a clip-on. He rose from behind his desk as we entered, and came around the corner, leaning forward with a hand outstretched.

"Miss Bracca, very pleased to finally meet you."

"Nice to meet you, too."

"Do you need anything? Water or tea?"

The hangover was making my mouth grow wool, and my headache was committed, so I nodded, which actually, physically, hurt. "Water."

"Cathy?"

"I'll be right back," Lumley told me.

She went out as Rodriguez motioned me to one of the two chairs in front of his desk. I took the backpack off my shoulder and let it rest against my leg, and Rodriguez went back to his seat, moving some paper. One short stack he slid toward me, with a thick pen.

"What's this?" I asked.

"It's the Currency Transaction Report. If you could just review the information, make any notes if something needs to be changed."

I looked at the top form, saw the words "Internal Revenue Service," and got immediately worried. "The IRS?"

"It's a formality, part of the way they regulate cash movement," Rodriguez said. "They're worried you're a drug dealer."

"No, just a musician."

"Same thing to them, maybe." He smiled, friendly. "It just tells them where the cash is going when it leaves the bank. Very simple in this instance, since you're both the withdrawer and the recipient."

I skimmed, saw that my personal information had been recorded, my full name, where I lived, my Social Security number. Nowhere was there a check box for "using money to pay kidnapper" or anything like that. The form didn't even need my signature, so I slid it back to Rodriguez, and he added the sheet to the stack on his blotter.

Lumley came back with a plastic bottle of water, and they both watched me, polite smiles in place, as I opened and drained it. Rodriguez handed me another form, this one a withdrawal request.

"Just fill it out like you would normally," he told me.

While I did so, he got up and opened a filing cabinet in the corner, and was back at the desk when I finished. I signed my name precisely, and he took the request and pulled a card from my file, and I realized he was comparing signatures. When he noticed me watching, he dipped his head apologetically.

"We have to be thorough."

"It's nice to know you're taking such good care of my money," I told him, although the care he was taking was starting to make me nervous.

But both he and Lumley brightened with the compliment, and I realized just how worried they were about losing my business. Rodriguez tucked the signature card back in my file, replaced the file in the cabinet.

"If you'll wait here," he told me, "we'll be back with the money. It won't take more than ten minutes."

"I'll be here."

They left, and I looked at the clock on the desk, then checked it against the watch on my wrist. The clock said it was eighteen minutes past eleven, but my watch said it was only a quarter past. I tried taking some calm breaths, telling myself that I had plenty of time to get back home before the call or whatever it was I was waiting on from the Parka Man. My stomach felt raw, and I wondered if draining the bottle of water had been such a good idea.

The door opened, and Lumley entered first, carrying a counting machine in both hands. She set it on the edge of the desk, ran the cord to the outlet in the wall. Rodriguez followed her, carrying a canvas sack with printing on the side, the name of an armored transport company.

"This is going to take another few minutes," he told me. "We need to make certain of the count."

Rodriguez set the bag in his chair and began pulling out stacks of bills, hundreds, one after the other. They were wrapped with paper bands around them, marking denominations of ten thousand dollars.

Lumley had switched the counting machine on, and it was humming slightly. He unwrapped the first bundle, and fed it into the hollow on the top of the machine, and the hum grew louder, and the bills began snapping forward. He fed another bundle, and another, and the paper kept flowing, and Lumley gathered the stacks and wrapped them in their bands again, setting them aside.

It took another fourteen minutes before they were positive they had six hundred thousand dollars in cash. Sixty stacks of hundred-dollar bills, bundled one hundred bills each.

"All yours," Rodriguez told me.

I opened my backpack and began shoveling the money inside. If they thought I was eccentric before, this confirmed it, and they watched, bemused, as I fought to get the last three bundles to fit. The zipper on the backpack stuck as I was trying to run it closed, and I had to muscle it before I could get the bag shut. Then I hoisted it on my arm, felt the weight pull on my shoulder.

Lumley offered her hand first, murmuring that if I needed anything else, I shouldn't hesitate to contact her. I told her I wouldn't, and appreciated all of her help.

It was Rodriguez who walked me to the door, saying, "You're going to want to take that someplace safe immediately. It's an awful lot of money to just be carrying around."

"I've got it covered," I told him.

He gave me his hand. "Pleasure doing business with you," he said.

Back at home, I switched on the porch light, then went down to the basement and the Fender amp, pulled the duffel bag free, then got the boxes of press packets out of the closet. On the floor, between guitars, I transferred the six hundred thousand in my backpack into the duffel, and it fit with room to spare. I closed the bag and hoisted it, trying to guess how much it weighed now. Definitely more than the Tele, that was for sure. I had to guess it was close to forty pounds.

The clock in the kitchen was reading three minutes to noon when I came back up, and I saw the empty bottle out where I'd left it the night before. I dropped it in the trash and got the Johnnie Walker out of the pantry, cracking the seal as I went to check the living room window. I pulled some of the heat into my chest, then looked out in time to see the Ford pull up.

Marcus and Hoffman had followed me to the bank, but when I'd emerged, they hadn't been in their car, and I'd made it home without them in my shadow. It didn't take Mozart to figure out what they'd done, that they'd stepped inside and had a brief word with Lumley and maybe even with Rodriguez. I doubted either banker would have given the detectives the exact amount I'd withdrawn, but it didn't matter. It was just one more piece to support Hoffman's theory.

She was at the wheel this time, and I could see her speaking into a radio as I took another drink, feeling the warmth crawl into my limbs. Marcus, beside her, was leaning around, to take a look at the front of my house. I thought about stepping out and offering Hoffman an apology for what I'd done, the way I'd behaved, for all of it, and knew it wouldn't do either of us any good. The only thing that would make it better would be me getting brave, telling them that it would happen today, that it would all be over soon.

But I couldn't, so I took another swallow, surrendering, and all I could think of was how certain the Parka Man had sounded when he told me he would know if I talked to the cops, how he knew people, how I should lie to them. They expected that, he'd said, and Hoffman had echoed him just the night before, already used to my string of lies.

When I thought about it some more it made me bring the bottle down and backpedal from the window.

I was crazy, I had to be wrong, but when I took the Quicks away from the equation, put the spying and the cameras and the pictures all to one side and Mikel and Tommy and the kidnapping on the other, it made even more sense. It explained why Tommy had been so worried for me, why he'd tried to warn me after Mikel's funeral, and why he hadn't given Hoffman and Marcus anything when he'd been arrested. It explained how Parka Man could get into my house, not once, but twice, how he could deactivate my alarm without me or anyone else knowing.

Why the Parka Man was doing what he was doing, I had no idea.

But now I knew who he was, I was certain. If I could find him, if I could find where he had Tommy, then there might be a chance. I had to make a plan, to come up with a plan. All I needed was a little time.

Then the phone started ringing, and there was no time left.

CHAPTER THIRTY-SEVEN

This is going to be real simple," the Parka Man said when I answered the phone. "Simple and quick. You want your daddy, I want my money. The sooner we finish, the happier we'll both be."

"I want proof he's alive," I said. "I want to hear him tell me he's all right."

"In a moment. Right now, you're going to listen carefully to the following instructions."

It felt like his words were swimming around in my brain, and I didn't know if it was the alcohol or the fear or the still-fresh realization of who he really was. The thought that I would accidentally blurt out his name came over me, and I knew that if I let it slip, Tommy was as good as dead.

"First thing you do is lose the cops," he said. "I don't care how you do it. Once you break the tail, you get on the MAX, you take it out to PDX. Just ride it straight out there, don't talk to anyone. Get off at the airport, then you take a cab, you go to downtown. You're getting out at the corner of Northeast Everett and Third. There's a bar, midway down the block. You go in there. At three o'clock, exactly, you get yourself a drink from the bar."

"MAX, airport, Everett and Third, bar, drink. Then what happens?"

"Be there and find out. And be there without company, or it's off, and your daddy never sees the light of day again."

It was the way he kept repeating it, as if I hadn't understood it, as if I hadn't lived the past three days with the fear of what he'd do to Tommy in my heart and head at every moment.

"I've got your cash," I said. "Now you put him on, you cocksucker, you let me hear his voice, right now, or you get nothing."

He chuckled. "You sure you want to make that threat?"

"You want the money, asshole?"

There was another chuckle, but not as amused, this time, and then a rustle. I heard labored breathing.

"Tommy?"

"Miriam?" His voice was thin, as if he'd gone without water.

"God, are you all right?"

Another rustle, and the Parka Man came back.

"Three o'clock," he said, and hung up.

For almost five minutes after he had cut the connection, I just stood in the kitchen, just stood there, thinking. Trying to find a way to get what I wanted, what I needed, without getting myself and my father killed. Because it was clear, so clear now, what he was going to do, what he *had* to do, if I was correct.

If Tommy knew who the Parka Man was, if Tommy knew he'd killed Mikel, then Tommy was dead as soon as he had the money. Which meant that by the time Tommy got in Charon's line, he'd find that his daughter was already crossing the Styx; no way in hell was this guy going to let me live after he had the cash. If he was going to tie up his loose ends, he'd tie all of them up, and that meant me, too.

For a morbid moment, I wondered if he'd try to make my death look like an accident. How hard would it be? Musicians die with changes in the seasons, and it wasn't as if I'd been living a very clean life. Maybe that was why he was having me come to a bar. Pour a bottle down my throat, the rest would be easy.

Maybe I'd get a tribute album, or fan pilgrimages to my grave.

Chapel's office was downtown, I remembered. I'd have to cover a couple blocks on foot to do what I wanted to do, but it was possible, and if everything went well, it wouldn't blow the schedule.

I grabbed the backpack, stuffed full, and the Taylor in its case, and went out to the garage, trying to get into the Jeep without Marcus or Hoffman getting a look at what I was doing, struggling with the weight. At first, it seemed like taking the car wasn't maybe the best idea, that perhaps I could try to go it on foot. But the way Hoffman and Marcus had always been covered, the way there'd never been a gap in the surveillance in front of my house, made me think that there were probably cops out back, too. They wouldn't have been doing their job if they were only watching the front door.

So I'd stick with the cops I knew. After all, they'd come this far with me.

It was twenty-six minutes to one when I pulled out, heading downtown, jockeying with the lunch hour traffic. I didn't try to switch lanes or speed up or slow down, nothing to get them worried. It didn't matter; they were already worried, and the one time I caught them close behind me, close enough to see them reflected in my rearview mirror, Marcus was grim behind the wheel, and Hoffman was again on her radio.

If there were others following me, I couldn't spot them. Another thing I couldn't control.

We crossed the river on the Steel Bridge, and it started to rain, spatters on my windshield that the wipers couldn't quite cope with, as if it wasn't sincere enough to require their best efforts. I turned at the light on Broadway, then again on Market, and pulled into the underground garage at Chapel's building. When I took my ticket from the dispenser, I could see the Ford idling near the top of the ramp.

Come on, I thought. Follow me.

The bar went up, and I pulled forward, winding farther down, past rows of parked Beemers and Lexi and Acuras, then through a forest of SUVs. I found a space on the lowest level near the elevator bank, got out with my backpack, and locked up.

There was no sign of the Ford.

This is not going to work, I thought, as I got into the elevator. I am fucked, and this is not going to work.

My hands were shaking when I punched the button for the tenth floor. I had to shove them into my pockets to keep them out of sight, and when the elevator stopped in the lobby, I was glad that I'd done it.

Marcus and Hoffman got on the elevator.

"This is a surprise," I said.

They didn't answer, just went to the back of the car, fitting in behind me. It was funny in its own way, how none of us was even bothering to pretend anymore.

We rode another four floors, and the car stopped once more, and two men in nice suits got on, talking anxiously about what the market had done in Japan that morning. They got off again at seven, and when the doors were again closed, I turned to face Hoffman.

"I was a total asshole last night," I said. "And I'm very sorry."

"Passive-aggressive *and* apologetic," Marcus remarked. "You're very talented, Miss Bracca."

"That's what they say." I was still looking at Hoffman. She was staring back, and I wasn't even certain she'd heard me.

Then the elevator stopped and we all got out, and they followed me into the offices of my attorney. Marcus and Hoffman waited near the back of the reception area while I approached Joy at the desk. She got to her feet when she saw me.

"Is Fred expecting you?"

"I hope so. He left me a message last night."

"Why don't you have a seat, I'll tell him you're here."

There was a clock in the room, hanging over a Tailhook poster, one I hadn't seen before. In this one, I was standing beside Van, with Click on a riser just behind us. The clock told me it was seventeen minutes past one.

It was reading twenty-nine to two when Joy, back at her desk, answered her phone, and then told me Mr. Chapel would see me now. I rose and joined her, and Marcus and Hoffman stayed put, unhappy with the situation. They wouldn't be kept at bay for long.

When we were out of the reception area and winding through the halls, I told Joy that what I really needed was a bathroom, and could she direct me to one. She veered off course, leading me to the restroom.

"I'll wait for you," she told me.

"No, don't do that." I gave her my best embarrassed grin. "Make me feel like a total princess, you have to wait for me while I pee."

She laughed, like I knew she would.

"I know the way," I said. "I can manage the rest."

"I'll let him know you'll be right there."

"Great, thanks," I said, and then went into the bathroom before she could say anything else, locking the door behind me. I stood with my back to it, listening, and I didn't hear her leave, but I didn't hear anything else through it, either, so it didn't mean much.

Thirty seconds, I told myself. Give her thirty seconds, then go. More than that, Hoffman and Marcus will barge in. Less, she'll still be there, waiting.

I watched the second hand move on my wrist.

Then I unlocked the door and took a breath, stepped out as if I knew where I was going and what I was doing. The receptionist had gone, and the only people in the hall were occupied with their own affairs, and paid me no attention. I set off toward Chapel's office, heard his voice, strained, coming from the area of Joy's desk. I didn't stop, hoping that he'd keep Marcus and Hoffman busy, but it still took me almost three more minutes before I found the fire door and my way to the stairs.

The latch echoed in the stairwell when the door shut behind me, and as soon as I heard it click shut, I started running, one hand on the rail, the other on the backpack strap, trying to keep it on my shoulder. I went fast, two, three steps at a time, too ambitious, and I almost fell twice, but I didn't slow down, and I sure as hell didn't stop. The hangover swelled in my head. Marcus and Hoffman wouldn't take long to figure out I was ditching them, if they hadn't figured it already, and the best I could hope for was that they'd go back to my car, thinking that's where I was headed.

Their bad luck that Portland has such a wonderful light-rail system.

There were two men standing in the rain, watching the ramp into the garage when I came out of the building, and I guessed they were cops, and turned my back to them before I had a chance to find out. Hoofed it across the street, my shoulders aching with the weight of the backpack, then jogged to the MAX stop. I made it by ten of two, and there was a train waiting, and I jumped on without paying the fare, working my way to the front of the carriage and dropping into a seat. It wouldn't be a problem until I was past the Lloyd Center, since fares in downtown were waived, but I didn't think I'd have time to hop out and pay then, either, and the thought that I might get caught only compounded my anxiety. It would be just my luck to have ditched the cops only to get picked up again for not paying public transportation.

It didn't happen, and I made the train switch and all the way to the airport without trouble. Halfway to PDX, I started looking around the car, wondering if maybe he was on board, if he was watching, but after a minute realized that was futile. I doubted he was actually following me; the runaround was more to make certain I didn't get any ideas, I supposed. Like I was going to start doing that at this late date.

Like I'd recognize him without his ski mask and parka, anyway.

The rain was coming heavier when I got off at the airport, and I swung through baggage claim and back outside immediately, heading for the cab stand. There were three people in line, and my watch was reading two forty-one, and the tremor in my hands was getting worse. I wanted a drink, settled for a couple drags of a cigarette, and got a Broadway Cab to take me back downtown.

"Third and Everett," I said.

The driver, already behind the wheel and pulling us into traffic, glanced at me in the mirror. "You mean Twenty-third and Everett, yeah?"

"No, I mean Third and Everett."

He started to argue, eyes on me in the mirror, then shrugged. If the strange white girl wanted to go to the heart of bum central, that was not his problem.

"Hurry," I told him.

Everett straddles the dividing line between Old Town Portland and Chinatown, and there are storefronts all around the area that date back to the turn of the century, and in some cases, earlier. I almost missed the bar, because I was late by my watch, and now even more frightened that I'd fucked everything up. The rain was coming down in sheets, cold and solid, like walking through a car wash, and I had to go down the block twice before I was certain I had the right place, an unmarked and smoked-glass door sandwiched between a porno shop and a Chinese antiques store.

Inside was everything you'd expect, dark and a little dank, with the bar along the left side, and booths along the right, and enough room between the two that I could fit, if I walked sideways. I was soaked to the skin, and the straps of the backpack had dug into my shoulders so hard it felt like my arms would go numb. I was shivering, and it wasn't the chill that was giving me goose bumps.

The bartender was a woman, alcoholically aged, trapped somewhere between forty and seventy, with drawn skin and gin blossoms on her face. She stared at me and I thought for a moment that she knew who I was.

"Jack rocks," I said, and dug out a twenty, slapping it on the bar.

She took the bill and grunted. My watch was reading six minutes past three. Rainwater dripped down my neck, and I could feel it soaking the back of my shirt. The fingers on my left hand had started throbbing again. There were only two other patrons in the bar, and both of them would have scared me if I wasn't already so preoccupied with other fears.

The door opened as I waited for my drink, and Brian Quick entered, soaked from the rain.

I turned hastily away, felt the panic claw at my heart. If I was right, he shouldn't be here, this didn't concern him. And if he was here, then I was wrong, and everything I was planning was worthless.

I heard him move to the bar, demand a bottle of beer, and the bartender snarled back at him to wait a fucking minute, then slapped my change down in front of me, planting my glass on top of it. I took the drink in a gulp. It was watered down, and if it was Jack Daniel's to start with, I was Nina Simone, but it lit a raw fire in my chest, and made me think it was what I needed.

Brian Quick received a bottle, focused on the television hanging over the corner of the bar. He could have been just another midday alcoholic for all the interest he had in the world around him.

I picked up my change, began folding it into my pocket, and saw a small slip of notepaper wedged between bills. I pulled it free, glancing again toward Brian, caught him taking a pull of his beer.

The paper read BACKROOM.

The door was set in the wall behind the final booth, and it opened into a storage room full of cardboard boxes stacked on metal shelves. I took a last look over my shoulder before pushing through, and the bartender was enraptured by the glowing box again, but Brian had twisted on his stool, watching me go. When I stepped in, I didn't see any lock for the door. A couple of kegs stood in a corner, and a single, naked bulb gave the only illumination. There was no one to be seen, and I thought I'd trapped myself, had started to turn around and head back out when I saw the other door, only about half-height, between two sets of shelves. The door was metal, old, and slightly ajar.

It opened into a chute of some kind, and there was a ladder propped against the wall. I looked down, and in the dim light saw a rough dirt floor maybe fifteen feet below. The walls on either side of the chute were stone, and the air smelled stale and perpetually wet. When I listened, I could hear the echo of water dripping onto stone.

There wasn't any more time. I adjusted my backpack, and slipped through the opening onto the ladder, feet first. The alcohol wasn't doing its job, and even when I gripped the rungs tight, forcing my injured fingers to close around the wood, they still kept shaking.

In the room above and behind me, I heard the door swing open, Brian coming from behind.

I'd been right about one thing. Whoever was doing this, they planned to leave me dead.

And they'd picked a perfect place to do it, a place where perhaps hundreds had died before me.

This was the Portland Underground, sometimes called the Shanghai Tunnels, and the reason that the City of Roses had earned the dubious honor of being called the Worst Port in the World. No one knew who had first constructed the tunnels, but they'd begun operation around the 1850s as a means to hold and move, to buy and sell, human beings. Thousands of men and women had disappeared through them during their days of operation, either taken by force or drugged into submission, dragged off the streets, most never to be seen again. It was a business, run by men called crimps, who would sell males as sailors and the women as prizes. They called their earnings blood money, and sometimes took as much as fifty dollars a head. Captains in port would request a crew, and the captured men would be drugged yet again, then loaded onto the ships this time to awaken in the Pacific, sold into slavery, on their way to ports like Shanghai and Hong Kong and Macao. Some eventually made their way home, voyaging for years to pay for their return. Most never made it home at all.

When I was sixteen, I'd written a report for school about the tunnels. I'd gone to the library and looked at microfilm of newspapers from the 1930s, read the accounts of men like Bunco Kelly and

Stewart Holbrook. The tunnels had reportedly been in operation into the early 1940s, and I'd had nightmares that they were still used, that I would be walking downtown and the ground would open in front of me, and I would be put in a cage and chained and sold to a harem somewhere.

Somehow, that seemed more appealing than what I was facing now.

I hit the bottom of the ladder, trying to find the source for the light. It was out of sight, around a bend, a soft glow that made the tunnel seem darker. The sound of the water was louder here, and there was a wind that raced along the stone, whining for attention as it found me and slid up my legs and down my shirt. The water on my back got colder, and the shakes got worse.

Above me, I heard the metal door swing open, hit the stone wall with a clang.

I put one foot carefully in front of the other, trying to remember how to breathe as much as walk, moving toward the light. My steps made echoes.

I was ten feet or so from the bend when he came around the side, setting a battery-powered lantern on the ground. He was dressed the same as he had been all the times before, still wearing the black mask. His hands were out and empty, and he seemed larger than he had before, and I stopped cold when I saw him.

"You were late."

I nodded.

He raised a hand and indicated the backpack on my shoulder. "Toss it over."

My voice sounded hollow and ethereal when I said, "I want my dad."

"Toss it over here."

In my jeans, my knees felt like they were turning to gelatin, trying to slide down my shins. I let the backpack slide off my arm, let the strap fall into my hand.

Behind me, Brian Quick said, "Half of that's mine."

The gun came out from beneath the parka as if it were a living thing, ready to leap on command, and it was up and pointed before I could begin to react. But not before Brian, apparently, because he shoved me hard to the side, snatching the backpack free with his other hand, and I hit the wall on my shoulder and bit back a cry.

The only thing that made the pain easier was that the Parka Man was now pointing his gun at Brian Quick.

Brian Quick, however, had brought a gun of his own.

"The fuck is this?" Parka Man asked. I thought it was directed at me.

"I'm your partner," Brian said, before I could speak. "I'm the guy who's made it easy for you so far."

"Is that so?"

"You killed her big brother, asshole. You killed her brother, but instead of cops coming after you, I've had them chasing after me. I gave you room to work."

"I didn't ask for your help."

"You got it anyway. How much you hitting her for? Fifty K? A hundred? We split it down the middle, right now, we never see each other again."

Parka Man didn't move, and neither did his gun. Unlike Brian, he held it in both hands, his knees bent in a slight crouch.

I tried to straighten up, using the wall.

"You fucking don't move, bitch," Brian snarled, adjusting his grip on his gun. His tongue stabbed out, wetting his lips. "You and me, we're not done."

"You're the pervert," Parka Man said. It came out soft, but there was no mistaking the realization in his voice. There was no mistaking the mirth, either.

"I'm no perv, asshole," Brian said, agitated. His hand was beginning to jump, and I wondered if he sampled the product he and his brother used to cook. "I'm a goddamn entrepreneur, I had a fucking sweet system going, then you came along and fucked it up."

"Did I?"

"Fuck you, man, I've got the money here, you want to take a shot? I fucking bought you time! We split this straight, fifty-fifty."

"No."

"Dammit, I fucking earned this, this is mine! I take half, at least I'm left with something!"

"You've already got something," Parka Man said. "You're still breathing."

Brian fired.

The gunshot was so loud it made my whole head ring, and I saw the Parka Man stagger back, and I thought that was it. I turned my back to the wall, started to push off it, driving toward Brian, knowing I was next, knowing he wouldn't wait, couldn't afford to count.

I was looking right at Brian when the bullets hit him. He had started to turn, and the first shot hit him in the side and made him bend, and then the second hit his neck, and made him twirl and spray. I faltered, catching myself, scrambling to reverse my balance and momentum all at once, and I fell backward, into the wall again.

On the ground, Brian's right arm twitched.

I covered my mouth, turned away, and Parka Man was back on his feet, one hand clapped to his chest. Through the black parka, I could see a fuzz of white. His mouth was moving, but I couldn't hear him, the gunshots still playing in my ears.

Parka Man gestured at Brian with his gun, then at me, and I understood that nothing had changed, that he intended us to resume where we'd been interrupted.

I stepped over to the body. Brian had fallen on the backpack, and I had to roll him to free it. I couldn't look at his face.

"We'll try this again," I heard the Parka Man say. His voice sounded strained, fighting pain. "Send it over here."

I used the strap, tossed it toward him. It landed short about four feet, and the thud echoed on the stone.

Parka Man reached for the backpack, leaning forward and down, and it was clear just from his body language that I didn't threaten him at all, that he was sure there was nothing I could do to him physically. I hated him for being right.

He knew something was wrong the moment he lifted the backpack, and I wondered if Brian hadn't ruined it for me, if he hadn't turned things so sour that Parka Man would lose his temper and send me bleeding to the floor, too. When he ran the zipper back, I could see the violence in the movement, the mounting suspicion. Once the backpack was open, he stared at the contents for a moment before turning it upside down and emptying it out. The sound of the paper hitting the dirt floor of that tunnel was like distant slaps, and it echoed like a blow against soft flesh.

Then he just stood there, staring down at the photos, the black-and-white promo shots, me and Click and Van, Tailhook triumphant together. I'd raided every press kit, filling the backpack to capacity, and the images slipped like a glossy puddle around his feet, reflecting the shadowy light.

"Is this supposed to be funny?" Parka Man asked me. "Is this supposed to be a joke?"

"I want my dad," I said. "You don't get shit until I get my dad."

He dropped the backpack, brought the gun up in both hands. "You get your father *after* I get my fucking money, not before!"

The shout made me wince, took a couple of seconds to echo away. The muscles in my chest were trembling, now, I felt like all of me would start to shake apart at any second.

Somehow, I said, "I want my dad. You don't get shit until I see him, until I see him walking away from you."

"Little Miriam, you're about to become little dead Miriam."

"You shoot me you get nothing, you did all of this for nothing."

"Where's my money?" he screamed.

"Somewhere else! Somewhere else, you kill me, you don't get it!" I was screaming back at him, just as loud, and certainly far more hysterical. "Where's my dad?"

He ran his thumb over the back of the gun, and there was a metal sound, clicking.

"Fucking kill you right here, little girl."

I closed my mouth, willed myself to keep breathing.

"Then do it," I told him. "Just do it and don't waste my time anymore."

The gun rose slightly, then settled on me again, and I saw the tension ride up his arms, saw his eyes readjust inside the hood, and I thought that this time he was going to go all the way. This time, I would die.

But he didn't shoot. Instead, he said, "Your daddy's just fine, Miriam. He's just fine, I'll let him go as soon as we're done."

"You're going to kill him as soon as we're done. You're going to kill me, too. I'm not the sharpest fucking tool in the shop, but I've figured out that much. So you have to decide something, you have to make up your mind. You want the money or don't you?"

"You're so sure you're a dead girl, why you willing to deal?"

The tremor was in my voice, and I hoped he bought it simply as fear, and not as something more. "Because it's a million dollars, it's cash, and with it you can go anywhere you want, wherever you want. I don't know who you are, and I don't care. I just want my father back. So we meet someplace, you pick where, but it's in public, someplace you can't shoot me, someplace you can't shoot him. And when I see him, when I see my dad walking away, you get your money."

He didn't respond and the gun didn't move, and I tried to get my breathing back under control, tried to slow it down, afraid I'd hyperventilate.

"You think I'm stupid?" he asked, finally. "You let this prick follow you, you think I should trust you?"

"I don't know about Brian," I said. "I didn't know he was there, and I swear I don't know how he found me, I don't know why he was here. I've got you your money, like I promised, that's all that matters. You can have it, but I want Tommy. Pick the place. I can have the money there in an hour, I swear to God. Anyplace you want, just in public, just bring my dad."

"We play this your way, I've got cops coming out of my ass before the money's in my hand."

I shook my head, desperate for him to believe me. "No! No cops, God, I don't care about the cops! This is about my dad and your money, that's all this is about!"

Again, he went silent, and this time, I did, too. There was nothing more to say to him. I'd dropped the score in front of him, shown him the parts, and either he'd play or he wouldn't, and I couldn't press him anymore. But he was thinking about it. Trying to find a way to have his cake and eat it, too.

"Five o'clock," he said, deciding. "Pioneer Courthouse Square, five o'clock. Be on the south side, the steps. I bring Tommy, you bring my money."

I nodded, hardly able to speak, and he lowered the gun and turned, and went away, his steps floating back along the stone, hiding in the echoes of the water, mingling with the memory of crimps and blood money deals, old and new.

CHAPTER THIRTY-EIGHT

I went to the Jeep first, still parked in Chapel's garage, and got the Taylor out of the back. There were no cops as far as I could see, but it didn't change the fact that I felt like I was being watched as I walked with the guitar case to the Starbucks on the corner of Morrison and Broadway, on the northwest corner of the Square.

Once inside, I got in line to get a cup of coffee. The shop was busy, with a mix of men and women, teens to fifties. The majority were high schoolers who'd come downtown to get an early start to their weekend; the rest professionals, out of offices a few minutes early, stocking up on caffeine before the commute home, or shoppers, ready to hit the boutiques in the nearby Pioneer Plaza.

Nobody was paying me any attention. I bumped one of the kids with my guitar, gently, playing at an accident, then offering an apology. The kid didn't even look back at me.

Van never had this problem, she could draw eyes to her without effort, and hell if I knew how she did it. Now, here I was, finally wanting—needing—the world's attention, and if I was on radar, it was as a soggy chick with an old guitar case.

When the barista, twenty-two at the most, handed me my java and change without even a flicker in her face, I realized what I was doing wrong. I went to sugar the coffee, keeping my head down this time, and avoiding eye contact altogether. One of the teens was stirring cream and cinnamon into a foamy drink in front of me, and I did the guitar move again, the nudge. This time I didn't apologize, and focused on my coffee.

It took him twenty seconds.

"Excuse me," the teen said. "Aren't you Mim Bracca?"

I hemmed, then sighed and nodded.

He grinned. He'd been in a group with four others his age. They were a mixed group, pretty clean looking, three boys and two girls, and as soon as I'd confirmed I was who they'd thought I was, they all surged forward, as if to take a better look.

"I love 'Queen of Swords.' "

"Are you feeling better? They said you were sick, MTV said you were sick."

"God, all that stuff about your brother and those pictures, I'm so sorry, that so blows."

"Is that your guitar? Of course it is, I mean, are you going to play? Are you playing somewhere?"

"I have all of the albums, all of them, I mean, I was a fan before you guys were popular."

I smiled and nodded and said, "Hey, yeah, thanks. Thanks a lot, that's wonderful to hear. Yeah, actually, I was thinking I'd do some playing."

More questions, more babbling, more attention. Half of the clientele belonged to me, as Graham would have said. My demographic, and the more I talked to them, the more pressed forward to listen.

I asked the young man, the first one, what his name was, and he looked so pleased and surprised that I cared, I almost felt guilty.

"Ray," he said, almost as if he'd forgotten it himself for a moment. "I'm Ray."

"I'm Ted."

"Lynn."

"Grace."

"Aidan."

"Deedee."

"Roxy."

"Shawn."

"Hi," I said. "I'm Mim."

They laughed, warmly, and I smiled with them, then made a show of checking my watch. "Damn. I've got to meet a guy on the steps."

A chorus of "ohs" and "wells" and sighs, the brush with fame apparently over.

"You guys really like the music?"

Nods and "yes" and "hell yeah" and "totally" and even a "you guys rock."

"You know, I'm working on something," I said, reluctantly. "I'd love to hear what you guys think. Can you give me twenty minutes and meet me down there?"

Ray, the young man who had found me first, took command. "Twenty minutes? Hell yeah, we'll totally be there."

"About five o'clock," I said.

Eager faces, more nods, and I told them I would see them shortly, and when I stepped outside, easily half of them were already dialing their mobile phones, calling their friends, telling them to hurry. Outside, there was no glimpse of Hoffman or Marcus, and no one in a black Columbia Sports Wear parka. The rain had all but stopped, and so had the wind, and people were lowering umbrellas, shaking them out as they hustled along the sidewalk.

I understood why he'd picked the location. Pioneer Courthouse Square is an open city block, red brick, and on its east side it faces the old Pioneer Courthouse. It's flat, but built on a slope, and tiers—or steps—run along its north, west, and south sides, descending to the open floor. There's no specific entrance to the Square, and no exit, and you can get in or out from any point with ease. Traffic runs along all four sides, one way, with the westbound MAX trains running up

Morrison and the eastbound ones coming down Yamhill. People loiter in the Square, people cut through the Square, people stop to chat in the Square. They come with lattes and chai teas, they buy hot dogs and crêpes from the vendors.

Now the Square was mostly empty, with pedestrians stepping around puddles as they moved through it. In another few weeks a Christmas tree would go up, and a month or so after that, the place would be packed for New Year's Eve. There would be pageants and fairs for those who had acquired permits, and people would come, because it was one of the most popular places in town.

He could come from any direction, leave from any direction. From any corner, he'd be able to take in all of the space. He'd spot me in an instant and I would never know, because I didn't even know what he looked like outside of a ski mask and black parka. If he didn't like what he saw, he could leave without even breaking stride. Those were his advantages, why he'd chosen this space.

I could only hope that they didn't outweigh my own, a growing mob of teenagers clustered in a Starbucks, watching me through the windows.

I took a seat on the south side of the Square, on the steps about four rows from the bottom, setting the guitar case to my side. The brick was cold and wet. The clouds had gone higher, but the sunset was making it difficult to gauge them. I didn't want it to rain; guitars like to stay dry.

I'd dropped a new set of strings in the case, so I got out the Taylor and replaced the missing E, thinking that Steven would be chewing my ass if he didn't see me replace the other five, too. But I didn't have time, and if he had been there and known what was happening, maybe he would have forgiven me. It took all of six minutes to get the string placed and tuned, and I put the Taylor away and shut the case when I was finished.

My hands weren't shaking anymore. I thought about lighting a cigarette, sat watching the people pass. Up at the Starbucks, the cluster of teens had emerged. The group had already doubled in size, and the mobiles were still going. Modern communication, letting all their buds know about my impromptu concert. All were trying not to be obvious about looking my way.

For my sake and theirs, I hoped they would be convincing.

Four minutes to five, by my watch.

A police car went by, driving up Morrison. It was the second I'd seen in the past three minutes. It was moving slowly, but that was probably due to traffic. I craned my head around, trying to see if there were others, and then I saw Marcus standing at the northwest corner, near Starbucks.

No, I thought. God no, please no.

Hoffman was at the northeast corner, the one in front of me, to my right.

They had to have picked me up when I'd gone back for the Taylor. They had to have been watching the car, knowing I'd come back for the guitar.

I checked the other corners, southeast and southwest, saw men and women loitering, talking. Which were cops?

I looked back at Hoffman, but she wasn't looking my way, watching as a MAX train came to a stop on Morrison.

They had the same problem I did, I realized. They knew they were waiting; they just didn't know who they were waiting for. Like me, the lack of knowledge trapped them. Parka Man would have to make the first move.

But there was no sign of him. I'd hoped he'd take my terms, that he'd decide the money was his first priority, that Tommy and I only came second. It had seemed to make sense when I'd conceived it: he would hesitate, then decide killing us could come later, after he'd secured the cash. I'd put his greed ahead of his self-preservation.

Apparently, I'd been wrong. Now, Tommy would be dumped in the Willamette, and some night soon, I'd wake up in the dark to find a gun at my head again. Only this time the photographs would be taken hours later, and by technicians who had maybe been to my house once already.

A new train pulled to the stop on Morrison, began kicking out passengers. I glanced at my watch, read a minute past five. The desire for a drink seemed to rise with the cold beneath me.

When I looked up, a man in a black parka was coming down the stairs on the opposite side of the Square. He was taking them slowly, one at a time, pausing after each, and after the third, he stopped and surveyed the area, and then his gaze snagged on me.

Even fifty feet away, Tommy didn't look good. He tottered unsteadily, as if drunk, as if he might lose his feet at any second. But it was him, and he was alive, and beneath the swollen bruises visible on his face, I saw him try to smile.

Despite it all, I smiled, too.

There was the splash of a foot in a puddle from behind me, and I felt the spatter touch my neck and cheek. In my periphery, I saw a man's knees as someone settled himself on the step behind me, to my left, and in the distance, on the corner, Hoffman turned my way, saw the same thing, but she didn't move.

The man pushed the guitar case with his toe.

"Don't turn around," he said.

Tommy was still standing where he'd stopped, maybe under instructions not to come any closer, not to leave. His feeble smile had vanished.

The man brought his head low, closer to my ear. "I've got a gun at your back," he said. "Any tricks, boom boom boom."

My fans were still at the Starbucks, now almost thirty of them, maybe more, and I looked their way. Ray, their leader, saw me, and it confused him. Then he checked his watch and gestured to the group, and they began coming toward me, loping down the steps.

"Where is it? Is it in the case?"

I reached out and flipped the locks, then lifted the lid, showing the contents. The Taylor lay in its bed of worn velvet, beautiful. I took it out, and rested it on my knee.

The kids were off the steps, coming toward me, grinning and joking and happy. Tommy hadn't moved, and across the gap, I saw his concern. Marcus was coming down from the sidewalk, making for him. Hoffman was standing still.

A pressure dug against my back, high on the right side, below my shoulder blade. The voice was a hiss.

"Dammit, where's my money?"

I didn't say anything, fighting my injured fingers into position. Ray, leading his group, stopped in front of me, and I lost the view of my father, of Hoffman. More than thirty of them, and a couple latecomers running our way, desperate to reach us in time to hear the show. Some began swiping pooled water from the steps, taking seats, smiling and murmuring.

The pressure against my back increased, and his mouth came lower, and I felt stubble brushing my ear. "Make them go away," he whispered. "Goddammit, make them go away or I'll shoot you right here."

"No," I said, and if the gathered crowd hadn't heard the threat, they certainly heard me say that, and several turned accusing eyes on the interloper at my shoulder. I lowered my head, checking my fingering, and pulled the melody I'd been fighting the last few days free from the Taylor.

"We're not early, are we?" Ray asked.

"You're right on time," I told him, letting my fingers wander the strings, letting the music come. "Everyone? This is Detective Wagner."

Everyone said hello to the man behind me, the man holding the gun on me. The pressure in my back sharpened for an instant, and he thought about doing it, then, I know he did. It took a second more before he realized exactly what I'd done, and that if he pulled the trigger now, he'd never get away with it. Even if my murder meant nothing, he'd have thirty fanatics to contend with, and all of them now knew his name, whether he denied it or not. They'd heard me, and they would remember.

"Do me a favor, Ray?" I asked.

Ray loved that I knew his name, it was in his face. He had blue eyes, and they adored me. "Anything."

"You see a guy in a parka behind you?"

Ray turned, and in the space between him and the others, I saw Marcus with an arm around Tommy, helping him off the steps and to the street.

"Just that guy," Ray said. "That the one you mean?"

Behind me, I heard Wagner shifting again, maybe getting ready to leave.

"That's my dad," I told Ray.

Wagner moved the gun from my spine to my neck, and it wasn't as cold as I remembered it this time. The teenagers needed a second, realizing, and then it started, and there was a cry, and they began scrabbling away.

Wagner dropped his hand onto my shoulder, taking my jacket in his fist, trying to pull me up. "Come on."

I started up, still holding the guitar. In front of me, Ray and his friends were backing off, confused and bewildered and terrified.

"Come on, you're coming with me," Wagner said again, harsher.

"No," I repeated, and I pulled forward, and his grip came away.

"I'll kill you."

I turned and looked past the gun, and met his eyes.

It was the same man. Older and sadder, maybe, but fear can do that to you. His mouth had gotten smaller and the muscles in his face had grown looser, and he'd lost hair as much as he'd lost dignity.

"You damn bitch," he said, and his voice cracked. "You damn bitch, you're as stubborn as your damn father, why couldn't you do this? Why couldn't you just let me have this?"

I just stared at him, not answering. Behind, all around, there was motion, voices, action, but it was fading, the world contracting to encompass only me and my guitar and an aging cop with his gun.

"You owed me this," he spat. "All I wanted was the money, all I wanted was what I was due. Damn you! You wouldn't have any of this if it hadn't been for me! You would be nobody if I hadn't done what I did for you and your brother!"

"You did nothing for us."

"I saved you, I protected you! You fucking think I didn't know who was behind the wheel? You think I didn't know who was lying, what really happened? I took your father away so you could have a goddamn *life*!"

There was a taste in my mouth, metallic and sharp. The gun in Wagner's hand was almost vibrating, his face twisting.

People shouting. Movement in my periphery, men and women in blue and in plainclothes, holding guns of their own. Someone was screaming my name.

"You killed my brother," I said.

"He didn't give me a choice!" The gun no longer wavered.

A voice told him to drop it, loudly. Another one told me not to move.

"You owed me," Wagner said, quietly. His eyes danced around, as if seeing the trap for the first time, seeing the teeth of it closing around his life. He brought his eyes back to me.

"You owed me," he said again.

Then he brought his other hand up, and the cops who had the shot took it, then.

The echo was louder than any audience had ever been as it caromed off the brick all around me.

CHAPTER THIRTY-NINE

This is the song I can never write, because I lie the way we all do, because I lie about the obvious, I ignore all the facts in favor of a more comforting fiction. The way Wagner and Brian and Chris Quick did. All of us creating fictions, making reality out of a fistful of rain.

Like Mikel in the pickup truck, and Tommy getting out to raise a fist at my mother for blocking the drive. Mikel not wanting to see that again, not wanting to be helpless one more time. Mikel, in driver's ed, thinking he knew enough, sliding along the seat and pulling the shift down to drive, looking over his shoulder.

Thinking he was in reverse.

The engine falls silent.

The girl feels weightless and dizzy, and doesn't remember turning to look at what has happened. She doesn't know if she is running or walking or floating to the entrance of the garage. She cannot hear the sound of her father opening the cab of his pickup, tearing at the handle in grief and rage, and she cannot hear the words her brother is mumbling and crying as he is torn from behind the wheel to sprawl on the glistening grass.

She cannot hear her father cursing and pleading, her brother's apologies turning him younger than even the girl herself.

Most of all, she cannot hear the sound that her mother is making, caught between the wheel and the ground.

She whirls away, but when she looks down the length of the driveway, she sees a spread of blood merging with the rainwater in the gutter.

Her father reaches for his boy and girl, but only the boy is rescued in the strength of that arm.

The sunlight vanishes behind a freshly loaded cloud.

It starts to rain again.

When Chapel arrived at the police station he made me go over the whole thing, then made me do it again for Marcus and Hoffman. They didn't need much from me; they'd already spoken to Tommy. It was Chapel himself who explained where Brian Quick had come from.

"He was in my office when you came by," my lawyer said. "He'd called, said he had information about the video taken of you, that he was willing to sell it to me for a nominal fee. He pretended he was the middleman, claimed there was raw video stored on some portable hard drives, that he could get hold of them very easily."

"We found them on Brian's body," Hoffman said.

"We'd like them destroyed."

"They're evidence."

"Then as soon as you're done with them, I want them returned to Miss Bracca."

"Brian was in your office?" I asked.

"That's why I kept you waiting," Chapel said. "Needed to move him to another room. I didn't want him seeing you. When Joy buzzed me that you were in reception, he must have heard it. I went to find him after you'd run off and he was gone, too. I can only assume he followed you."

"Or got out ahead of her, followed her then," Marcus said.

"Possible."

"Way we're looking at it now, Brian had a falling-out with his brother. Probably about just what to do with the video. Chris was the tech head. If he had decided to write the whole thing off, all he had to do was delete the drives. We're thinking Brian killed him to keep that from happening, to keep his brother from destroying his big payday."

"Then you pulled up," Hoffman told me. "And Brian recognized the vehicle, thought it was his chance to make that money."

There was silence in the room for a minute.

"Are you charging her?" Chapel asked them, going back to business.

Marcus chuckled. "We're thinking of slapping a fine on her, for playing in the Square without a permit."

"She can go," Hoffman said. There was no smile. "Her father's been taken to Legacy Emanuel."

"How bad is it?" I asked.

"Couple cracked ribs, some broken fingers, a lot of soft-tissue damage. He'll be laid up for a few days. The worst of it is dehydration. Wagner didn't provide much in the way of bread and water."

Chapel rose, waited for me to follow him. I didn't move yet. Instead, I said to Marcus, "I want to thank you."

"You could have avoided all of this," Marcus said. "All you had to do was tell us the truth."

"I was scared Wagner would find out."

"He probably would have," Hoffman said. "He still knew people in the department. But we'd have stopped him anyway."

I nodded, and then all of us, Chapel, Marcus, Hoffman, and myself, went to meet the press.

There were questions, so many questions, and reporters, too many reporters, and they wanted to know all of it, everything that had happened. It took most of an hour for the press conference to run its course, and Chapel had instructed me to stay quiet for the most part, until the end, when I read a statement he'd prepared about how glad I was that my ordeal was finally over, how happy I was that my father was okay, and how sad I was that Mikel was dead.

When I was asked about rejoining the Tailhook tour, Chapel said, "Miss Bracca's going to be taking some time off to recover from the events of the last two weeks."

When I was asked about the pictures, Chapel said, "No further questions."

Saturday morning I went to see Tommy. He was in a room with two other patients, in bed and awake. The bruises on his face were purple and black, and he had stitches on his lip, heavy with dried blood. When he tried to smile at me, the stitches pulled, and he had to stop.

"I've been lying here, wondering if you'd come by. Wondering what you'd call me when you did."

"I was thinking of sticking with Tommy."

"This guy, Steven, he must have been some guy."

"He was."

"I'm glad you had that. I'm sorry he's gone."

I pulled up a chair, dropping the magazines I'd brought him on his stomach. He set them aside, turning his head to look at me.

"The detectives, they've told you what I said?" Tommy asked.

"I came to hear it from you."

Tommy felt the edges of his mouth for fresh blood before answering. "Ran into Wagner by accident. He'd known I was out. I'd given Mikel's number and address for my own when I registered for unemployment. I was at my meeting, I go to an AA meeting up in the northwest, by the synagogue up there, and he was there when I came out one night. He must have followed me from Mikel's but he didn't say, he didn't say much of anything.

"Just that he had done me a favor, and he felt he was owed something for it. That it must be nice having a daughter who was so talented and so pretty and so rich. I told him all that was in spite of me rather than because of me."

He stopped, looking up at the ceiling. I used the pitcher on the stand to pour him a cup of water. He drank it slowly.

"Go on," I said.

"He said he wanted money, that he could make things bad for me if I didn't get it for him. He said, since my daughter is so rich, she can spare some money. Not too much, he told me. Maybe fifty thousand. She'll hardly miss it."

"I hardly would have."

Tommy rolled his head, meeting my eyes. "I told him I didn't talk to you, I hadn't talked to you for fifteen years. He said he didn't care. He said it'd be easy to hurt you, that it wouldn't take much. Someone famous, he said, it never takes much. Just some smack planted in your house, an anonymous call, that would be all he needed to do. He said he probably didn't need to plant anything, the media would destroy you."

"That's why you came to see me," I said.

Tommy took another drink of water, then settled against his pillows. When he went on, he picked a spot on the ceiling to speak to, not me.

"I just . . . I told myself I just wanted to see you, with my own eyes. Not on a television, not in a magazine. It went so badly, and you started shouting, you started offering me money, and I had to get out.

"I was so angry. I kept blaming you, kept thinking I should just take the money like Wagner wanted, that it would serve you right . . . and I hated myself for even thinking that. So I did what I always did when I hated myself. Not right away, I had to work myself up to it. But that Friday, I couldn't find a job . . . and I started drinking. And you know how that goes."

I did. "Was Mikel there?"

"I went out to buy more beer. When I got back, he was dead."

"Wagner told you he'd shot him?"

He shut his eyes, and his Adam's apple bobbed in his throat. "He said he'd come by to see what was taking me so long. Mikel recognized him. Wagner said he attacked him, he laughed about it, said it was funny that my drug-dealer son was more concerned about protecting his family than I was. They fought, and Wagner shot him."

We both fell silent.

"I had to hate you," I told him. "Do you understand that? I had to blame you for everything you took away, because I didn't want to give you the credit for anything I have. But Mikel never would have done time, Tommy. No judge would have sentenced him for a mistake. He was a kid, a scared kid who made a stupid mistake, that's all. He never meant to hurt anyone."

"You knew."

"I remembered."

Tommy shook his head. "Wagner wasn't anything. He did us a favor. I wasn't a good parent, and that wasn't going to change. A good parent doesn't beat his wife and doesn't drink until he passes out and he doesn't take drugs. A good parent doesn't pour her bitterness on her children, deny them pleasure because she's had it denied to her. We were destroying your life."

"You gave me my life. You gave me my first guitar."

"A piece of shit Silvertone in a house with a mother who would never let you play it."

"You're the one who gave me music, Tommy."

"That's not all I gave you."

That afternoon, I finally went to Joan's and helped go through Steven's stuff, and we finally had it out, she finally let all the anger loose. I took it and gave none of it back, because I deserved it, and when Joan was finished we both could finally share the grief each of us had been holding in for so long. We had dinner at Riyadh's, ate kafta patties and falafel, and I told her about everything that had happened. She held my left hand in hers, examining my fingers.

After dinner I dropped her at her home, then went back to mine, eager to be warm and safe. The million dollars was still in the duffel, and I thought it was stupid as hell to just leave it there, but there wasn't anything I could do with it until Monday morning, when the bank opened again.

I thought about calling Hoffman, and decided against it.

Instead, I plugged the Tele into the VOX AC-30 and worked on some exercises, trying to speed my fingers along their recovery, and when I was tired and happy, I went up to the kitchen for a smoke and a drink, to celebrate my job well done.

It was Monday afternoon when I came to, lying on the kitchen floor, half-naked and feeling more than half-dead. When I managed to start moving to survey the damage, it shocked me. The kitchen was a mess, and the living room, and the music room.

The Taylor was in fragments on the floor by the foot of the stairs, strings and splinters, neck snapped from body, utterly beyond repair. Marks on the banister and the pads on the floor showed where I'd struck the instrument again and again, battering it apart.

I sat on the bottom step, staring at the corpse, and I tried and tried and tried, and I couldn't imagine why I would have done such a thing. There was no reason, none at all.

Just seeing that Halloween pumpkin I'd carved with my mother, how I'd shattered it against the door of our house when the police had taken my father away.

Van called me that night, from Glasgow. I was at the sink, a cigarette in my mouth, bottle in my hand, trying to accept the rest of my hangover, and the ring sliced through all of the noise like it was made especially for my suffering. When I answered, I was surprised it was her.

"You have a minute?" Van asked.

I shut off the tap and said, "Sure. How're you doing?"

"How're you?"

"Turned a corner," I told her.

"That's really good to hear."

There was a transatlantic pause.

"Clay's not working out," Van said.

"I'm surprised."

"He just doesn't have what it takes. He's got chops in the studio, Mim, but you put him onstage, he's like furniture. If you heard what he was doing to your arrangements, you'd cry."

"I'm sure it's not that bad."

"No, it's that bad, Mim, it really is. Graham and I were talking, and Click, too, and we're supposed to be playing a couple gigs in the Midwest starting Wednesday, then on through the South. We were wondering if maybe you could meet us in Chicago."

I looked at the row of bottles on my counter.

"I can't."

"If you're angry, if you're holding a grudge, I can understand why you'd be doing that. But this is about the band, and we can't keep putting Clay—"

"You were right to send me home, Van."

"What?"

"I said you were right, and I need to stay here, now. I need to dry out, I need to learn how to stay that way once I get there. I'm hoping that by June I'll have it mastered. Until then, call Birch, or someone else."

She gave me more of the transatlantic silence.

"I have to do this," I told her.

"Good luck," Van said.

I hung up, went back to dumping the last of my bottles down the drain.

*   *   *

Tuesday morning, I picked up Tommy at the hospital. He was expecting me to take him straight to Mikel's, but I told him first things first, and drove him over to a shop on Hawthorne that I liked, called Guitar Crazy.

I bought him a used Taylor acoustic.

ACKNOWLEDGMENTS

The technical aspects of this book were many, and those who contributed their time and knowledge are too numerous to name. That being said, special thanks must go to the following:

The members of *Audio Learning Center:* Chris Brady, Paul Johnson, and most particularly, Steven Birch. Wonderful musicians all, talented beyond compare, and each generous to a fault. To Steve in particular, thanks for everything, from the first steps to the final lap. Shameless plug for their album *Friendships Often Fade Away.*

Special indebtedness to one of the most fabulous couples it has been my pleasure to know—Judd Winick and Pamela Ling, M.D. Unique insight, brutal honesty, great humor, and yes, I know it's not so much a visual tremor as a verbal tic, but it's so much more *dramatic* when it's written that way.

To Nunzio Andrew DeFilippis, who leapt for the over-the-wall catch and made the save not once, not twice, but on three separate occasions. Like the ladies before her, Mim loves you.

Thank you to Gerard V. Hennelly, without whom no acknowledgment would be complete. You know dangerous things, and are always willing to share. Thanks as well to Nancy Hess, for taking the time to speak with a total stranger, and better, to speak honestly.

To John W. Patton and Courtney Dreslin; the former for taking time better spent at better tasks to research the hypothetical, and to do so very thoroughly; the latter for not only fielding the first questions, but enlisting the former in answering the second ... and third ... and fourth ...; additional legal thanks to Harvey Mittler and N.M.R., and to Brad Meltzer, for pointing the right way.

To the Cats at Oni Press—Joe Nozemack, Jamie S. Rich, and James Lucas Jones—break out the reading pants.

To Matthew Clark, for patience.

And finally, to Jennifer and Elliot. I'm back. Sorry I was gone so long.

ABOUT THE AUTHOR

GREG RUCKA was born in San Francisco and raised on the Monterey Peninsula. He is the author of several novels, including four about bodyguard Atticus Kodiak, and of numerous comic books, including the Eisner Award–winning *Whiteout: Melt* and *Queen & Country*. He resides in Portland, Oregon, with his wife, Jennifer, and their son, Elliot.